ICING

Allison

Books by Pamela Burford

Jane Delaney Mysteries
Undertaking Irene
Uprooting Ernie
Perforating Pierre
Icing Allison
Preserving Peaches
Simmering Stu
Liquidating Larry
Scrapping Scarlett
Jane Delaney Humorous Mystery Series: Books 1-3 Box Set

Romantic Suspense
Snatched
Going Commando
Storming Meg
A Case of You
Twice Burned (Double Dare book 2)

Contemporary Romance
Rags to Bitches
In the Dark
Snowed
Too Darn Hot
The Boss's Runaway Bride (a novella)

The Wedding Ring matchmaking series:
Love's Funny That Way
I Do, But Here's the Catch
One Eager Bride To Go
Fiancé for Hire
The Wedding Ring Matchmaker Series: Complete Four-Book Romantic Comedy Box Set

ICING
Allison

A Jane Delaney Mystery
Book 4

Pamela Burford

Paperback edition published 2018 by Radical Poodle Press
Copyright © 2017 by Pamela Burford

ISBN 978-1-939215-78-9
Ebook ISBN 978-1-939215-79-6

Interior design by BB eBooks
Cover design copyright © 2017 Patricia Ryan
Author photograph copyright © Jeff Loeser

www.pamelaburford.com

for Myra

1

So-Called Fun

YOU'RE PROBABLY WONDERING what I was doing trekking through secluded woods on a bitterly cold winter day, following a dangerous man carrying a scary-looking chainsaw. Okay, when you put it like that, it does seem kind of stupid. And for the record, I'm not the one who says he's dangerous. That would be my ex-husband, Dom, but Dom tends to be overprotective.

Plus I had my own history with this particular bad boy. Martin McAuliffe and I had been in a tight scrape once, of the life-threatening variety, and he'd shown his true colors then.

Right about now you're thinking that big, brave Martin came to the rescue of frightened little Jane. The fact is, *I* saved *his* life. Just to, you know, set the record straight.

If I was in danger from Martin, then so was Sexy Beast, my seven-pound apricot poodle. Sexy Beast—SB for short—was having a grand old time, trotting along with us, sniffing all these wonderful new smells, and watering the trees. He wasn't too crazy about the little plaid parka I'd put on him. Well, it was *cold*.

Oh, did I forget to mention? The dangerous man was also carrying two pairs of ice skates. I happen to know what was in his backpack, because he'd teased me with the contents in order to entice me to, well, willingly spend time outdoors in winter. He'd gone to my favorite deli to pick up our lunch: thick roast beef sandwiches and potato salad. Then he'd swung by Patisserie Susanne for pastries, including my all-time favorite, chocolate croissants, and sealed the deal with a thermos filled with hot chocolate. I mean, really, the man does not fight fair.

Sexy Beast wouldn't go hungry, either. I'd brought along his favorite treat, Vienna sausages. Plus some water and one of those cute collapsible doggie water bowls.

And before you start thinking this was some kind of date, let me assure you it was nothing of the sort. There was zilch going on between me and Martin. He wasn't my type. I'm not attracted to sexy-as-hell bad boys with mysterious backgrounds. I'm too mature for that.

You can stop snickering.

"Why couldn't we go to an ice-skating rink?" I asked. Well, it might've been more of a whine.

"A skating rink when the temperatures have been in the single digits for days?" he called over his shoulder. "Nature is our skating rink."

"I never knew you were such a nature lover," I said. "And why won't you tell me what the chainsaw is for?" I knew it wasn't to cut down a Christmas tree. Christmas had come and gone. The new year was one week old, and as Martin had pointed out, it was toe-numbingly cold and had been so for a depressingly long time.

Though I wasn't about to admit it, it was actually refreshing to be doing something outdoors, and the view didn't hurt. The sight of the padre's nice firm posterior encased in snug jeans was as bracing as the weather.

Oh, you thought I was talking about the view of the pristine woods. Yeah, that was nice too, especially with the frozen lake coming into view. It hadn't snowed for a couple of weeks, but here and there patches of old snow lay on the trail. I tried to ignore that I'd been to these particular woods before, had viewed that particular lake before. Although now that I was getting a clearer, calmer look at it, I saw it was more modest than I remembered, somewhere between a small lake and a very large pond.

That other visit to this particular nature preserve had been several months earlier when I'd arrived bound and gagged in the trunk of my own car. I'd barely managed to avoid being shot and dumped in that picturesque lake. Of course, it had been July then and the woods had been thick and green.

Martin had been shaken by my close brush with death. Well, heck, so had I. I wondered if his choice of these woods for our jolly winter activity was a way of helping me confront and get past that episode, kind of like getting back on the horse again.

The air had that sharp, clean smell you get only when it's bitterly cold. I was dressed warmly, and so was Sexy Beast, but my fingers were starting to get numb despite my gloves. I figured I'd generate some heat once I was out there skating—if, that is, the ice was safe. We paused at the edge of the frozen lake. It looked inviting, but…

"How do we know it's thick enough to hold our weight?" I asked.

This was Martin's cue to set down the skates and fire up the chainsaw. The obnoxious racket was Sexy Beast's cue to bark like hell. "It's been so cold for so long," he said, "there can't be much doubt. And just look at that ice. Clear and blue just like we want it. But just to be sure…"

He strolled a few yards onto the ice while Sexy Beast's mounting hysteria warned he was taking a foolish risk. I had to agree. What on earth would I do if he fell in? He placed the tip of the chainsaw on the solid surface and sliced straight down through it. Water sprayed as he repeated the procedure, creating a small hole. He set down the saw and extracted a metal measuring tape from his jacket pocket, which he extended and inserted into the hole, hooking the metal tab under the bottom of the ice.

Martin's grin crinkled the corners of his eyes, which were the same pale blue as the ice. "A little over seven inches. We're good to go. Put those skates on."

"That doesn't mean it's that thick everywhere."

"When did you become such a worrier?"

When I almost became fish food in this very lake, I wanted to say.

He ambled all the way to the center of the lake and repeated the exercise, then held up seven fingers.

"Is that really deep enough?" I called.

"You tell me," he shouted, with a devilish grin. "Does it take more than seven inches to satisfy Jane Delaney?"

Automatically I looked around to make sure no one was within earshot, but of course we were the only ones in the whole dang preserve. "Couldn't you have just used a chisel to test the ice?" I asked. "Maybe a cordless drill?"

"Where's the fun in that?" He grabbed the chainsaw and walked back toward me. He wore a sheepskin-lined leather bomber jacket and a black watch cap pulled down over his short, sandy hair.

I parked my behind on a large rock and examined the skates Martin had rented for me that morning at Vargas Sporting Goods. They were my size. Well, of course they were. The padre seemed to know everything about me, sneaky SOB that he was. I was used to it by now.

Why do I call him the padre? you ask. This goes back to last spring when we first met. Martin had been impersonating a priest at the time. And before you start thinking what a shameless thing that is to do, in the interest of full disclosure I must admit that I was trying to steal a piece of jewelry from a corpse during the wake. As it happened, Martin beat me to it. I guess he has more experience being shameless than I do.

As bad as it might sound to be swiping something from the recently departed, let me assure you it was just business and completely on the up and up. Okay, maybe not *completely*. Irene McAuliffe—yeah, she was related to Martin, kind of— had hired me to retrieve the brooch before it ended up six feet under the gently rolling turf of Whispering Willows Cemetery. The brooch actually belonged to her, you see. Or something like that.

I can hear you thinking, *Wait, what? Someone actually paid you to steal from the dead? Is that a* thing *now?*

For me, it is. My name is Jane Delaney, but I'm better known as the Death Diva. People hire me to do all sorts of things to, for, or on behalf of their dearly departed.

Oh don't make that face. We're talking pretty benign stuff. Well, most of the time. You need someone to scatter cremated ashes? I'm your gal. How about delivering flowers to the cemetery or ordering a tombstone or writing an obituary? You know those memory boards you see at wakes and visitations, with photos of the deceased in more animated times? I can't tell you how many of those I've made. I do all those things, plus some that might not immediately pop to mind.

For example, I've arranged for the cryogenic preservation of a loved one's head so that decades from now scientists can, I don't know, attach it to a sexy young body, as a great big *nyah nyah* to all the poor saps who'd allowed themselves to be buried or burned once their bodies gave out. I've taken a deceased person's cremated ashes on a cruise to Alaska because he always wanted to go, but his wife got seasick. So not only did I get a free cruise, but I actually got paid to do it. Is this a great career or what?

Martin tied his skates and got onto the ice while I was still struggling to lace up my first one. Then after I got them on I still had to take care of Sexy Beast's feet. I produced a set of little dog booties from my own small backpack and managed to get them on his little paws while he jerked and twitched and did everything in his power to thwart me. He'd never worn footwear before, but I mean, he was going onto the ice, and I didn't want his sensitive little feet to freeze.

I watched my dog stumble around the frozen ground kicking his feet out, trying to dislodge these strange things that I'd forced on him. "I'm not trying to torture you, SB," I said. "This is for your own good."

The look he gave me questioned my sanity. *I knew you'd go crazy on me eventually, I just didn't think it would happen so soon.*

"You know, he doesn't need those," the padre called from the middle of the lake. He was skating beautifully, sailing across the ice with strong, graceful movements. I could've sat there and watched him all day if I weren't worried about frostbite. "Dogs have excellent circulation in their feet. You're just annoying him."

I ignored Martin, got to my feet, and made my ungainly way onto the ice. "Come on, SB, let's go have some so-called fun."

Sexy Beast was still trying to shake off the boots, but he managed to follow me onto the ice, where he proceeded to stumble and slide. He really did look pathetic and I wondered if Martin was right.

I started to skate, or I should say I tried to remain upright while shuffling my feet in a forward direction. Sexy Beast's sullen glare took in my skates and his own boots. He admitted a long-suffering sigh but soldiered on, tottering after me, except when his feet splayed in all directions and he belly-flopped onto the ice. He was definitely earning that Vienna sausage.

A poltergeist grabbed one of my skates and yanked on it. I landed hard on my keister. Sexy Beast managed to get his front paws up onto me. His dark little eyes stared straight into mine. I knew he was thinking about his nice cozy bucket bed in the kitchen and his fuzzy toys. I was the alpha female, I was supposed to take care of him, and he was probably wondering if he'd have to haul me off this frozen lake by my collar.

Martin skated toward me. "You weren't kidding about being a lousy skater."

"Can we stop now?" I asked. "I'm ready for hot chocolate."

"You have to earn it. And these have to go." He bent down and tugged the booties off SB's feet.

"Put those back on him," I said. "He needs them."

Martin shoved them deep into his front jeans pocket. "You're welcome to fish them out." Another impish grin.

The look I gave him said, *Keep dreaming.* Reckless Jane wanted to go ahead and shove her hand into his pocket, grope around for those booties, just to see his reaction. Sensible Jane knew that would probably be a bad idea. *But why?* Reckless Jane asked. *After all, you've known the padre for almost a year.* Okay, more like nine months. We'd survived a really hairy situation once, as I've mentioned. And yeah, maybe I still didn't know anything about Martin's background, but I trusted him and liked him. Well, most of the time. So why shouldn't I go ahead and, you know, take things a little further?

Sensible Jane had an answer for that. Well, of course she did. She's so boring and predictable that way. *Bad boys might be exciting in the short term,* Sensible Jane sniffed, *but they're no good for long-term relationships.*

So? Reckless Jane countered. *What's wrong with a little short-term whoopee?*

While this battle waged inside my cranium, Martin positioned himself behind me, hoisted me by my armpits, and grabbed hold of my waist. Sexy Beast began barking at this fun new game.

"What are you doing?" I squawked.

"Trying to turn you into a skater." He started to skate slowly, guiding me ahead of him. "Don't fight me, Jane. Relax."

I wasn't fighting him, I was just a little flustered, unaccustomed as I was to this much physical contact with him. I tried to obey him, tried to relax. There was nothing intimate about what he was doing, after all. Right?

Reckless Jane told me to shut up and enjoy it.

Sexy Beast happily trotted after us, unencumbered by the ridiculous boots. Oh, he slid a few times until he got his bearings on the ice, but overall he seemed to be enjoying himself. He avidly sniffed the frigid air, tail wagging.

Martin guided me around the edge of the lake, slowly picking up speed. My skates did try to fly out from under me a couple of times, but he held me steady. Meanwhile he offered bits of advice, which I tried to obey. It's not that I have no athletic ability, I was a softball champ in high school, and okay, so that was a long time ago, more than two decades if I'm being honest. But skating is just something I never quite got the hang of.

Now, as we made our way around the frozen lake, I was kind of glad I'd never quite gotten the hang of it. I decided I was enjoying the feel of Martin's hands on my waist, his strength and power as he propelled us both over the ice, his breath warming the back of my neck.

I kept looking down at my skates, trying to keep them going in the right direction, trying to prove to Martin that I wasn't completely hopeless, which is why I saw her first.

A shrill scream rang out over the lake and reverberated through the woods. Only belatedly did I realize it had come from me. I found myself on my hands and knees, staring down into a pale face under the ice. Her eyes were open. Her mouth was open. Her long black hair streamed in all directions, frozen in place. She wore a red jacket and gray gloves.

I recognized those eyes. I knew that lovely, still face.

Martin knelt next to me. He said something, I have no idea what. I could hear nothing past my own roaring pulse. SB was all over me, trying to comfort me. He didn't know what was wrong, he only knew his pack mate was in distress.

"We have to get her out of there!" I cried. I looked at Martin, his handsome features grim as he stared at the woman under the ice. I grabbed the collar of his leather jacket. I tried to shake him. "Get your chainsaw, Martin. We can get her out. It might not be too late."

He pulled me hard against him, held me tight, tucked my face into his chest as if to spare me a sight that would forever haunt me. I fought him for a few seconds before collapsing against him, grateful for his steady presence, grateful I wasn't alone.

He didn't say it. He didn't have to. It was already too late for Allison Zaleski.

2

In Which Jane Has Everything So Under Control

MAIA ARMSTRONG SLID A PAN of rolls into the oven. She asked, "Who's the one documenting the buffet table for posterity?"

I peeked outside the kitchen to the dining room, where the table had been loaded down with chafing dishes and trays of salads and sandwiches. Sure, it was an appetizing spread, but this was, after all, a funeral reception. There's a time and place for everything, and it would be nice if the guests remembered they were there to honor the deceased, not to update their snack status on social media.

"She was at the funeral home and cemetery too," I said, watching a young woman snap pictures with her phone. "Taking selfies during the graveside service, can you believe it?"

Maia made a face. "Classy."

The murmur of conversation drifted from the living room. About a dozen people had arrived so far. We were expecting forty. We were in Allison Zaleski's home, a rambling two-hundred-year-old farmhouse in Crystal Harbor's historic district.

"What do you need me to do?" I asked Maia. She was a popular local caterer there in Crystal Harbor, a town on the North Shore of Long Island. The two of us often collaborated on assignments that combined my area of expertise—dead folks—with her area of expertise: delicious vittles. Well, it's only natural. Food has always played an important part in the grieving process. There are worse times to break bread with loved ones than when you're all hurting from the loss of one of your own.

Maia was in her mid-thirties, with dark, catlike eyes and a cloud of Afro coils, tied back today with a pretty paisley headband. She was popular for a reason. Not only was her food the absolute best, but she was unfailingly professional in her dealings with clients. Our friendship had begun seven years earlier when she'd made the decision to move her budding catering business from a less affluent community to well-to-do Crystal Harbor.

"Well," she said, "if you could find a place for all these boxes, that would be great." She indicated the stacks of bakery boxes piled up all over the kitchen, brought by Allison's friends and neighbors, most bearing the distinctive gold-and-white label of Patisserie Susanne. Yes, the same wonderful French bakery where Martin had bought the chocolate croissants that were supposed to be part of our skating lunch four days earlier when we found Allison's body. Will you be surprised if I tell you neither of us ate a bite that day? Martin had ended up tossing our lunch into the trash.

"*I'll* do that." It was Kari, coming in from the living room. Karina Faso was my ex-husband Dom's oldest child, by his second wife, Svetlana. Kari was only sixteen, but she was a go-getter, and Maia had started employing her part-time as an assistant on weekends. The girl was tall, like her father, and with the same dark brown eyes. She had long, golden brown hair, pulled back now in a neat braid.

"These belong in the butler's pantry." Kari hefted a stack of boxes and headed for the pantry, which had connecting doors to both the kitchen and dining room.

"You can put some of those in the freezer," Maia told the girl.

"I'm way ahead of you."

The aroma of coffee mingled with the yeasty perfume of baking rolls in the big country kitchen. Allison Zaleski had had quite a sense of style, no surprise when you consider that she'd been a gifted amateur photographer. Her artistic eye spilled over into her personal space. The irregular walls of the old kitchen were painted in broad vertical stripes of ivory and marigold yellow. The original beamed ceilings and rough plank flooring had never been replaced, nor had the enormous stone fireplace. The state-of-the-art appliances didn't detract from the many homey touches, including a roughhewn, whitewashed display cabinet filled with charmingly rustic handmade pottery: plates, platters, bowls, and mugs with irregular edges, dimpled surfaces, and unusual earth-toned glazes.

I recognized the style of this pottery, although I'd never seen so much of it in one place. The young couple who created it had a studio on Main Street next to Janey's Place, the health food restaurant that belonged to Dom. Yeah, named for me a couple of decades earlier when we'd been dating. I'd been introduced to the pottery couple, but I could never remember their names and was too embarrassed to ask again. To me they were Pottery Man and Pottery Lady. Allison must really have loved their work to buy so much of it. And I had to admit it looked great in her eclectic kitchen.

More pottery hung on the sides of the cabinet and sat on a sideboard beneath it. My gaze was drawn to a little ceramic mushroom, three or four inches tall. I picked it up and examined it. It was crafted in the same rustic style as the rest of the pottery, with a pale speckled glaze. There were several holes in the top and a cork plug in the bottom. A salt shaker, I realized. Or a pepper shaker, one or the other. Where was its mate? I turned it upside down and shook it. Empty. It felt good in my hand.

I was still examining the little shaker when Allison's mother, Joleen Gleason, entered the kitchen, carrying yet another bakery box, handed to her by a guest. She looked around for a place to set it down. Every surface was taken up with food in various stages of preparation. It was organized mayhem. Well, maybe not that organized.

"I'll take that, Mrs. Gleason." It was Kari, entering from the butler's pantry.

"Why, thank you." After Kari disappeared back into the pantry, Joleen said, "Such a nice girl." She had a strong Texas accent. Allison's had been much milder, which made sense considering she'd moved to New York in her youth. Joleen was tall, as her daughter had been. Her iron-gray hair was cut in a practical bob that stopped just short of her shoulders. The strain of the past few days showed on her face, but I had yet to see her cry or fall apart. She and her husband, Douglas, maintained a dignified stoicism.

I was about to place a comforting hand on Joleen's back but then thought better of it. My gut told me this reserved woman wouldn't appreciate such an intimate gesture from someone she wasn't close to. Not that we were strangers. I'd met Allison's parents the previous June when Allison herself hired me to do the very same thing I was doing today: organize a post-funeral reception. Back then it had been for Allison's late first husband, Mitchell Zaleski, who'd died tragically in a hiking accident.

And now here we were again, mourning another accidental death that had occurred during a supposedly healthful outdoor activity. There's a lesson in there somewhere.

And yeah, the lesson just might be that the healthiest thing you can do is laze around in front of the TV with some pizza and a bottle of orange soda and leave the outdoor stuff to the risk takers. Which happened to be kind of my specialty. The pizza and soda thing, I mean, not the risk-taking thing.

Allison and Mitchell had been married for six years. He'd been close to sixty when he died, decades older than his young wife. At least it couldn't be said he'd died young. Allison, on the other hand, had been only thirty-one, beautiful and statuesque. She'd had black hair, worn in a long, sleek curtain with blunt bangs. Her most striking feature, however, had been her violet eyes. I recalled thinking, when I first met her, that she looked like a young Elizabeth Taylor.

She hadn't remained single very long following Mitchell's death. Three months later she'd married Nick Birch, an unemployed actor several years her junior. From what I could tell, Nick was taking Allison's death hard.

The Gleasons had remembered me from Mitchell's funeral and asked me to help make arrangements. I'd been present at both the funeral home and graveside service that day, making sure all went according to plan while Maia got the refreshments ready for visitors.

Joleen was looking around the kitchen as if seeking something to do.

"Mrs. Gleason," I said, "everything here is under control."

"We've got this." Maia was arranging cookies on a platter. "You don't need to do anything."

"I'm not used to not doing anything. What's that you have there, Jane?" Joleen asked.

Only then did I realize I was unconsciously rolling the ceramic shaker between my hands. I showed it to her. "I'm thinking this must be part of a pair. You know, a salt-and-pepper set. I don't see the other one."

"That's cute," Maia said.

"You're right," Joleen said, "that's the salt shaker. The pepper is darker and smaller. I haven't seen it in a while. It probably got broken."

"That's too bad." I set the shaker back on the sideboard.

"They made the set especially for her," Joleen said, "you know, that nice young couple that do the pottery. Allison loved mushrooms. If you like it, why don't you keep it," she added. "It could still be used for salt or spices or whatever."

"Oh, I couldn't," I said, reflexively.

"Don't be silly," she said. "You can ask Nick if you want, but I'm sure he won't mind. What on earth is he going to do with half of a salt-and-pepper set? He'll probably throw all of this away." She swept her arm toward the pottery cabinet, her expression dour. "I'm sure it's not his style."

I'd fallen in love with the silly little thing, but still I hesitated. Maia made the decision for me, with a muttered, "Good grief, Jane, she wants you to have it." She grabbed the salt shaker, wrapped it in a paper towel, and shoved it into my purse, which hung on one of the kitchen chairs.

I thanked Joleen, who said I was very welcome and headed back to the guests.

"I'd better get out there too," I said. "Let me know if you need any help."

"I have Kari," Maia said. "No worries."

I greeted people as I passed through the dining room. Most of them were friends and neighbors of mine there in Crystal Harbor. I said hello to Lacey and Porter Vargas. Porter owned a chain of sporting goods stores. The Crystal Harbor store is where Martin had rented our skates four days earlier. His wife, Lacey, owned a lingerie shop called UnderStatements. Porter was in his mid-fifties but looked younger, with an athletic build and dark hair just beginning to go gray. Lacey, on the other hand, looked her age, although she dressed well and took care with her appearance.

"Do they know what happened?" Lacey asked.

"The best they can figure," I said, "is that Allison went for a walk in the preserve a couple of weeks ago and ended up on the frozen lake, but the ice was too thin. She fell in and couldn't get out. The cause of death was drowning."

"It didn't get really cold until the end of December," Lacey said. "I guess the ice just couldn't support her weight."

Porter frowned. "That doesn't sound like something Allison would do, taking a risk like that."

"She used to work for you, didn't she?" I asked.

He nodded. "When she was younger, before she met Mitchell."

"They met at the store," Lacey said. "Mitchell came in for some camping supplies and they hit it off."

Allison's first husband had owned a ski resort in upstate New York. The couple had had plenty in common, despite the age difference. They'd both been sporty, outdoorsy types, always hiking, kayaking, camping, and of course, skiing. They'd been devoted to fitness and had participated in several triathlons in their respective age categories.

I glanced into the living room and spied the young woman who'd been taking selfies at the cemetery, and snapshots of the buffet table. She stared at her phone, her thumbs a blur as she tapped the screen. I nodded in her direction and lowered my voice. "Do you know who that is?"

They looked. "Sure," Lacey said. "That's Skye Guthrie, Allison's best friend."

Skye had black hair worn in the same style as Allison's, but that's where the physical similarities ended. Skye was about five foot three, a good six inches shorter than Allison had been, her figure somewhat rounder. She had a pronounced midwinter tan, which I suspected owed more to chemicals than an island vacation. She wore a black dress, the kind normally associated with the term *little black dress*. A cocktail-party dress, short and low-cut. Not the kind of thing you expect to see someone wearing at her best friend's funeral.

But who was I to judge? In my two decades as Death Diva, I'd seen far worse. This Skye Guthrie might not be the most sophisticated creature, but I'm sure she'd loved her deceased friend.

"Oh my God," Skye crowed to everyone within earshot, "my picture of the casket already has forty-two likes."

Come on, work with me, I wanted to tell her. *I'm trying to give you the benefit of the doubt here.*

The doorbell rang and I excused myself to answer it, passing through the cozy living room, where a fire blazed in the hearth. Here, as in the rest of the house, Allison's photography was on display. There were plenty of nature pictures, attesting to her love of the outdoors. My favorite was an arresting image of creamy-white oyster mushrooms growing on a fallen tree in the woods. The overcast sky, the low photographic angle, the shallow depth of field, all lent the picture an otherworldly feel.

There were also photos of people, singly and in groups, taken all over the world. She'd had a fondness for photographing strangers, but she wasn't sneaky about it. It was clear she got to know her subjects before turning her camera lens on them. The result was intriguing, often quirky images full of humanity. Her photographs of architectural detail were a revelation. It was as if Allison Zaleski had seen things that other people, including me, simply passed by without notice, and the results were often striking.

I entered the small vestibule and opened the front door. I recognized the couple who stood on the front porch, their breath smoking in the cold air. They'd been at the funeral home and cemetery. I ushered them inside and accepted yet another white bakery box. "Let me take your coats," I said. "I'm Jane Delaney. I'm helping the family today."

"Lou Yates." The man stripped off his overcoat and helped his companion shed hers. "This is my wife, Brenda. She's Allison's... well, Mitchell was her dad."

"Oh." Somehow I managed to juggle both their coats and the bakery box. "So you're Allison's stepdaughter." I regretted the words instantly. Brenda and her husband were in their mid to late thirties, several years older than Allison had been.

Brenda's only response was a sour look, quickly squelched. She was of average height and build. She had shoulder length chestnut hair and wore a conservative dark green sweater dress. Lou wore a dark suit and tie. Both of them appeared ill at ease.

Clearly they didn't know anyone else there.

I signaled to Porter and Lacey to join us, and introduced them. Skye Guthrie glanced furtively at our little group, then quickly redirected her attention to her phone. Porter apparently thought Allison's best friend should meet her stepdaughter. He pulled Skye into the conversation and made introductions. Both women seemed ill at ease as they shook hands and murmured polite greetings. This close to Skye, I noticed that the roots of her hair were conspicuously pale, medium brown rather than the shoe-polish black of the rest of her hair.

I deposited the bakery box in the kitchen, and the Yateses' coats in the small bedroom we'd set aside for that purpose. In the hallway I bumped into Sophie Halperin, who was the mayor of Crystal Harbor as well as one of my closest friends. She lived in another historic nineteenth-century home not far from there. Sophie was a pugnacious, amply padded woman in her mid-fifties and one of the best people I knew.

"Have you seen Nick?" I asked her. Allison's young husband wasn't in the dining room or living room.

"Last I saw him, he was headed in there." Sophie pointed to the closed door of Allison's first-floor home office.

"Thanks," I said. "I'll catch you later." I listened outside the door for a moment and heard nothing. I quietly knocked and peeked inside. The curtains were drawn against the afternoon sunlight, the room dim. Nick Birch sat slumped in an upholstered easy chair, nursing a small glass of clear liquid that I suspected was not water. He was ridiculously good-looking, with longish dark-blond hair, whiskey-colored eyes, and the kind of bone structure romance authors write about.

"I don't mean to intrude," I said. "I didn't see you out

there and… well, I just wanted to check up on you, see if you need anything."

"I guess I should be…" Nick tossed his hand in the direction of the doorway. "I just needed some time."

"No problem." I started to withdraw.

He stopped me. "No, don't go, Jane. Sit with me a few minutes." He gestured toward the chair opposite his.

I closed the door and sat. Nick had shed his suit jacket and tie. His white dress shirt looked like it had been sewn onto his toned torso. I assumed Allison's money had paid for the bespoke clothing—that is, the money she'd inherited when her first husband died. As far as I knew, Nick's acting career had yet to take off. There'd been a soda commercial some time ago. Several people had mentioned that commercial to me. Clearly it was the highlight of his career thus far.

He sipped his vodka. "How are her folks doing?"

It seemed an odd question for the young widower to be asking of the hired help. Then again, he'd been the Gleasons' son-in-law for a scant four months. He and Allison had married in September. He probably didn't know her parents well.

"They appear to be holding up," I said, "but it's hard to tell."

He nodded at that. "Cold fishes."

"I wouldn't say that. They're reserved is all. I guess they're trying to get through this as best they can."

Nick waved away the excuse. "Joleen and Doug have always been that way, at least toward me. I know they think I married Allison for her money."

In my admittedly bizarre line of work, I'd become accustomed to virtual strangers in the throes of grief revealing personal information they would never have mentioned under ordinary circumstances. I was accustomed to it, but it still made me uncomfortable. The best strategy, I'd learned, was to quietly allow the individual to unburden him or herself without comment. Naturally, I would never share anything I learned. I was like a priest that way, or a doctor. It was part of the Death Diva code of honor.

There is *too* a Death Diva code of honor. I should know, I made it up. You can do that when you're the only Death Diva.

"Well, all her assets are mine now. Two-thirds anyway. The other third goes to…" His vague gesture told me that either he forgot or it hadn't been important enough to learn in the first place. "Anyway, it's got to be making her folks crazy."

I know it would make *me* crazy if the freeloading pretty boy my widowed daughter had married on the rebound three months after her first husband's death managed to inherit two-thirds of her multimillion-dollar estate.

Nick swirled the vodka in his glass, to the accompaniment of clinking ice cubes. It occurred to me he was awaiting a response, some sort of validation. He needed reassurance that he was somehow entitled to his sudden windfall.

The closest I could offer was, "Mr. and Mrs. Gleason are still reeling from their daughter's death. I doubt they're thinking about who's inheriting what."

He drained his glass and sat staring into middle distance. I was about to take my leave when he said, "She was supposed to be in Australia."

"Excuse me?"

"Allison booked this adventure trip," Nick said. "Three weeks horseback riding somewhere in Australia where there are mountains or desert or something. She was always doing stuff like that. That's where I thought she was. And all the time she was in that damn lake."

"When was she supposed to go to Australia?" I asked.

"The day after Christmas."

I did the math. Twelve days. Allison's body had been discovered nearly two weeks after she was scheduled to fly halfway across the world. I said, "Didn't you worry when you didn't hear from her?"

He shook his head. "She didn't keep in touch much when she was away on these adventure trips. The idea was to throw herself into whatever she was doing and take a break from the real world."

"So this is why you didn't report her missing," I said.

Nick brought his glass to his lips and stared at the bare ice cubes for a moment, as if wondering where the vodka had gone. He set the glass on the side table.

My brain was whirring. I knew I shouldn't pursue it, but I couldn't let it go. "So when she left to go for a walk in the woods, you thought, what, that she was going to the airport?"

After a moment he said, "I wasn't up yet. I kind of slept in that day."

"Oh." What kind of man "sleeps in" when his wife is about to take a long trip like that?

"Christmas didn't go so great," he said. "Well, Christmas Day was okay. We went to Allison's folks', had a nice dinner and everything. But after, when we were back home, we fought."

I really didn't want to hear this. Nick was clearly a bit tipsy, and I strongly suspected he was going to regret opening up to me like this. I cast about for a graceful way to end the conversation and slink out of there.

"She found out I lost my job. I never even wanted it, it was all her idea. I mean, she's got all this money, this huge place." Nick made a broad gesture meant to encompass the sprawling farmhouse. "And I'm supposed to stock merchandise in some stupid sporting goods store? For what, to prove I'm not some bum living off my woman? To her, my acting career was BS. It was worth nothing. Just 'cause it's been a little slow lately."

A little slow? If Nick had appeared in anything other than that long-ago soda commercial, I never heard about it.

"So you worked for Porter Vargas?" I asked. That was the only sporting goods store in town.

He nodded miserably. "Porter's an old pal of Allison's. She asked him to take me on. He did it as a favor to her, but I could tell the guy had no use for me."

"Why did he let you go?" I asked.

Nick rolled his eyes. "I'm chronically late, he says. I take too long for lunch. I make too many mistakes. But the main thing, and the reason a stupid job like that could never work out for me? I need time off for auditions. I mean, *that's* my career, you know? Acting. Not inventorying his damn hockey sticks and crap. He could never get that through his thick skull. Neither could Allison."

"How did Allison find out you lost your job at Vargas?" I asked.

"She called Porter. Checking up on me like I'm some kind of untrustworthy little kid," he said. "And he tells her he canned me five weeks ago."

Five weeks? The man doesn't tell his wife he's been out of work for five weeks? Not that he's untrustworthy or anything.

"So we had it out," Nick said. "Then she closed herself up in here for a while, editing pictures or whatever, and went to bed. I was still too wound up to sleep, so I stayed up for hours playing video games and getting loaded."

"And you slept in the next morning," I said.

"Yeah, till like noon, maybe a little after. She had to be at the airport by then, and I'd planned to drive her, but she didn't wake me up. She must've still been angry."

"So you assumed she got to the airport under her own steam?" I asked.

"Her car was gone," he said. "I figured she left it at one of those long-term parking places near the airport. She sometimes did that."

"But she never made it that far."

He shook his head. "After her body, you know… after she was found, the cops located her car at the nature preserve. Her luggage was in the trunk."

Obviously Allison had been on her way to the airport and decided to stop at the preserve and take a walk. "I was just talking with Porter a few minutes ago," I said. "He seems to think Allison wouldn't have taken that kind of risk. I mean, going out on the frozen lake like that without checking it for safety. What do you think? Does that sound like something she'd do?"

He shrugged. "Who knows? We didn't do stuff like that together."

"You never went hiking with her?" I asked.

"Hiking, mountain climbing, all that outdoorsy crap…" Nick lifted his glass, sucked an ice cube into his mouth, and crunched it. "It's just not my thing, you know?"

So. Unlike husband number one, Nick didn't share Allison's love of fresh air and vigorous outdoor exercise. I had to wonder what had attracted Allison to Nick. I mean, sure, he was easy on the eyes. More than easy—Nick was so handsome, it was almost painful to look at him. Could that be the whole story? I hadn't known Allison Zaleski well, but she didn't seem like the type of woman to commit her life to someone as... well, as shallow as Nick Birch.

Which wasn't really a fair assessment on my part. I knew him even less well than I'd known Allison. I was going on first impressions. Still, I like to think I'm a good judge of character. In my line of work I often have to make prompt assessments of people, particularly when the client requests some unusual or even borderline illegal service.

Perhaps her marriage to Nick could be explained simply by the fact that she was on the rebound following sudden widowhood. My curious nature sought answers, but my practical nature simply wanted this assignment to go smoothly.

I decided I'd heard enough of Nick's personal woes. I stood and lifted his empty glass. "Can I bring you another one of these?" It would be a watered-down refill if he took me up on the offer.

He pushed his fingers through his honey-colored hair. "No. Thanks. I'll get back in there in a minute." He waved me away.

More people had arrived while I'd been sequestered with the young widower. Friends and relatives of Allison's now mingled in small groups throughout the first floor. Kari was in the living room, collecting dirty dishes. I took the tray from her and held it while she piled it with plates, glasses, and flatware.

A large palm caressed my back. I knew who it was even before I looked over my shoulder. My ex-husband, Dom Faso, gave me a warm smile and a kiss on the cheek. He was a couple of inches over six feet, with dark, wavy hair and bottomless espresso eyes—not classically handsome, but bristling with sex appeal. At least I'd always thought so.

"Here, Janey, let me help you with that." He tried to take the laden tray from me, but I held on to it.

"Thanks, I've got it." *I'm not a guest here*, I wanted to tell him, but he knew that. Dom's just a nice guy and wants to help where he can.

At this point you're probably thinking we're pretty friendly for a divorced couple. It's not just me, Dom gets along great with all his ex-wives. Oh, didn't I mention? I'm just the first of three ex–Mrs. Fasos. We divorced seventeen years ago after eight months of marriage. No, come to think of it, it will be eighteen years next month. How time flies when you're miserable watching your former husband, whom you regretted leaving even before the divorce was final, cycling through two more wives and fathering three kids who should have been yours. The fact that Dom was fully aware of my misery only added to it.

Bitter? *Moi?* Whatever gave you that idea?

Martin claimed I never got over Dom, which might explain why the padre refrained from putting the moves on me. Or it might just be that he wasn't interested. Of course, he was awfully flirtatious for someone who wasn't interested. But I digress.

Just because Dom and I were the best of friends and we talked all the time and shared confidences and he still visited my parents and we'd almost kissed a few months earlier, that did not mean I was still hung up on him, despite what Martin said. What did he know?

What's that? You want me to tell you about the almost kiss? It didn't happen, that's all you need to know. I didn't let it happen because of the woman now joining Dom and placing a proprietary hand on his elbow. That particular hand, her left one, sported a blindingly sparkly diamond that irked me every time I saw it.

Just so we're clear, I fell in love with Dom when he was a poor kid trying to scrape up enough moolah to buy a food truck—the first incarnation of what would morph into the stunningly successful Janey's Place health-food restaurant chain. No, that's not true. I fell in love with Dom in eighth grade when I first set eyes on him during Mr. Bender's third-period Spanish class.

When we got married, Dom was too poor to buy me a gold band, much less a diamond. And yes, the cheap silver ring he put on my finger all those years ago is still in my jewelry box, black with tarnish.

Bonnie Hernandez and I greeted each other politely. She looked sleek and sophisticated in a formfitting navy silk dress and a string of ferociously expensive South Sea pearls—a gift from Dom, natch. Her dark hair was cut in a short, fashionable style.

I looked like what I was, the hired help, wearing my usual work uniform of gray skirt suit, white blouse, and faux pearls. *Faux* sounds so much swankier than *fake*, don't you think? Plus I was carrying a tray loaded with dirty dishes, the go-to fashion accessory for the well-put-together Death Diva. My strawberry-blond hair was trying to spring free of the French twist I'd coerced it into, and doing an admirable job of it.

I gave Bonnie a smile that oozed sincerity. Or something. "How's the new job going, Chief?"

"Just fine, thanks."

She'd recently been promoted from detective to chief of

police, following a scandal involving another detective, his buddy the then-chief, and a drunk dispatcher who happened to be the chief's mistress.

From outside, Crystal Harbor might appear to be a starched, well-mannered New York bedroom community, but we have our share of scandals, and that one was a biggie. It shook up the entire police department, leaving my ex's future missus in charge of the whole shebang.

Besides being elegant and well put together, Bonnie was young, in her early thirties, whereas I'd be facing the big four-oh in March. Of course, my age didn't seem to bother a certain hot Parisian I'd met a couple of months earlier. The thing about hot Parisians, though, is that they tend to live in Paris. Talk about geographically undesirable.

Bonnie tucked herself a little closer to her fiancé. "I was so sorry to hear about Allison." Her speech carried a hint of her native Dominican Republic.

"Did you know her?" I asked. My tray full of dirty dishes was growing heavier by the second. Why hadn't I let Dom be a gentleman and take it from me? At that moment I was at a loss.

"She had that gallery show last month in the city. That's where we met." Bonnie's gaze lit on the framed pictures on the walls. "Her work was exquisite. I tried to commission her to photograph Frederick, but apparently portraits of pets were beneath her. Oh, she didn't put it like that, but..." She shrugged. "I didn't take offense."

Frederick was Bonnie's blue-ribbon-winning standard poodle and the reason—okay, one of many reasons if I'm being honest—for Sexy Beast's inferiority complex.

"Well, I have to, um..." I indicated the tray.

"Yes, of course," she said. "Don't let us keep you."

"Help yourself to the buffet," I said, and hurried to the kitchen, where I helped Kari empty and refill the dishwasher. Maia, meanwhile, made trips through the butler's pantry to the dining room, replacing empty platters with full ones.

A young couple entered, carrying several foil-wrapped plates and a plastic deli container filled with some dark liquid. It was the pottery couple, who'd crafted all the ceramic pieces on display in this very room. I'd seen them at the funeral home and cemetery also. I greeted them and set the offerings on a counter. Whatever they'd brought, it was still warm. And it smelled heavenly.

"It's empanadas," Pottery Lady said, "with a beef filling and a dipping sauce. I hope that's okay. I didn't know the Gleasons hired a caterer." Her eyes were red-rimmed and it was clear she'd been crying. She had long blonde dreadlocks tied back with a scarf, and wore gray corduroy overalls over an ivory sweater that appeared to be handmade. A tiny gold stud adorned her nose just above one nostril.

Maia answered her. "It's more than okay. We're drowning in bakery boxes. It was so thoughtful of you to bring something homemade."

"It was Allison's favorite." Pottery Lady's voice was thick. "I used to make these for her when she came over."

Her husband—at least I assumed they were married—put his arm around her shoulder. Pottery Man was quite tall, with reddish-brown hair and a bushy beard. His hairline was trying to make a run for it, despite his youth. Both of them appeared to be in their mid to late twenties.

Maia lifted the foil on one of the plates, revealing crispy fried turnovers. "Oh, they look wonderful. I'll put them out now while they're still warm." She stacked the plates and carried them into the dining room.

I decided on total honesty. What? It's been known to happen.

"I know we've been introduced," I told the couple, "but I can never remember your names and I'm always too embarrassed to ask." They'd called me by name when we said hello, so the memory lapse only went one way.

The man smiled and tipped his thumb toward his chest. "Beau Battle." He indicated his wife. "Poppy Battle."

I tried to think of some mnemonic trick to avoid being humiliated by having to ask again. Poppy Battle… I envisioned a red flower waving a scimitar and rushing toward the enemy line. Hmm, that one might need a little work.

I said, "I get the feeling you and Allison were close."

Poppy nodded. She appeared to be controlling her grief with an effort. "She was a good friend, one of our best friends here in Crystal Harbor."

"Then you must know Skye Guthrie," I said.

"Yeah, I know Skye." Poppy left it at that. I got the feeling she wasn't a fan of Allison's best friend.

Beau said, "We should go find Joleen and Doug." His wife nodded and they went in search of Allison's parents. I figured they must indeed have been close to Allison to be on a first-name basis with her folks.

I was kept busy for the next hour getting visitors settled, helping Maia with the food and beverages, and making sure Allison's closest family members were comfortable and had everything they needed. I saw Joleen and Doug sitting near the fireplace in a quiet huddle with Poppy and Beau, ignoring the animated conversation around them. The women held hands, their eyes glistening. It was clear they were talking about

Allison, reminiscing.

Watching them, I felt my own eyes tear up. I glanced around for Skye and spied her in a corner, giggling with another young woman as she displayed something on her phone. I'd yet to see the person who was supposed to be Allison's best friend exchange one word with the grieving parents.

Sten Jakobsen had arrived a short while ago. He was a local attorney, over seventy but still practicing general law. Sten was very tall, about six four, his blond hair and trim beard gone mostly white. He was suitably dressed, as always, in a dark pinstriped suit and somber tie, wearing his ever-present wire-rimmed glasses.

I spotted him now standing alone near the dining room windows, holding a small plate with some cut fruit on it. As I watched, Nick approached him and started a conversation, gesticulating with yet another glass of vodka on the rocks. The room was too crowded and the noise level too high for me to make out their words. Nick spoke animatedly to the older man, while Sten glanced around uncomfortably as if concerned about being overheard.

I busied myself tidying the food set out on the dining table, gradually making my way closer to Nick and Sten, straining my ears for snippets of conversation.

Okay, yeah, I was curious. So sue me.

Skye Guthrie appeared just as curious, staring fixedly at the two men as she nibbled a sandwich: smoked turkey and brie on a croissant.

"… Just a hint," Nick was saying. He was smiling, mock-punching Sten's shoulder. "I'm not looking for a final number right now. Can't you just ballpark it?"

Sten kept his volume low as he leaned toward the younger man, but his signature slow, precise delivery and deep basso profundo voice helped me make out his words. "This is not the appropriate time or place to discuss it."

"Ah, come on, man, I'm dying to know—"

"Come to my office Monday morning at ten as we arranged," Sten said.

"I have a right to know." Nick was starting to get loud. Heads were turning toward them. People started whispering. "And you have no right to keep this information from me. You're her lawyer. You drafted the will. I know you know how much she left me."

Sten was a dignified person. The last thing he'd want is to cause a scene during a client's funeral reception. It was clear Nick wasn't going to wait until Monday morning to find out how rich he was. Sten set his plate on a side table. "Where can we speak privately?" he asked.

Nick looked gleeful. "That's what I'm talking about! Come on." He finished off his vodka and shoved the glass at Kari as she set out a fresh platter of grilled veggies.

Sten looked grim as he trailed the young widower through the house and down the hallway to Allison's office. The reason I know this is because, you guessed it, I kind of followed them.

Oh, like you wouldn't have done the same thing. You want to hear about this or not?

Nick closed the office door after them. Meanwhile I meandered closer, doing important Death Diva work like straightening pictures and inspecting the carpet runner for wrinkles. I heard nothing from behind the door for close to a minute, even with my ear very close to it. Okay, with my ear pressed to it.

Nick's booming voice made me jump. I heard *"No way!"* and *"That's not possible!"* and a lot of very bad words, shouted at high volume.

Skye shoved me out of the way and yanked the door open. I'd been so intent on eavesdropping, I hadn't noticed her lurking behind me. "What did he say, Nick?" she demanded, at full volume. "How much are you getting? Tell me!"

"Jane?"

I turned to see a worried-looking Joleen coming down the hallway toward me. Her husband trailed after her, along with Poppy and Beau. Meanwhile the door to the office stood open and Nick was still hollering and cursing.

"She put me in her will," he yelled. "Right after we got married. She left most of it to me."

I caught Beau's eye. "It's nothing. I'll take care of it. Why don't you just get everyone…" I flapped my hand.

He seemed to get the message. So did Poppy. The couple steered Allison's parents back toward the living room. "Jane has this under control," he told them.

Oh yeah, I thought, *I have this so under control*. I slipped inside the office and shut the door behind me. "Guys, I need you to hold it d—"

"I saw the damn will," Nick snarled, getting right in Sten's face. The lawyer didn't blink. "She showed it to me. I get two-thirds. I don't know what you're trying to pull, old man, but you won't get away with—"

"Allison recently changed her will." Sten's voice was steady, the pace of his speech as leisurely as always. I'm sure he'd handled far tougher customers in his nearly five decades of legal practice. "I am assuming you have not seen the revised version."

Nick gaped at him, his face blotchy with rage. Had I really considered this guy painfully handsome? "She cut me out? I don't believe it. Allison wouldn't do that. She loved me."

"He's the *husband*!" Skye screamed, her own face practically crimson. "He has *rights*!"

"Normally that would be the case," Sten drawled. "In New York a spouse has what's called a 'right of election' to one third of the estate."

Nick turned to me. "Can this guy talk any faster?"

"I don't think so," I said.

"So he gets a third," Skye said. "That's still a lot, right? I mean, Mitchell left her about twelve million bucks, right?" I could see her doing the math in her head.

If you're wondering why Skye cared so much about Nick's inheritance, what her stake was in all this, then all I can say is, you're pretty slow on the uptake. I figured it out right away, just listening to the two of them harangue Sten. I mean, think about it. What would prompt a wife to cut her husband out of her will? What's the first thing that pops into your head? Oh, come on, the darn thing's waving sparklers and screaming into a megaphone.

Now you're getting it. And with her best friend, no less.

"A third's better than nothing," Nick said. "I can live with a third."

"I said *normally* a spouse is entitled to that amount," Sten said. "A spouse can choose to forfeit the right to inherit."

"Well, I don't choose to forfeit anything," Nick said with a smirk. "Why would I do that?"

"You already did it," Sten said, "when you signed your antenuptial agreement before the wedding."

Nick frowned in confusion. "My ante-*what*? What are you talking about?"

Sten switched to the less lawyerly term. "Your prenuptial agreement."

Skye wheeled on Nick. "You signed a *prenup*?"

"No, wait a minute." Nick raised his hands as if to forestall the inevitable. "That was just a formality, you know? Like, if we got divorced I couldn't take all her money."

"That prenup," Sten said, "included a waiver of your right of election. Allison was under no legal obligation to leave you any of her assets."

"You idiot!" Skye shoved Nick's chest, hard. "You slipped up. She found out about us."

"No! I never said a word. There's no way she could have known."

"Wake up, Nick!" Skye got right in his face. "She was going to divorce you."

"No way! Allison loved me." Uncertainty turned the statement into a whine. He turned to his late wife's lawyer. "Is it true? Did Allison want a divorce?"

Sten said, "Anything I discuss with my clients is confid—"

"Tell me!" Nick cried. "I have a right to know."

Sten remained silent, his expression stoical.

It was answer enough. Nick's eyes bulged. A vein throbbed in his temple. I tensed, ready to throw myself at him if he went after the older man. "I was tricked into signing that prenup," he said, spittle flying. "I want to see that thing right now."

"You have your own copy," Sten said. "If you'll recall, you did not see the need to engage a separate attorney to protect your rights. However, I insisted you do so, specifically to forestall a future challenge to its legality. Does any of this sound familiar, Nick? We are talking about events that occurred only four months ago."

"Then my lawyer was incompetent," Nick blustered. "I'm going to get this thing overturned."

Skye stabbed a finger at Sten's chest while he stood tall and sober. "And then we're going to sue your sorry ass. You're going to lose your license to practice law. When you pull slimy crap like this, there are *consequences!*"

Nick pulled her to him, wrapped his arm protectively around her shoulders. "Don't get so worked up, bunny," he told her. "Think about the baby."

This just kept getting better and better.

Oh, please. With everything these two were throwing at Sten, I wasn't allowed to get my snark on? Not even a little? Boy, are you strict.

"Your attorney was perfectly competent," Sten told Nick. "The document was fully explained to you, and you expressed comprehension of its contents. Naturally, you are free to pursue a challenge, but it would be expensive and you would lose."

Skye threw off Nick's arm as if his touch revolted her. "So who did she leave it all to?" she demanded.

"The beneficiaries have yet to be notified," Sten said. "Until they are, I have no intention of divulging—"

She interrupted him with a savage curse and flung open the door, startling a gaggle of eavesdroppers, who leapt back as one.

"Bunny," Nick pleaded, "stay here with me. I need y—"

"*Go to hell!*" She shoved past the gawkers and sprinted down the hallway.

3

A Fungi to Guess Passwords With

THAT NIGHT I GOT ready for bed around eleven o'clock but realized I was too wound up from the events of the day to go to sleep. I tied the sash of my fuzzy yellow robe and padded back downstairs in my slippers. Sexy Beast followed me, grumbling. He's a creature of habit and believes in retiring punctually at a civilized hour every night. But his strong pack instinct won't let him sleep alone while his alpha female is rattling around downstairs, getting into all sorts of mischief and risking attack by whatever beasts and intruders he imagines might crawl through the window in his absence.

In the kitchen I poured myself a small shot of excellent añejo tequila, a gift from Martin during the summer when he'd been trying to talk me into letting him bunk at my place for a while. Okay, that's not strictly accurate. By the time I'd discovered his intentions, he'd already moved in. The insanely expensive tequila had been intended as both a distraction and a bribe. If I tell you it worked, will you think less of me?

You were supposed to say no.

And for the record, the padre had slept in the first-floor maid's room and never once tried to slip into the master bedroom. I would have been ready if he had. You may take that any way you want.

"Cheers, SB." I took the first small sip and shivered as a trail of golden heat streaked down my gullet. Sexy Beast emitted a snort of disapproval. He can be so prissy sometimes.

Suddenly I remembered the mushroom-shaped salt shaker Allison's mom had given me. My purse sat on the granite kitchen island. I rooted around in it, located the little piece of pottery, and unwrapped it. It looked even prettier and more distinctive by itself, away from the rest of Allison's pottery collection.

Well, no reason not to use the shaker for its intended purpose. I retrieved the cylindrical box of salt from a cabinet and pried the small cork from the bottom of the shaker. That's when I got my first surprise.

Stuck to the inside surface of the cork was a blob of soft putty, the kind people use to attach posters to walls. The end of a small metal object was stuck into the putty. I peered closely at it, turned it this way and that. It appeared to be a flash drive. Jeez, these things were getting smaller all the time. This one was just over an inch long.

I plucked the flash drive off the putty, which had kept it from rattling around in the shaker. I'd have to call Joleen in the morning and arrange to get it back to her.

I set the little object down on the granite and stared at it. For a long time. Yep, that's what I'd do, all right, return this thing to Allison's parents pronto. No matter who ended up inheriting her belongings under her revised will, it rightly belonged to them and, based on the pains their daughter had taken to hide it, probably contained information of a personal nature.

I certainly wasn't going to insert this flash drive into my

computer and check out the contents. That would be a violation of Allison's privacy. Right?

I picked up the tiny thing and turned it in my fingers. I set it back down. On the other hand, it was entirely possible the contents of this drive might be shocking or hurtful to her folks. I mean, it could be anything. Did Joleen and Doug really need to see, I don't know, their daughter's sex tapes? Not that she'd seemed the type, but what did I know? I'd met the woman precisely twice.

Her parents had hired me to assist with the funeral arrangements and stuff. Okay, I just added that *and stuff.* There was nothing in our agreement about *stuff.* But I felt an ethical and moral obligation to minimize the pain they were going through in any way I could. It was another part of that Death Diva code of honor I mentioned earlier.

An unwritten code of honor can really come in handy at times like this.

And yes, I was curious as hell, but that wasn't the only reason I carried the little device into the maid's room, which I'd turned into a sort of cozy office. I turned on the floor lamp. The room contained a daybed, an overstuffed chair, and a small antique lady's desk, currently occupied by my laptop computer.

Without giving myself time to reconsider, I sat at the desk, opened the computer, and inserted Allison's flash drive into one of the USB ports in the side of the machine.

A window popped up, demanding a password. I muttered a naughty word. Well, of course she would have password-protected the drive. After all, she'd gone to the trouble of hiding the thing in a darn salt shaker.

I leaned back, drummed my fingers on the desk. That was

it, then. I'd scarcely known the owner of this drive. There was no way I could guess her password.

My fingers stopped drumming. But I knew someone who might be able to. Hadn't the padre deduced my own computer password last spring when he'd let himself into the nasty little basement apartment I'd been living in back then?

No, I hadn't given him a key! I'd just met the man, for heaven's sake. Back then I didn't know about the adorable set of lock picks he never left home without.

And yeah, so my password had been my wedding anniversary. Pitifully easy to guess. What's that you say? You chose your anniversary as your password after having been divorced for how many years? It's just that I'm sentimental, that's all. I already told you, I'm not still hung up on Dom. I mean, he's getting married again, right? For the fourth time! How could I possibly still be hung up on him?

Okay, you know what? Let's move on to something else. Like what the heck is on this flash drive. I was curious before I'd tried to peek at the contents. Now that I'd been presented with an impregnable roadblock in the form of a password, I was *rabidly* curious.

I'd left my cell phone on my nightstand. I sprinted upstairs for it, a process that took longer than you might think, considering the size of my house: five bedrooms, six and a half bathrooms, home theater, gym, et cetera. It was your basic mini mansion, squatting on five of the most exclusive and expensive acres on Long Island.

If you're wondering how I could afford such luxurious accommodations after having lived in the aforementioned basement apartment in a working-class neighborhood far from this rarefied burg, the answer is, I couldn't afford it. Irene

McAuliffe left me the house in her will. Or more accurately, she left it to Sexy Beast during his lifetime, after which the property would be mine. And she asked me to be his guardian, which meant I got to live there with him. What can I tell you? That was Irene. She also left enough money to maintain the property, but I still had to work for a living. Overall, not a bad deal.

I called Martin as I resumed my seat in front of the computer, setting the phone to speaker and placing it on the desk near me.

"How'd the funeral go?" he asked by way of greeting.

"You missed the fireworks," I told him. "It turns out Allison disinherited the boy toy she married a few months ago."

"I heard. He was banging the bestie."

"Are you at work?" I asked. "Sounds like it." I heard a hum of voices in the background, conversation and laughter. Martin tended bar at Murray's Pub, a popular local watering hole that had been a Crystal Harbor fixture since the late nineteenth century. No doubt it was hopping on this Saturday night. He lived in the apartment over the bar.

"Hold on a sec." I heard him take someone's order for a Manhattan and a glass of Pinot Noir.

I said, "Well, did you hear—"

"That the boy toy and the bestie are looking forward to a blessed event?" he said.

I wasn't surprised the news had gotten back to Martin. Even before he started tending bar at Murray's, he'd had a way of knowing everything that went on in town. I said, "Listen, I need your help with something."

"I get off at two," he said. "Wear that green lace teddy."

He knew about the teddy? I'd bought it ages ago. It still had the tags on. I'd get to use it one of these days. Or nights, rather. And yeah, the padre was an irrepressible flirt. I think you've learned that by now. As for his knowing the contents of my closet, well, the infuriating man came and went as he pleased. Remember that set of lockpicks? I'd gotten used to it. Well, sort of.

"I need you to crack a password," I said.

"For what?" He didn't sound at all surprised. I wasn't sure how I felt about that.

"A flash drive."

"Whose flash drive?" he said.

"Allison Zaleski."

He didn't hesitate. "Did she have a pet?"

"Just the new husband," I said.

"Try his name."

I typed *Nick* into the little box and hit Enter. "That's not it," I said.

"Try all lowercase and all caps."

I did. "Nada. Let me try the first husband, Mitchell. He was the, you know, *real* husband." That one didn't work either.

"Did she have any kids?" the padre asked.

"Nope."

"I assume you've tried password?" he asked.

"That's why I called you," I said.

"No, I mean the word *password*," he said. "You'd be surprised how many people use that as their password."

"For real?" I tried it. "No."

"Welcome," Martin said. After a few moments he said, "Jane? You still there?"

"I thought you were talking to a customer. You want me to try the word *welcome*?" I asked.

"Yep. And *qwerty*."

"What?"

He spelled it. "The first six letters on your keyboard. That's another common one."

"Nope. Maybe she was too smart for these obvious passwords." It was probably some completely random and unguessable combination of letters, numbers, and symbols.

"There are a few more we can try," he said. "What kind of car did she drive?"

"I don't know. I never went into her garage."

"Favorite movie?" The sound of rattling ice in the background. "Color? Hobby?"

I perked up. "Photography. She was a serious shutterbug."

"Try any words associated with that," he said. "*Camera, snapshot*, stuff like that."

After we'd exhausted photography-related words, Martin made a bunch of other suggestions, including obvious strings of numbers and, yes, her birthday and wedding anniversaries, which I didn't happen to know.

"I can come around tomorrow," he offered, "see what I can do."

"Thanks, but don't bother. Maybe it's just as well. I really shouldn't be snooping like this."

"That's a joke, right?" he said.

After I hung up, I sat staring at the screen and that tormenting little password prompt. "Come on, Allison, talk to me," I muttered. "What are some of your favorite things?" This line of thinking installed that song from *The Sound of Music* in my cranium. I shook my head vigorously, determined to keep it from turning into an earworm.

I kept at it, trying her parents' names, the words *pottery* and *ceramics*, and all the words I'd already tried in combination with numbers, including her street address. I knew it was a losing battle, knew I should go to bed and start fresh in the morning, but at that point I was too invested to stop.

What were some of her favorite photographic subjects? I thought of her nature shots. The picture of white mushrooms growing on a fallen log popped into my head. It wasn't the only photo of mushrooms adorning the walls of her home. I thought of the little ceramic mushroom that had concealed the flash drive. What was it Joleen had said? Allison had loved mushrooms.

I typed in *mushroom*, singular and plural. Nothing. All caps. All lowercase. I tried tacking on *123*, her street address, and other alphanumeric combinations. Was there another word for *mushroom*? *Fungus*, I typed, and *fungi*. Another one came to me. I typed *shrooms*.

Bingo. I was in.

It took a moment for my mind to register it. My fingers hovered over the keyboard, frozen in place, as if one wrong move could undo what I'd worked so hard to accomplish. "I don't believe it," I breathed.

I was looking at a list of files contained on the flash drive, a couple of dozen of them. The file extension indicated they were videos. A stab of alarm shot through me. *Please don't let these be sex tapes*, I mentally pleaded. But I'd come too far to abandon this project without even checking them out. Within seconds I was viewing the first video, dated the previous June.

At first I saw only an upholstered chair, the same easy chair Nick had occupied earlier that day in Allison's office. Then I saw a female figure from the back as she moved from the camera to the chair and sat on it, tucking her feet under her. It was Allison Zaleski. She wore a summer nightgown. Her hair was pulled back in a ponytail. Her lovely face, free of makeup, appeared sad, almost drawn.

At first she simply stared into the camera lens. As the seconds dragged on, I sensed her mental struggle. She didn't know how to begin. Finally she said, "I can only do this if I'm talking to you, Jim. You're the only one I was ever able to open up to. Even Mitchell…" She looked away briefly as if fighting to govern her emotions.

When she once more faced the camera, she said, "I buried him three weeks ago today. I never thought I'd find someone to love, I mean truly love, after you. Please don't be jealous. If I hadn't lost you so long ago… well, the whole trajectory of my life would've been different, wouldn't it?"

I knew I should turn off the video at this point. Allison no doubt meant for this to be kept private. She certainly hadn't meant for me to view it. I can't say why I felt compelled to continue watching. My motive wasn't voyeurism. As soon as she'd started speaking, I felt an undeniable connection.

"Mitchell's daughter, Brenda…" Allison shook her head sadly. "I tried so hard with her. She and Mitchell had been estranged since he divorced her mother. She blamed him, of course. This is going back decades. I thought I could help heal the rift. Brenda and Lou have three kids, and Mitchell barely knew them, barely knew his own grandchildren."

I thought about Brenda Yates, whom I'd met earlier at the reception. We'd engaged in a little small talk. Brenda was a part-time bookkeeper for a group of doctors. I sensed she hated the job. She and Lou had three kids, all under the age of eight.

"I managed to get them together a few times," Allison said. "Birthdays, Christmas, that sort of thing. Mitchell was hopeful at first, that he could finally have a relationship with his daughter, his grandchildren. Brenda, though, she just kept this wall up, accused him of trying to buy her children's affection with presents. God knows what she was telling the kids about us when we weren't around. They never did warm to him. Or to me, but that would take a miracle, considering how Brenda feels about me."

Allison gave an incredulous shake of the head. "You're not going to believe this, Jim. She thinks I killed him. Brenda thinks I murdered her father."

My heart banged. This was taking an ugly turn.

"We were hiking in this gorgeous forest upstate." Her voice was husky with emotion. "Mitchell… he wanted me to take his picture in front of this steep ravine. It would have been a spectacular shot—the trees, the stream. The sky was startlingly blue. I was about to take the picture when he backed up suddenly. He must not have realized how close he was to the edge. He lost his footing and—" She broke off, with her hand over her mouth.

My eyes filled. What a horrible way to lose your spouse.

As I watched, Allison composed herself. "Brenda claims I pushed him. She even tried to get the police involved. The way she sees it, I married a much older man for his money. Mind you, she didn't concoct this accusation until after she found out he left everything to me. Although how she could've expected to inherit anything after pushing him away for more than twenty years is a mystery." She looked pensive. "His grandchildren, though, they had nothing to do with that."

Allison was silent for a minute. I watched her expression

gradually soften. "There's this guy. No, that doesn't sound right. He's not… It's not like that. Not so soon after… He's just this sweet guy I met while taking pictures at this old-timey restoration village. It's a bunch of old buildings that were all moved to one location. They have a few houses, a general store, a church, a one-room schoolhouse, that kind of thing. They hire people to dress in Colonial clothes and work in the village."

I knew the place she was talking about. It was a popular destination for families with young children.

"He plays the blacksmith," Allison said with a little smile. "He's good at it. I mean, he learned how to forge iron and everything. He was making a horseshoe. It was really hot in that little blacksmith shop." An embarrassed smile. "All right, so I'm a sucker for a good-looking guy sweating over a coal fire. Not that it's like that," she repeated. "Nick is just a friend, a sweet guy, like I said. He understands my pain. I can talk to him. If the situation were different, if I weren't grieving, then maybe there could be something more."

And yet Allison had ended up marrying this "sweet, understanding guy" a mere three months after making this video.

"Please don't be jealous, Jim." She took a deep breath, her eyes glistening as she stared straight into the camera lens. "I don't know why I say that. It's not like you could ever see this video. There isn't a day you've been gone that I haven't thought about you. I still miss you so much."

Allison kissed her fingertips and extended them toward the camera lens, her eyes welling. Then she got up and approached the camera. The video ended.

4

Drinking Out of Tiny Cups

BRASS BELLS TINKLED as I entered Crystal Harbor Ceramics, which was located on Main Street next to Janey's Place, the flagship store of Dom's health-food empire. I held the door for Nina Wallace, who was exiting with one of those ginormous baby strollers that cost more than my car.

You think I'm kidding. I have little doubt Nina paid more for her infant's luxury conveyance than I did for my used—excuse me, pre-owned—Mazda sedan. Poppy Battle hovered behind her, wincing as she watched her wedge the huge thing through the doorway. Six-week-old Laura lay oblivious and adorable inside her cushy chariot, bundled against the cold in a nest of pink cashmere and shielded from the light snow flurries by a clear plastic stroller cover.

Nina and I offered each other brief, polite greetings. Outwardly she was the very epitome of the affluent suburban matron: mother of three, president of the Crystal Harbor Historical Society, always elegant and well put together. But scratch the surface and you'd find questionable behavior and even more questionable values. She was far from my favorite person, and I knew darn well the feeling was mutual.

It was Monday afternoon, six days since I'd discovered

Allison Zaleski in that frozen lake. Stepping into the pottery studio was like entering another world. Welcome warmth enveloped me. An earthy, spicy scent pervaded the space, thanks to a little incense burner in the corner. Exotic hangings adorned the whitewashed brick walls. The handcrafted wares were displayed on a variety of antique furniture: bookcases, dressers, desks, even a church pew.

"Nina insisted on pushing that huge stroller through the whole place," Poppy said. "Nearly took out a tea set and a stack of plates."

"The proverbial bull in a china shop."

"And then she didn't even buy anything." She leaned in toward the straw bucket tote that hung from my shoulder. "Well, hello there, cutie."

Sexy Beast's ride was a lot more humble than baby Laura's. I took him everywhere in that tote. Poppy gave him scritches and was rewarded with licks. He whined to be let out.

"Do you mind?" I asked her.

She lifted him herself and set him on the floor, which was covered with a variety of antique rugs. "How much trouble can a little guy like this get into?"

Oh, you'd be surprised. On the other hand, a seven-pound poodle would have his work cut out for him even reaching the goods on display, so I figured it was a risk worth taking.

Poppy's overalls today were patched blue denim, which she'd paired with a red sweater. "What's his name?"

"Sexy Beast."

"Cool," she said. "Is he named for the movie?"

"He sure is." I was impressed. Most people didn't make the connection. "His first owner was a film buff."

Poppy spread her arms, indicating the handmade

merchandise. "Are you looking for anything in particular?"

"To be honest, I wanted to ask you something. It's about Allison. I know you were close."

Her expression sobered. It was easy to see she was taking her friend's death hard. She turned and gestured for me to follow her. "Do you like tea? I have every kind of herbal. I might have a little something for Sexy Beast, too."

"Hear that, SB? Treats!"

That was a word he knew. He willingly stuck by my side as I trailed Poppy to the back of the store, where there was a small round table with four chairs. I appreciated her offer, but to me, herbal tea is another way of saying potpourri soup. "Nothing for me, thanks," I said, shucking my cream-colored anorak and draping it over the chairback. "I'm a coffee drinker."

"Give me half a minute," she said. "I have some cold-brew concentrate. The kettle's already hot. Sit."

Sexy Beast and I obeyed in unison as Poppy disappeared into what I assumed was some kind of break room, leaving the door open. I knew the actual studio, where the pieces were crafted, was located at the back of the building, along with a kiln. The Battles gave pottery classes there, and other artists paid them to fire their work.

I heard muted conversation and a moment later Beau emerged and greeted me. His plaid flannel shirt and white painter's pants were spattered and streaked with gray-brown clay. There was even some in his beard.

I said, "Nice day for mud-wrestling."

He grinned, gesturing to his begrimed clothing. "Like it? Potter chic. The latest craze." He pulled up a dainty, needlepoint-upholstered chair and sat, which posed no risk to the chair since the mess was confined to his front. "Poppy said you had a question about Allison."

"I thought you guys would be the best people to ask," I said. "Well, except for Skye, but she's kind of... distracted at the moment."

Poppy called from the other room, "Skye Guthrie? Why would you ask her about Allison?"

"They were best friends," I said, and watched Beau's left eyebrow rise. "Weren't they? That's what Porter Vargas told me."

"Probably because that's what *Skye* told *him*," he said. "She liked to spread it around that they were tight, but the truth was, she met Allison at some party about a year ago and latched on to her like chewing gum. Allison could never shake her off. She was too nice."

"That's about the size of it," Poppy called from beyond the doorway. "Cream? Sugar?"

It took me a second to realize she was asking how I take my coffee. "Oh, nothing," I said. "Just black."

She entered carrying an old-fashioned hammered aluminum tray, which she set on the table. SB, who'd been lying quietly at my feet, perked up. He couldn't see the contents of the tray, but he could smell them, far more accurately than we mere humans could.

"Such a good, patient boy!" Poppy exclaimed. She tilted a small pottery bowl toward me. It held a little chicken, cut into tiny pieces. "Is this okay for him?"

"As long as it's not spicy," I said. "You'll have an adoring slave for life."

SB gobbled up the chicken in about two seconds and whined for more. I declined Poppy's offer of a refill.

"Sorry, kiddo," I told him, "you've had enough." Yeah,

that's just what I needed to endear me to this nice young couple: my dog barfing on their carpet. I took a sip of coffee. It was very hot and very good, perfect on a frosty day like this. "So Allison just kind of tolerated Skye?" I plucked an oatmeal cookie off a charmingly irregular ceramic plate.

Poppy nodded. "I think there was some hero worship going on."

"You mean like the hair?" I thought of Skye's dyed black tresses, cut in the same style as her friend's.

"Plus she emulated the way Allison dressed," Poppy said, "in her own low-rent way. If Allison bought a particular wine, or raved about some movie, Skye was all over it. It's like she was trying to remake herself in her friend's image."

"What does she do?" I asked. "I mean, you know, for a living."

"Works part-time in a cell-phone store." Poppy shrugged. "If she has any other source of income, I don't know about it."

"Skye stole a lot more than Allison's sense of style." Beau stirred honey into tea the color of spoiled cranberry juice. "She didn't get knocked up on her own."

The affair and Skye's pregnancy were public knowledge at this point. Word had spread at the speed of light following that brouhaha during the funeral reception.

"What was it you wanted to ask us?" Poppy said.

"It's about someone Allison used to... well, an old friend of hers. Or maybe more than a friend. Did she ever talk to you about someone named Jim?"

Wordlessly the couple consulted each other. They shook their heads. Beau said, "I can't recall her ever mentioning anyone by that name. Why?"

I was ready for this. Which isn't to say I didn't feel rotten lying to them. It was a white lie, but still. "A couple of people at the funeral asked where Jim was. I figured he might be someone important, that maybe he should be, you know, notified about her death." There had been a couple of references in her videos to the two of them having attended high school together.

I asked myself why I was here, pumping these people for information. After all, I'd hardly known Allison. What right did I have to the intimate details of their dead friend's life? I'll admit I was more curious than I had a right to be, but I couldn't help it. In the day and a half since I'd discovered Allison's flash drive, I'd viewed the first ten video diary entries, and I was beginning to develop a strong emotional connection to her. She'd held nothing back when making the videos. And okay, so they were apparently meant for her eyes only, as a sort of catharsis, I suppose, or self-therapy, but it's as if she were speaking directly to me rather than to the mysterious Jim, who I suspected had died a long time ago.

I was watching the videos in order. The last one I'd viewed had been made in September. I hadn't yet gotten to Allison's discovery that her new husband and her friend were having an affair. What I *had* seen was Allison falling for, and marrying, a sexy younger man shortly after her husband's death. *Don't do it*, I wanted to shout. *You're too emotionally fragile to make a life-altering decision like that.*

Sten had apparently agreed. He'd insisted that Allison have her bridegroom sign a prenuptial agreement. The document dictated that Nick would not be entitled to alimony in the event of divorce and that he relinquished any right to inherit. She'd balked at first, pointing out that her wealthy first husband hadn't demanded a prenup, but Sten had been persistent and eventually she'd let him craft the document. Nick had signed it without much fuss and, yes, after consulting his own lawyer.

I learned other things from the videos. I learned that Allison had grown up poor in some dinky West Texas town and had moved to Massapequa, Long Island, with her parents at age fourteen. She'd been insecure and unpopular and it had been a tough transition.

I learned that Allison and Mitchell had wanted children. It's why they'd bought that big old house. When she'd failed to become pregnant, she'd consulted a specialist and begun fertility treatments. This was in the late spring, right before Mitchell's tragic death.

In the videos I'd viewed thus far, Allison had made only one or two references to Skye. That alone should have told me they weren't as tight as Skye claimed.

Allison touched me, it's as simple as that. In many ways she reminded me of myself, not least because of her unfulfilled desire for children. I was certain that, given the chance, she and I could've been good friends.

Poppy said, "You should ask Allison's parents about this Jim. I'll bet they know who he is."

"It's not that important," I said. "I don't want to bother them with this after all they've been through." Which was true. Also, the Gleasons would certainly want to know which funeral-goers had been asking about Jim, which was not a question I cared to dance around.

Naturally, Poppy's next words were, "Who was asking about this Jim?"

I began mentally dusting off my dancing shoes but was saved by the bell.

No, seriously, the brass bells hanging on the door of the

shop chose that moment to jangle. Beau hurriedly rose and headed for the front of the store. The reason for his haste became apparent when I spied Norman Butterwick. Norman was well into his nineties, with a head of thick white hair and a dapper sense of style. He always carried one of his collection of antique walking sticks, with which he tended to gesticulate enthusiastically. Which wasn't normally a problem, but in this particular instance we were back to that bull-in-a-china-shop thing. Beau kept a sharp eye on the cane as he helped Norman choose a gift for his granddaughter's birthday.

Poppy leaned toward me conspiratorially. "Thank God Allison moved fast to change her will. Can you imagine if she hadn't? That bastard would have inherited everything."

"Two-thirds of everything, according to Nick," I said, "which is still a bundle. She must have known about him and Skye. When did she find out about the affair?" I asked.

"Just a couple of weeks ago, but she figured it had been going on the whole time they were married, if not before." Poppy had lowered her voice to keep from being overheard by Norman, though I doubted his ancient ears were up to the task of eavesdropping. Then again, he was the most youthful nonagenarian I knew, despite a short-term memory that refused to play nice. There was nothing wrong with his long-term memory, however.

"She caught them at it," Poppy said.

"Seriously?" I winced, thinking how horrible that must've been for Allison, remembering her giddy excitement in the videos as she talked about the new man in her life, how much she was coming to care for Nick. How sweet he was to her, how understanding of her grief and her need for time to come to terms with it. Well, not too much time as it turned out. Sweet, sensitive Nick had managed to snag a very wealthy wife when she was still reeling from the loss of a man she truly loved, a man who, despite the age difference, had by all accounts been her soulmate.

"Allison came home early from one of her adventure trips." Poppy sipped her tea, which was a pale straw color and smelled like perfume. "She'd wanted to surprise him. She's the one who got the surprise. They were out on the back porch, in the hot tub. Really going at it."

"What did they do once their coitus was interruptus?" I asked.

"Oh, they never knew she was there. She saw them through the kitchen window. She quietly left the house and came back when he was expecting her."

"Well, I give her credit for self-restraint," I said. "No way would I have been that calm and collected."

"That was her way," Poppy said. "She saw the big picture. Confronting them right then and there might have felt good at the moment, but it would've tipped her hand."

"And given him time to regroup, to try to turn things around." I imitated a whiny wayward spouse. "'She means nothing to me, honey. It'll never happen again.'"

Poppy nodded. "Allison was a chess player. She had an organized mind. To her it made more sense to work behind the scenes and quickly do what needed to be done—a kind of surgical strike—than to let the whole thing blow up with drama and accusations and pleading and all that messy stuff."

Okay, maybe Allison and I weren't as similar as I had thought. Messy stuff is my bread and butter. Messy stuff has a way of tracking me down, bitch-slapping the heck out of me, and forcing me to play by its rules.

"Come on." I rose. "Let's go say hi to Norman."

As we approached the front of the store I heard the old

man say, in his strong, patrician voice, "Sarah likes to drink things out of tiny cups. Espresso, sake, that sort of thing."

"Well," Beau said, "we have plenty of things like that, or we can make something to her specifications."

"Oh. I didn't think of that. Perhaps a gift certificate, then?" Norman noticed me and we hugged. I lifted Sexy Beast so he could pet him. I knew what his next words would be. I'd heard them countless times, though I'm sure he didn't realize he was repeating himself.

"This isn't a dog," he said in his teasing way. "Father had a dog back in the late thirties that would have put this little fellow to shame. Her name was Candy. Splendid English setter, white with liver ticking. Best gun dog I ever knew. And so sweet-tempered. Well, I doubt the grouse thought so."

SB, accustomed to being unfavorably compared to "real" dogs, emitted a resigned grumble.

Poppy turned to Norman. "Would you like some tea and cookies?"

"No, thank you, dear," he said. "I can't stay long."

"I can bring a chair over for you," she said.

He waved away the suggestion. "Not necessary, but I appreciate the offer."

"So," she said, "you want to buy a gift certificate."

He looked surprised. "I do?"

"That's what you said," I reminded him.

"Oh, yes, of course. I recall now," he lied.

"How much?" Beau asked.

"Five hundred should do it," Norman said.

The Battles shot each other wide-eyed looks. "Wow. Okay," Poppy said.

"You must really love your granddaughter," Beau observed.

"Who?"

"Your granddaughter?" he said. "You're here to get her a birthday present? She likes pottery? And, uh, drinking things out of little cups?"

Norman frowned in concentration, and I could almost hear Beau wondering if he'd just blown a five-hundred-dollar sale. The old man produced his cell from the breast pocket of a tweed sport jacket that had probably been custom-made for him half a century before smart phones were invented.

He jabbed at the screen with a gnarled forefinger. "My great-grandson Jason put a note-taking 'app' on this gadget." And yes, he gave "app" air quotes. "No, I stand corrected. It was Evan who did that. Jason put that evil-clown game on it. Terribly clever. One battles the clowns with shotguns, grenade launchers, what have you. The higher one's ranking, the more bizarre and deadly the weaponry." He pointed his finger at SB and made *pew-pew-pew* shooting noises. The dog yawned. "I must admit I'm quite addicted. Ah, here it is."

The rest of us exchanged guarded glances. Was Norman going to stand there all afternoon slaying evil clowns? I snuck a peek at his phone's screen. Happily, I saw the note-taking app, set to a list of names and dates.

"What is today's date?" he asked.

"January thirteenth," I said.

"Yes, then it's Sarah's birthday coming up." He pocketed the phone and slid a credit card out of his wallet. "She loves handmade ceramics. And drinking out of tiny cups."

"I'll fill in the gift certificate." Poppy took his credit card and started toward the back of the store. "Five hundred, you said, right?"

"Make it a thousand," Norman said.

She skidded to a halt. "Are you sure?"

Beau gave his wife a pointed look. *The man wants a*

thousand-dollar gift certificate, his look said. *We do not question thousand-dollar gift certificates.*

"Why?" Norman asked. "Too stingy, you think?"

Poppy made a strangled sound as she groped for a response.

"It sounds perfect to me," I said, and made shooing motions to Poppy. As heir to the KrunchWorks snack-food empire, Norman was worth tens of millions. And he was expert at managing his fortune, a skill acquired long ago at his daddy's knee and unaffected by any lapse in short-term memory.

While waiting for Poppy to return, we chatted about Norman's artwork, which was currently on display at the local library. The old man was a gifted painter. His landscapes were in high demand.

"Are you into the barter economy at all?" Beau asked him.

"I'm not familiar with that concept," Norman said, "but it sounds most intriguing."

"It's basically what it sounds like. You barter with someone for goods and services and leave the green stuff out of it. I'm totally into bartering—like maybe one of your paintings for some of my pottery?"

Norman thought about that a moment. "But then, how does one calculate sales tax and income tax on such a transaction? The IRS must have some opinions on this barter economy."

"Uh…" Beau had no ready answer for that. I happened to know from experience that the IRS did indeed want their cut when you exchanged, say, a professional-mourner gig—don't judge me!—for a half-dozen mani-pedis.

"Okay, well," Beau said, "it's just something to, uh, keep in mind for the future."

Poppy returned with a gift box, beautifully wrapped. "I

tucked the gift certificate in with a set of demitasse cups that I think your granddaughter will like. I hope that's all right."

Norman paused in the act of signing the credit card receipt. "Well, let me pay you for the cups, dear."

"I wouldn't think of it," she said. "Do let her know we'd be happy to make her something special."

We said our goodbyes and Beau held the door open for the old man. It was snowing in earnest now. Fortunately, Norman's driver had managed to park right outside the store. We watched as he ushered his employer into the nice warm vehicle and drove off.

"That's the way to get around." Poppy turned to her husband. "Where's *my* chauffeur?"

"Keep those thousand-dollar sales coming," he said, "and who knows what's in our future?"

I said, "Maybe you can barter pottery for driving."

"We bartered with Allison," Poppy said. "We needed someone to take pictures of our pieces, someone who really knew what they were doing."

"For our portfolio," Beau added, "and our website. She was our official photographer, I guess you'd say."

"I've been to your site," I said. "The photography is outstanding. Which isn't surprising. I saw some of Allison's pictures in her home. She was extremely talented."

"She never went anywhere without a camera," he said. "I mean, a real one, not just her phone. She had a bunch of them."

Poppy said, "We never could have afforded a photographer of Allison's caliber, and she loved our work, so the swap was a win-win."

So that's how Allison ended up with all that pottery—through bartering with the Battles. "And I'm sure the IRS got a piece of the action," I teased.

Beau winked. "There's a mug set with your name on it if you promise not to squeal on us."

The brass bells tinkled and we turned to see Joleen Gleason enter the store. "It's really starting to come down out there," she said in her homey Texas accent before exchanging greetings with us. I was still holding Sexy Beast. Joleen went through the motions of patting his fuzzy little cap of hair, but you can tell when someone's not a dog person. She was just doing it to be polite. She accepted Poppy's offer of tea and we all settled around the table in back. I reached into my tote bag for a dog biscuit, which SB happily gnawed while Beau brought out more cookies for the rest of us.

"You look very nice today," Poppy told Allison's mother, who'd removed her snow-dusted coat to reveal a businesslike gray dress and pumps. Not the most practical footwear, considering the weather.

"We were at the lawyer's earlier," Joleen said.

"Sten Jakobsen?" I asked.

She nodded and sipped her tea—regular black tea with lemon and sugar. "To discuss Allison's will."

"Oh," Poppy said. "I hope that… went all right."

"She left two-thirds of her estate to me and Doug, in the event she predeceased us." Joleen said this matter-of-factly, but I detected tension in her speech, her bearing, as if the effort to control her emotions was costing her. "She left nothing to my son-in-law," she added.

Apparently the Gleasons had inherited the portion that was originally earmarked for Nick, the result of Allison's last-minute alterations to her will.

Beau said, "I guess he'll have to move out of the house."

"We'll give him a decent amount of time to find a new

place," Joleen said. "I wanted to offer him, well, something, some money, but Doug won't hear of it."

Can you blame him? I thought, but managed to hold my tongue. Looking at Poppy and Beau, I could tell they agreed with Allison's father. Nick was a selfish loser. He'd betrayed his wife, and with someone who was supposed to be her friend. More than enough reason, in my book, to let him slink off with nothing.

I was dying to know who had inherited the other third. I didn't expect Joleen to assuage my curiosity. She and her husband both seem to be reserved, private people. I figured I'd find out soon enough, considering how fast news spread in Crystal Harbor.

Joleen set down her tea mug. "This isn't a purely social visit. I have a favor to ask."

"Anything," Beau said. "Like we told you the other day, we're here for whatever you need."

Joleen's eyes welled. "And I appreciate that more than you can know. So does Doug." She reached into her purse and produced a small leather box. It appeared old and somewhat battered. "I was going to ask you and Poppy to do this, but now that I've run into Jane, I'm thinking this would be right up her alley."

"Of course," I said. "What can I do for you, Mrs. Gleason?"

Joleen undid the little latch on the box and opened the lid, revealing an antique gold pocket watch. We all admired it, especially Beau, who lifted it out and examined it closely.

"This is awesome," he announced. "Family heirloom?"

"Yes," Joleen said, "but not my family. This watch was Mitchell's. It belonged to his great-grandfather."

We passed the watch around from hand to hand. The gold

case and the glass face were a little scratched from long use, but it was magnificent.

"Well, it's yours now," Beau said. "Would you like us to help sell it for you?"

"Oh no," Joleen said. "It wouldn't be right for us to keep it. This belongs to the Zaleski family. Mitchell has a daughter, Brenda. I want her to have it."

None of us stated what we all had to know, that Allison's late first husband and his daughter had been estranged and that he'd disinherited her. I admired Allison's parents for wanting to get this family keepsake to her despite that.

I asked, "Would you like me to deliver this to her?"

"I'd be so grateful if you would," she said. "Allison and Brenda didn't get along, and it would be, well, awkward for Doug and me to give her this. But I'm thinking a third party…"

"I'm happy to do it," I said.

"Just add it to your invoice," Joleen said, referring to the work I'd done on the day of her daughter's funeral.

"I wouldn't dream of taking payment for this," I said. When Joleen started to object, I held up my palm. "Please, Mrs. Gleason. Let me do you this small favor."

In truth, I felt guilty about Allison's video diaries. No one but me knew I had them. I doubted anyone else even knew they existed. By rights they belonged to Joleen and her husband. Someday I'd get that little flash drive to them, in the not-too-distant future when I suddenly "discovered" it in the salt shaker. But first I had to finish viewing all the videos. It was like a compulsion, an addiction. I wasn't proud, but that's how it was.

"Thank you so much, Jane." Joleen replaced the watch in its box and handed it to me. "That's a burden off my mind."

5

Losing Her Head

BRENDA GOT RIGHT down to business. "You said my father left me something?"

We were sitting in her living room, which was decorated in a bland contemporary style. Plenty of pale leather and chrome. Even the framed painting over the white mantel was boring: an abstract seascape in pale tones that echoed both the room's furnishings and the crystal sailboat that perched in front of it, as if to complete the nautical scene. The only hint of warmth was a scattering of children's toys in the corner.

It was the following morning. I'd phoned Brenda shortly after leaving the Battles' pottery studio.

"Actually," I said, "this is a gift from Allison's parents." I wanted to make that clear. If Brenda thought I was delivering something bequeathed to her by her father, she'd assume Allison had withheld it during the seven months since his death. "They thought you should have it."

I handed over the little leather box. I watched Brenda open it, watched her wary expression soften. She lifted the watch out and examined it, much as Beau had done yesterday. "This is my great-grandfather's watch," she breathed.

"Your great-great-grandfather's, I believe," I said.

She considered a moment. "You're right, I was off by a generation." She replaced the watch in its box and set it on the mirror-topped coffee table. "Please thank the Gleasons for me. No, I really should do that myself. Do you have their address?"

An old-fashioned snail-mail thank-you note. Let it never be said that Brenda Zaleski Yates neglected the social niceties. She'd politely offered me coffee when I got there, and I'd declined. It was clear neither of us wished to prolong this meeting.

"Sure, I'll give it to you." I took my phone out of my purse and located the Gleasons in my contacts. She produced a notepad and pen, and I jotted the address.

Brenda stared at it, thinking. Something was troubling her. Then again, I had the sense that something was always troubling this woman. Brenda Yates was not a happy person.

"This was very generous of Allison's parents," she said, "considering… well, considering the terms of the will. They couldn't be very happy about that."

I didn't know how to interpret her words. How could the Gleasons be unhappy about becoming instant multimillionaires? Granted, they would have preferred that their daughter had lived and that they hadn't inherited a thing from her. But displeased by the terms of the will? Why would Brenda assume that? Unless she was unaware of Allison's bequest to her parents, in which case it was not my place to enlighten her.

Brenda was studying my face. "Do you know that Allison left two thirds of her assets to her parents?" she asked.

I nodded. "That's all I know."

"She left the other third in trust to my children," she said. "I just found out yesterday."

I couldn't conceal my surprise. Brenda looked away. Spots of color stained her cheeks. "Also, she took out a million-dollar life insurance policy," she said, "naming me as beneficiary."

"That was very generous of her," I said. "How old are your children?"

"Lou Junior is eight, Meghan is six, and Ethan is three," she said. "Yesterday when I met with Mr. Jakobsen, he told me that she'd done all this—the trusts and the insurance policy—right after Dad died. Because that's what Dad would have wanted, supposedly. But I know better. She was trying to find a way to live with her guilty conscience."

Okay, I couldn't just sit there and listen to this. I said, "You can't really believe that Allison was responsible for your father's death."

She looked at me sharply. "How do you know about that?"

Oops. I'd learned about Brenda's crazy accusation from Allison's secret video diary. "Word gets around."

"How?" she said. "The cops upstate are the only ones I spoke to about it, besides… Well, no one who knows about it would have spread it around."

I did some quick cogitating. "What, you think the cops upstate aren't going to talk to the cops down here, where your father lived? And for sure they questioned people who knew Mitchell and Allison. I mean, once something like this is set in motion, well, you can't expect to keep it quiet." *Can I go now?*

Brenda shook her head, clearly disgusted by the thought of town gossips making her private business public. "The police didn't take me seriously, even though I had evidence. It was an accident, they said. As if any of those yokels could be bothered to conduct a serious investigation." She met my gaze, her face a mask of pure hatred. "She found out Dad was going to divorce her. That's why she killed him. She would've been left penniless.”

I knew I shouldn't, but... "Penniless?" I said. "After six years of marriage? Allison would've gotten something in a divorce. Alimony, a cash settlement. Something. Your father told you he was planning to divorce her?" I was under the assumption Mitchell and his daughter hadn't communicated, except for birthdays and holidays, when Allison had more or less forced them to interact like a real family, for the sake of Brenda's three children. Of course, I was basing that only on Allison's video diary. The actual situation might have been more complicated.

According to Allison, Brenda didn't initially suspect foul play after her father's death. She'd concocted the accusation only after discovering Mitchell had left everything to Allison and nothing to her—or to his grandchildren, a lapse that had bothered Allison and which she'd apparently decided to correct by placing four million bucks in trust for them.

Brenda said, "What I discussed or did not discuss with my father is no concern of yours." She stood. "I believe we're done here. Thank you for bringing the watch."

THIS VIDEO WAS made in November. Allison sat on the upholstered chair in her home office as usual. Her hair was down and she wore a moss-green turtleneck, jeans, and high black boots. Her face showed strain.

"I found this in my mailbox today, Jim." She held up two small items.

I squinted at my computer screen. "I can't see what you've got there, Allison," I said.

As if she could hear me, Allison got up and approached the camera, holding the objects closer to the lens. One of them was a Barbie doll, dressed in a snappy daytime outfit of floral pencil skirt and sleeveless rose-colored top, her unnaturally arched feet clad in high-heeled white plastic sandals. She would have been all ready to meet the other Barbies at some trendy lunch spot except for one thing: She had no head.

The other object Allison displayed was—you're way ahead of me here, I can tell—Barbie's head. The long hair had started out blonde but was now thoroughly streaked with black. I pictured someone going at it with a permanent marker. The hair in front had been chopped into irregular bangs.

Allison resumed her seat. "I found it like this, in two pieces. Nice, huh? Think someone's trying to send me a message?" She tossed the broken doll out of the frame. It sounded like it landed in a wastebasket. "I showed it to Nick. He says he knows nothing about it. He thinks some kid is having fun. If it were Halloween, I might agree with him, but that was two weeks ago."

"God," I said, "I hope you showed this to the cops."

"I know what you're going to say, Jim," she said. "I know you. 'Did you go to the police?' No, of course not. They would've laughed me out of the station. I mean, please, we're talking about a doll."

A doll that someone took pains to make resemble Allison Zaleski before decapitating it and presenting it to her like a dead mouse on her doorstep.

The cat analogy felt accurate. Cats are born predators. Whoever had executed this sick joke, if that's what it was, possessed predator instincts. He or she wanted to freak Allison out. Despite her forced nonchalance, it was easy to see the effort had succeeded.

I might agree with Allison that this stupid practical joke was no big deal were it not for a piece of knowledge I possessed that she did not, namely that a mere six weeks after making this video, she would be dead. Granted, her death had been accidental, but this felt wrong on a gut level.

"That's all I wanted to do tonight," Allison said, "show you the little present someone left me. It makes me feel better, even though I know you'll never see this. Over and out."

6

A Clear Case of Police Brutality

NORMALLY MURRAY'S PUB would have been half-filled at best on a weeknight in the dead of winter, but this was Wednesday, trivia night, always a popular draw for the locals. Sadly, my team had come in last place, thanks to the fact that my tardy arrival had forced me to join up with a trio of middle-aged Japanese tourists who spoke zero English. And yeah, it would have been nice to get a heads-up about that one in advance. I chose the team name: Gotta Have a Sensei Humor.

Keiko, Akira, and Jinsei had discovered Murray's in some online list of "iconic American bars that have been doing business in the same spot since well before you or anyone on the planet drew breath." I know this because they all proudly showed me the site on their phones. What my teammates lacked in language skills, they made up for in enthusiastic participation. The more scotch they knocked back, the louder and more raucous were their random responses to the questions Maxine Baumgartner, the owner of Murray's Pub, called out.

First-place honors went to a team called Wait, This Isn't Speed Dating?, who won a fifty-dollar bar tab. They had a ringer in the form of Mayor Sophie Halperin, a certified geography whiz who nailed the round called Countries That Ain't There No More. She did pretty well with Political Assassins Throughout History, too. The other two rounds were Name That Song (The Monkees edition) and Crazy Moms from Film and TV.

I liked my new Japanese pals. We had a lot of laughs despite the language barrier. They invited me to accompany them to the next stop on their All-American pub crawl. I heard the word "McSorley's" and deduced they were on their way to the venerable Lower East Side pub, which had been established seven years before Abraham Lincoln took office. I politely declined amid a lot of bowing and watched them stumble happily out into a half foot of snow.

I sidled up to the bar—you're not allowed to sidle up to anything else; I believe there's a law on the books—and waited for Martin to finish filling a pitcher of beer for Mal Wallace, Nina's husband, who was enjoying a boys' night out with his buddies. He'd probably catch hell later for not staying home and giving Nina a break with the baby. Normally I might be on her side, but I mean, everyone in Crystal Harbor knew that little Laura had been fathered not by Mal but by a notorious figure from the town's recent past. So I was willing to, you know, cut the guy some slack.

"Here you go." The padre slid a small cognac glass in front of me, half-filled with a clear golden liquid.

I brought it to my nose and sniffed. "Martin, you know I can't afford the good stuff." This was my favorite añejo tequila, and I knew how much Maxine charged for a single shot of it. I shoved the glass back at him. "Give me a shot of well tequila. Plus some salt and lime to kill the taste."

He slid the glass back across to me. "This *is* well tequila,

Jane. Bottoms up." Martin was looking particularly studly tonight in a black turtleneck with the sleeves pushed up, which advertised his well-developed forearms. Normally he wore his blond hair buzzed practically to the scalp, but he'd let it grow out since the summer, presumably to keep his head warm. The short strands had an appealingly rumpled look as if he'd just rolled out of bed. My fingers itched to smooth them down.

Instead I took hold of the snifter and glanced around to see if Maxine—Max to her friends—was in the vicinity. The pub's owner might have something to say about her bartender swapping out cheap well tequila for the kind that costs ten times as much.

"You worry too much." The padre grinned.

I shrugged. "It's your job on the line."

"Max would never can me," he said. "I bring in the customers."

What he meant was that he brought in the *female* customers. Max had known what she was doing when she hired Martin. The man was single-handedly responsible for a startling and no doubt unhealthy increase in alcohol consumption by female residents of Crystal Harbor. I'm sure he was very proud of himself.

I took a sip and groaned from the sheer, sensual perfection of it.

He said, "Say, 'Thank you, Martin.'"

"Thank you, Martin." I sipped again.

Bracing his arms on the bar top, he leaned toward me and said in a quiet growl, "Do I know how to take care of you?"

My giggle morphed into a piglike snort which caused a mouthful of hideously expensive liquor to shoot out of my stinging nostrils. Well, I mean, come on. When a guy this hot says something that suggestive, what do you expect me to do?

Okay, you know what? It's easy for you to sit there now and tell me what I *should* have said. And for the record, I don't say things like that. I'm a lady.

And no, it is none of your business when I last had a hot date.

I turned and surveyed the thinning crowd. Only a couple of booths remained occupied, and the customers in one of them were getting ready to leave. It was nearly eleven and most of the bar-trivia contestants had to get up early the next morning for work. I waved to Denny Pinheiro, who was on his way out the door. Denny owned a company that cleaned up crime scenes and other icky stuff. We helped each other out with referrals.

The barstools were now empty except for a couple who sat at the far end. The back of the woman's head was toward me. Black hair. Fake tan. Sparkly top. Short, tight skirt. Spike-heeled boots. I recognized Skye Guthrie's voice before she turned and polished off her drink. It was only after she signaled Martin for a refill and I saw him tip a bottle of rum into her glass that I realized she was downing something with a heftier kick than straight cola.

Okay, I'm not the preggers police or anything, but really? That was not cool, no matter how far along she was. Did she think that just because she wasn't showing yet, it was okay to get hammered?

The padre was well aware of Skye's delicate condition. He served the drink and rejoined me, accurately interpreting my questioning look. He leaned in closer, keeping his voice low. "I can't do anything about it, Jane, it's the law. I can't refuse to serve her unless she's visibly intoxicated, which she's not." He appeared none too happy about the situation. And yes, there was one of those signs behind the bar that read DRINKING ALCOHOLIC BEVERAGES DURING PREGNANCY CAN CAUSE BIRTH DEFECTS.

"How many of those has she had?" I asked, as Skye leaned toward her date to snap a grinning selfie.

"That's her third."

The woman could hold her liquor, I'd give her that. Sure, she was laughing shrilly and playfully smacking her companion's shoulder, but I chalked that up to her personality, not the booze. The guy was tipsier, probably trying to match her drink for drink. I didn't recognize him and wondered if she'd met him using one of those hookup apps, the kind where you swipe left (ugh, no) or right (oh yeah, baby) on a prospective date's picture.

"Oh good," Martin said dryly, "I was hoping there'd be at least one messy scene tonight."

I followed his gaze and saw Nick striding purposefully from the entrance toward where Skye sat cozying up to her date. I hadn't thought the handsome young widower had it in him to look haggard, but that's the word that popped into my head at that moment. There were puffy circles under his eyes. He looked like he hadn't slept, or shaved, since the funeral four days earlier. He didn't appear to notice me or Martin, or the other two remaining customers chatting quietly in a booth.

One of those customers was Howie Werker, a friend of mine who'd been promoted to detective during the recent shakeup in the police department. He was with a woman I didn't recognize. She wasn't his wife, Lillian, and Howie wasn't the type to cheat, and even if this crackerjack detective *were* the type to cheat, he sure as heck wouldn't do it on trivia night at

Murray's Pub in full view of dozens of his friends and neighbors.

Drawing on my own vaunted powers of detection—hey, I've been known to make a few good guesses!—I concluded that this lady just might be Crystal Harbor's newest police detective. I knew the department had hired someone from the outside and that she was named Sugar or Candy or something like that. She certainly didn't look like a Sugar or a Candy. Which is to say she appeared more professional than a cloying name like that would suggest. Her curly brown hair was pulled back into a messy bun. She wore eyeglasses with fashionable burgundy-colored frames, and funky little brass-and-glass earrings shaped like owls. Okay, not *too* professional.

Nick grabbed Skye's shoulder and spun her to face him. "What the hell are you doing, Skye?" His bloodshot gaze took in her drink, her date, her swipe-right getup. "I've been trying to get in touch with you. You keep dumping my calls, ignoring my texts."

She jerked out of his grasp. "You don't own me, Nick."

Martin's body language was deceptively calm as he wiped down the bar near the squabbling pair. I knew him well enough to discern he was on high alert, prepared to leap over the bar if this dreary little scene threatened to escalate into violence. He caught Howie's eye and I saw something pass between the two men, an unspoken communication. The female detective—Honey? Cupcake? Pumpkin Spice Donut?—appeared just as watchful.

If Skye expected her drinking buddy to confront the interloper and toss him out of the pub, she was to be disappointed. The fellow frowned at her. "You told me you're single."

"I *am* single!" She jerked her thumb toward Nick. "This guy's out of my life."

"How can you say that?" Nick demanded. "You're having my baby, in case it slipped your mind."

The barstool Skye's date was sitting on became suddenly electrified. What else could explain the speed with which he sprang off of it?

She latched on to his arm. "Don't go!"

"I don't know what your game is," he said as he extricated himself and grabbed his coat off one of the hooks near the entrance, "but I didn't sign on for any baby." He had his phone out of his pocket before he'd even opened the door. He was either opening a rideshare app or, more likely, on the prowl for another, more reliable late-night hookup. One without a bun in the oven and a baby daddy stalking her.

"Hey!" Skye called after him. "Who's going to pay for these drinks?" She followed this up with a string of ripe cussing as the door closed on her date's back.

"Skye, come on," Nick pleaded. "You should be taking better care of yourself. You shouldn't even be here."

"Now you're telling me where I can go? What I can do?" She tossed back the last of her rum and Coke and turned to Martin. "Give me another."

"I'll need you to take care of the tab first," the padre said. "Sixty-one bucks."

This triggered a fresh bout of foul language. Nick produced his wallet and slapped a few bills on the bar. "You're just upset, bunny," he told Skye, "and confused. Let's get out of here. Come home with me. We can finally stay together all night in my bed. Won't that be nice? And in the morning I'll make you breakfast, something good for the baby like, uh, ham and eggs or something. The baby needs protein, right?"

"I'm not going anywhere with a loser like you," she said. "Hey, bartender! Where's my drink?"

Martin gave Nick his change. "Ran out of rum. I can give you plain Coke if you like."

"Don't lie to me, scumbag." Skye pointed to the half-full bottle he'd recently poured from. "There's plenty left."

Martin turned to me. "Jane, do you see any rum in that bottle?"

I squinted at it. "Looks empty to me."

"Me too," Howie volunteered from across the room.

"Ditto," said Cream Puff.

Having initially appeared perplexed by the sudden epidemic of Booze Blindness, Nick finally caught on. "There's no more rum, bunny. Come on, let's go."

"You idiots all think you're so smart," she said. "Give me bourbon. Make it a double. On the rocks."

"Okay, I'm getting you out of here," Nick said in a surprising display of assertiveness. He tried to ease Skye off her barstool, but she fought him, punching and kicking and even biting him in response to his gentle coaxing.

Apple Fritter slid out of her booth and approached Skye. She flipped open her badge wallet to display the gold shield. "Miss, I'm Detective Cookie Kaplan."

"Thank God you're here," Skye crowed. "This bastard refuses to serve me. That's against the law, right?"

"I just witnessed you assaulting this gentleman." Cookie indicated Nick.

"*He* assaulted *me!* Didn't you see? He's trying to force me to leave. I don't want to leave. I want to stay here and drink." She turned to Martin again. "Bourbon. Now!"

The padre busied himself arranging glassware.

"I'm going to fight that prenup, bunny," Nick said. "I've got a new lawyer and he's working an angle. I'll tell you about it later."

"How are you going to pay for a lawyer?" Skye sneered.

"That's the best part," he said. "I don't have to pay him now. He'll take a piece of whatever I end up with."

"How big a piece?"

"Uh… I think he said thirty percent," he said. "Maybe forty."

Skye thought about this. I could almost hear the calculator in her head clicking away. "And that's all you'll owe him? The rest is yours?"

"Yeah!" He wore a proud grin. "Once that prenup is out of the way, I'll get my one third, minus the lawyer's cut. Not bad, huh?"

Skye faced him directly, as if to claim his full attention. "And you're sure he doesn't want any money up front? No retainer or anything?"

"Well, I mean, the guy has expenses, you know? I have to cover whatever he lays out. It's only fair. Dispensations, I think he called it."

Martin said, "Disbursements."

"Right!" Nick said. "Disbursements."

Skye's expression hardened. I sensed she had not had an easy life and was accustomed to bad news. "How much?"

"Just fifteen thousand. That'll cover every—"

"*Fifteen grand?*" She gaped at him. "Where are you going to come up with that kind of bread?"

"I thought… well, you said you had some money put aside…"

"You have seriously lost it if you think I'm handing over my life savings to some crooked lawyer who's just out to fleece you."

"It's an investment," Nick whined. "Can't you see that, bunny? Think about how much we'll have once that prenup is history."

Skye's face contorted with disgust. "After Allison died, all you could talk about was how rich we were going to be. I should've known all along it would never happen, not with a loser like you calling the shots. Story of my life."

"You're just hormonal," he said. "It's normal. I've been reading up on pregnancy. Your emotions are all over the place. I get that. I'm here for you, bunny. We're in this together. Don't pull away from me now. I need you. We need each other. And the baby needs—"

"I'm so sick of hearing about the baby!" She punched him in the chest. He stood there and took it.

"Miss," Detective Cookie Kaplan said, "if you don't want to be arrested for assault, you'll need to leave the premises immediately."

"This is police brutality!" Skye hollered back, while Nick struggled to shove her arms into her coat. "I'm going to report you to your boss. They'll take away your badge. Yours, too," she told Howie, who was still sitting in the booth, serenely sipping his beer and munching on Cajun curly fries. "For not doing anything to stop this blatant injustice."

She continued to squawk as Nick escorted her out of the pub. The only remaining patrons were the two detectives.

"We'll be out of your hair in a few minutes," Howie told Martin.

"No rush, take your time."

I introduced myself to Cookie, who had a firm handshake and a ready smile. She asked me to join them and became my friend forever by pushing the basket of fries in front of me as I took a seat across from her.

"Beer, Jane?" the padre asked from behind the bar, where he was shutting down the register.

"No, thanks. I'm still working on this." I indicated my tequila.

"I've heard of you," Cookie said. "The Death Diva, right?"

"Yeah, well, it's not as gross as most people think." You can imagine the reactions I was accustomed to dealing with.

"Oh, I think it's really cool," she said. "You saw a need and you created a whole career out of it. Totally original. What's not to love?"

I decided I really liked Detective Cookie Kaplan.

"You know," I said, "I'm glad I ran into you guys. There's something that's kind of bothering me. It's probably nothing."

Howie said, "Usually when I hear those words, it's not nothing." He gestured for me to continue. Howie Werker was a tall, tasty, dark-skinned man in his early forties. Not to mention buff: He ran marathons in his spare time.

Okay, don't get too excited. He's married, remember? And I happen to really like his wife. Not that I'd mess around with a married man under any circumstances. I sort of had the chance a couple of months ago with Dom and I put on the brakes. Not that Dom is married, but he's engaged. More or less. To my knowledge, he and Bonnie have yet to set the date. And no, I don't know what that means or how I feel about it, so let's just drop the subject, okay? Sheesh.

"It's about Allison Zaleski." I popped a curly fry into my mouth.

"What a tragedy, to die so young and in such a horrible way." Cookie shook her head. "I never met her, but everyone who did says she was nice."

Howie said, "That had to be rough for you, finding her like that. How are you doing, Jane? Are you all right?"

My eyes stung with a burst of raw emotion I was helpless to suppress. My reaction shocked me. I thought I had this whole thing under control. It's not as if I were a stranger to death and dead bodies. But this was different. Allison haunted me. I saw her when I closed my eyes to sleep. I saw how she looked under the ice, almost like one of her own photographs. A figure under glass, serene, unmoving.

And then there were her videos. Just a couple of gal pals schmoozing, sharing confidences. That's what it felt like anyway, watching them.

I grabbed a paper napkin and dabbed the corners of my eyes, mumbling an apology.

Howie slid his arm around my shoulders and gave me a brisk, wordless hug. He glanced up and said, "You were there too."

Only then did I notice Martin had joined us, sliding onto the bench next to Cookie. He nodded grimly.

I cleared my throat. "So, um, here's the thing. I probably shouldn't be telling you this."

"Our favorite words," Cookie said, lightening the mood. "Do proceed."

"Well, I've been watching these, um, video diaries Allison made." I didn't tell them how I'd come across the videos and I hoped they wouldn't ask. I mean, they *were* cops, and I was in possession of something that didn't strictly belong to me. But I'd known Howie a long time. He'd had my back during a couple of sticky situations. So I figured I wasn't about to get hauled to the hoosegow. This despite the bar-trivia team name these two had assigned themselves: Let Us Win or We'll Arrest You.

"So when you say 'video diaries,'" Cookie said, "that means, what, she made them for herself?"

"Yeah, I guess so. She's the only one in them and she's just, you know, talking. Well, it's like she's addressing this guy Jim, but he's definitely past tense. I think he's dead. Anyway, one of these videos contains something that's kind of disturbing."

"Disturbing how?" she said.

"Something was left in her mailbox," I said. "A Barbie doll. Headless. Well, that's not accurate. The head was there, it just wasn't attached to the doll's body."

The detectives looked at me. They looked at each other, then they looked back at me. "Okay," Howie said, "that's creepy, sure, but…" He shrugged, and I read his mind. *What are you getting yourself so worked up about?* Maybe he thought finding Allison's body really had sent me over the edge. He added, "That's the kind of prank a kid might pull."

"Okay." Cookie leaned forward, forearms on the table. "Tell me more about this Barbie."

Thank you! I was liking this woman more and more.

"Had someone messed with it in any way?" she asked. "Altered it? I mean, besides yanking the head off."

Howie looked suddenly interested. I could tell this possibility hadn't occurred to him, and that bothered him. Martin, meanwhile, simply sat and listened. I knew I could trust him not to spill the beans about how he'd helped me hack into Allison's flash drive.

"Well, that's the thing," I said. "Someone *had* messed with it. It was a blonde Barbie, but the hair had been colored black."

"Dyed?" Howie asked.

"No, like with a Sharpie. It was crudely done. And they chopped off some of the hair to make bangs."

I didn't have to state the obvious. The doll had been changed to look like Allison Zaleski.

"Okay, I have to say this," Cookie said. "That woman who was here a little while ago? Beating up on her boyfriend?"

"*Ex*-boyfriend, by the looks of it," Howie said. "That was Allison's husband, by the way, the guy that hustled her out. Nick Birch. I notified him when her body was found."

"No kidding." Cookie's eyebrows shot up. "Looks like Nick's been a very bad boy. Anyway, that woman obviously did the same thing to her hair that someone did to that doll. The dye job, the bangs."

"Her name is Skye Guthrie," I said. "She was a friend of Allison's. She wants everyone to believe she was her best friend, but I've watched a bunch of these videos and Allison only mentioned her a couple of times, and not in a best-friend kind of way. More like a 'here's this hanger-on I have to tolerate' kind of way."

Cookie said, "A hanger-on who claims to be your bestie and makes a baby with your husband. Lovely."

"So you can see why I was concerned, right?" I said. "I mean, someone made this doll look like Allison—a decapitated Allison—and left it in her mailbox."

Howie and Cookie consulted each other via silent detective woo-woo.

"That's kind of threatening, right?" I said. "It rattled Allison, I'll tell you that."

"Well," Howie said, "she didn't report it to the police, as

far as I know."

"No," I said, "she threw the doll away. It's long gone. She thought you guys wouldn't take it seriously."

"When did this happen?" Cookie asked.

"The video's date-stamped November twentieth," I said, "so probably that same day."

She said, "Do you know if she showed the doll to anyone else?"

"Just Nick, as far as I know. He told her he knew nothing about it."

"You know that Allison's death was an accident, right?" Howie said. "I mean, I think I know where you're going with this."

"I'm not going anywhere with it," I said. "It's just disturbing, like I said."

Martin finally spoke up, addressing Howie. "Question. How did Nick react when you gave him the news? About Allison."

"He was stunned," Howie said. "Distraught."

"You do know he's a professional actor," Martin said.

"I know he's an actor. As for how professional..." Howie rocked his hand. "From what I hear, Leonardo DiCaprio has nothing to worry about."

"Still," Martin said, "it's something to keep in mind."

Cookie turned to me. "What would you like us to do, Jane?"

Now that she was asking me directly, I felt a little embarrassed. What Howie had said was true. The authorities had judged Allison's death to be purely accidental. She'd drowned. There'd been no evidence of trauma or anything suspicious. She'd been alone in the woods and had made the fateful decision to walk across ice that turned out to be too thin to support her weight. Then she'd fallen through and had been unable to make it out.

Only a sip remained of my tequila. I lifted the snifter and drained it. "Would it be possible for you guys to look into this a little? Like ask a few questions, see if anyone, I don't know, had it in for Allison?"

Howie leaned back. He was thinking about it.

Cookie didn't have to give it much thought. "Sure, no problem. I don't know how much time I can give it, but I'll make some discreet inquiries." She gave Howie a significant look.

"Sure, okay," he grumbled. "I'd only do this for you, Jane. Don't expect anything to come of it."

"I know, I know," I said. "It was an accident."

7

Pick a Card, Any Card

"I DON'T KNOW how I let you talk me into this," Lenny Ahearn said.

"I didn't have to do much talking," I said. "The pile of cash Wendell dangled in front of you was pretty darn eloquent."

His grunt conceded the point but said he didn't have to like it. We stood in the rear of one of the visitation rooms at the Leonard T. Ahearn and Sons Funeral Home, where a wake was in progress. Several dozen friends, relatives, and fans of the late Wendell Webster crowded the front of the room, viewing Wendell's remains. It should come as no surprise, given what I do for a living, that my business relationship with Lenny went way back. Many of my assignments took me to this very funeral home, and we regularly referred customers to each other.

"I don't know," Lenny fretted, "I try to maintain a dignified atmosphere at this place. In the end, all you have is your reputation, right?" He tossed his hand toward the business end of the room, where Wendell was laid out.

I guess *laid out* isn't entirely accurate in this case since the dearly departed wasn't lying in a satin-lined coffin. A wake like that would have been altogether too prosaic for the likes of Wondrous Wendell, sleight-of-hand magician extraordinaire. Wendell was a showman to the end. When the octogenarian's "bum ticker" had presaged his imminent demise, he'd engaged me to arrange a sendoff that would not soon be forgotten.

Wendell's body had been posed in a sepulchral tableau vivant in the place of honor where his coffin should have sat. The funeral-home staff had done an amazing job, despite Lenny's reservations. Wendell sat behind a cloth-draped table on which playing cards had been fanned out. Behind him hung a red velvet stage curtain embellished with his stage name in lights: *Wondrous Wendell.*

His white hair was slicked back as usual. He wore his customary performance attire of salmon-colored suit and a bowtie imprinted with playing cards. Dark sunglasses had not been part of his magician's getup, but he wore them now, at Lenny's insistence. Likewise, Wendell had never, to my knowledge, performed on a stage flanked by RIP floral arrangements, enough to perfume the entire room. Well, I guess there's a first—and in this case, last—time for everything.

The magician's pose was eerily lifelike. He sat forward a little as if playing to his audience. One hand rested on the tabletop. The other was raised, displaying a card: the seven of spades. His smug grin, even with the opaque sunglasses, conveyed an unmistakable query: *Is* this *your card?*

A handful of mourners dabbed at their eyes. Whether their tears sprang from grief or irrepressible giggles, it was impossible to say. Many snickered openly and offered irreverent commentary. Most simply goggled in astonishment. For their part, Wendell's fellow magicians appeared to admire their late colleague's sense of style. They sized up the display as if contemplating how to outdo it when their time came.

I must say, I'd never seen so many cell phones at a wake. Everyone in attendance, it seemed, felt compelled to snap pictures of Wondrous Wendell's final, sold-out performance. No doubt the images were already flooding every nook and cranny of social media.

Wendell had known precisely what he'd wanted and had been willing to shell out boatloads of cash to make it happen. I'd been the go-between, negotiating with Lenny and finally managing to convince him to make the magician's final wish a reality. Lenny wasn't the only one making a tidy profit. My commission would keep me in Fruity Pebbles and orange soda for years.

I nudged the funeral director. "This thing is going viral even as we speak, Lenny. I'm telling you, after today you're going to have people banging down your door, wanting to attend their own funerals."

I couldn't tell whether that prospect cheered Lenny or appalled him. He was in his late sixties, his remaining hair mostly still dark. His black suit failed to conceal a slight paunch.

Norman Butterwick approached us, and Lenny stiffened, bracing himself to defend this vulgar parody of a wake.

Norman gestured toward the front of the room with his walking stick, this one crafted of ebony, by the look of it, with a handle of silver and inlaid mother-of-pearl. "Never in all my years have I witnessed a spectacle like this."

"Well, Norman," Lenny said, "we, uh, we strive to accommodate our clients' wishes, no matter how, uh… that is, we try not to judge—"

"I want you to do this for me." He wagged his cane toward Wendell again.

"What?"

"Oh, not posed with playing cards, of course." Norman chuckled at the absurd notion and offered a more reasonable one. "I'd be standing at my easel, painting one of my landscapes. I'd be wearing my painting apron, holding a brush…" He demonstrated the pose he was going for: head tilted to one side as he gazed contemplatively at the work in progress, paintbrush raised, poised for action.

I nudged Lenny again. "What did I tell you? You're a trendsetter." To Norman I said, "The problem is, this kind of thing isn't compatible with the green burial you arranged."

Norman's white eyebrows pulled together in confusion. "Green burial? There must be some mistake. I look dreadful in green."

Lenny spoke up. "'Green burial' refers to natural disposition of the remains in a way that minimizes environmental impact. You requested a simple shroud with no casket."

"You don't say!" Norman said, as if he were learning about this intriguing concept for the first time. "I like the sound of that. Let's do both, the artist pose followed by the green burial."

"I'm afraid that's not possible. This kind of, uh, thing—" Lenny gestured limply toward Wendell "—requires embalming, which isn't permitted in green burials."

"Ah. Well then," Norman said, "I shall give the matter some thought and apprise you of my decision."

As Norman returned to the front of the room, I gave Lenny a reassuring pat on the back. "Don't worry, by tomorrow he won't even remember this conversation."

"Well," Lenny said, "at his age, if he's going to change his mind about what he wants done with his remains, he'd better do it soon."

"You do know that Norman's parents both lived past a hundred, right?" I said. "You could have him flip-flopping on you for a decade or more."

An amused male voice interrupted us. "Why the long face, Lenny? Did Wendell miss his last payment?"

It was Ben Ralston, a local private investigator and a pal of mine. Ben was a middle-aged Black man, a bit on the short side but powerfully built. After retiring from the Crystal Harbor police department, he'd established Ralston Investigations. From what I could tell, he'd done pretty well for himself.

Once we'd gotten hugs and handshakes out of the way, Ben said, "So. Lenny. That's a hell of a job you guys did with Wendell. He looks like he's about to jump up and give us all a heart attack."

"It was quite the, uh, undertaking." The funeral director stretched his mouth into something meant to resemble a smile.

Ben leaned in closer and said, softly, "You can tell me. The guy's still alive, isn't he?"

"What? No, of course not."

"Jane…" Ben's expression urged me to level with him. "I know you set this thing up. Wendell sitting there having a big laugh, right? When's he planning to let everyone in on it? Is he going to take it as far as the cemetery?"

I said, "Ben, do you really think a guy Wendell's age could sit there in that position, holding up that card, for hours on end?"

He turned to Lenny, lowering his voice further still. "You put some sort of support in his sleeve, didn't you? Something to keep his arm steady."

"I'm sorry to disappoint you, Ben," Lenny said, "but Wendell Webster is deceased."

"If that's true," Ben said, "then hell yeah, I'm disappointed, 'cause I have fifty bucks riding on it."

"Oh, don't tell me," I said. "Are you guys betting on this?"

Ben's shrug said, *What did you expect?*

A strange sound squeaked up Lenny's throat. "Gambling… *here*…" he moaned.

I scanned the crowded room. "Okay, where are Christopher and Kevin? They'll put a stop to this." They were Lenny's sons who worked with him, in case you thought the name Leonard T. Ahearn and Sons Funeral Home might be some kind of exaggeration.

"They're up there taking bets," Ben said. At Lenny's stricken look, he added, "Don't worry, they're making sure the house gets a cut."

Lenny took off at a sprint, bulling his way through the mourners. Ben followed at a leisurely pace, chuckling at the mayhem he'd set in motion. Lenny was probably reconsidering the *and Sons* part of his business plan.

I was about to follow him into battle—I mean, I did have some responsibility, having arranged this bizarre wake—when Dom strolled up.

"Every time I think your Death Diva stuff can't get any weirder," he said, "you prove me wrong."

"I'm just giving the clients what they want," I said. Which is my general policy, except in cases where the client wants me to do something illegal, immoral, or too gross for words.

"Where've you been keeping yourself, Janey?" he asked. "I've missed you."

Oh no, he did not get to do that, not after our history. "You saw me five days ago at the funeral," I reminded him. "Your fiancée was there too, remember? Speaking of which, you two must be awfully busy getting ready for the wedding."

He sighed. This was not where he wanted the conversation to go. Too bad.

"When's the happy day, by the way?" I asked. "I haven't received a save-the-date, but maybe I'm not invited. I mean, Bonnie probably doesn't want your ex there. Oops, I mean your three exes."

"Of course you'll be invited," he said. "You know that."

I did know that. One thing about Dom, he strove to maintain a cordial relationship with all his ex-wives, even the one who wasn't one of his baby mamas. Which, in case you haven't been paying attention, happens to be yours truly.

Not that I'd planned it that way. I'd always dreamed of being a mother and had anticipated, when Dom and I had married eighteen years ago, that I soon would be. In hindsight, that's a conversation we probably should have had before the wedding. Turned out my young bridegroom had zero interest in becoming a daddy. It's what caused our breakup.

Then along came Svetlana, wife number two, who basically took the decision out of his hands, presenting him with his first two kids in rapid succession before it even occurred to him to ask, *So you* are *on the pill, right?* Wife number three, Meryl, gave him his third child. A happier, prouder papa, you never saw.

Yeah, that's right, my mistake had been letting my husband have a say in whether to reproduce.

"You didn't answer my question, Dom," I said. "When's the wedding?"

He looked uncomfortable. "We haven't set a date."

"Still? How long have you been engaged?" I was just torturing him. We both knew the timeline. Dom and Bonnie had been engaged for a year if you didn't count a brief hiatus the previous summer during which he'd tried to persuade me to remarry him. The fact that he'd promised me time to think about it and then promptly gotten reengaged to Bonnie while I was doing said thinking still stuck in my craw. Okay, he'd sort of apologized for that, but still.

"Come on, Janey, it's been a long time since we had dinner together," he said. "How does tomorrow sound? I've heard great things about a new place in Greenlawn."

Right. Greenlawn, which was a good fifteen miles from Crystal Harbor. None of our friends and neighbors were likely to spot Dom dining with a woman who was not his fiancée in Greenlawn.

"I have a busy day tomorrow," I said. "I'd rather stick closer to home. Let's go to the Harbor Room." Which was a venerable local eatery and bound to be crammed with people who knew us. I enjoyed watching him squirm.

No, that does not make me a bad person. Dom deserved to squirm. He was the one trying to arrange a nice, intimate, romantic dinner—otherwise known as a date—with his ex, in a location remote enough to keep from fueling the insatiable Crystal Harbor gossip mill. I didn't doubt he loved Bonnie. I also didn't doubt his desire to keep his options open.

Sorry, Dom, this *option isn't cooperating.*

"The Harbor Room..." he said. "Come on, aren't you bored with that place?"

"You love their dinner salad with beets and goat cheese," I said. "I heard you telling Bonnie about it. Hey, have her join us! The more the merrier."

Dom wasn't stupid. The look he gave me said, *Okay, you win.* I didn't doubt he'd try again, but perhaps he'd put a little more effort into it, be a tad more subtle. Which he had to know would do him no good. I'd already made it clear he could expect neither hanky nor panky from me while he was in a committed relationship with someone else. For that matter, I couldn't see him trying to sleep with me while he was engaged to Bonnie. Dom had his faults, but he was no cheating cur. I figured he was just trying to keep the kettle simmering, make sure my interest in him didn't wane in light of my own newly invigorated social life.

Because, let's face it, the tables had turned. *I* was the one with the options now, which he well knew. He'd been so complacent for so long, confident of my pitiful unrequited longing for him, our unfulfilled might-have-beens. It had to irk the heck out of him to see Martin cozying up to me, flirting with me. Dom had tried on numerous occasions to warn me away from the bad boy with the mysterious past, but would I listen? It was so much more fun not listening.

And then there was Victor Dewatre, the aforementioned French hottie. Not only was he leading-man handsome, but he was young, in his early thirties. I'd met Victor back in September when he'd arrived in Crystal Harbor following the murder of his brother, Pierre. He'd been my houseguest for a month while the investigation unfolded, which didn't please Dom at all. Well, to be fair, Victor had been a suspect in his brother's murder, so one could say Dom was concerned for my safety. One could also say he was feeling a wee bit possessive.

Dom had to be wondering whether Victor and I had become intimate during that long month. We hadn't, but I had no intention of telling Dom that. It was none of his business. Besides, like I said, it was his turn to be miserable. Victor had invited me to visit him in Paris and take a side trip to his family's bed-and-breakfast inn in Provence, and who knew what would happen between us then?

Okay, I was pretty sure what would happen, and I'm not embarrassed to tell you I was looking forward to it. I mean, have you *seen* Victor?

Likewise, Dom must be curious as to whether the padre and I had done the deed, which, as I've mentioned, we had not. For my part, there was that "precisely how bad is this bad boy?" thing. For Martin's part, he assumed—okay, not without reason—that I was clinging to the hope of a happily ever after with my ex. I suspect he wanted no part of something that messy.

The bottom line was that for the first time in eighteen years, Dom was being kept on his toes, as far as Ex–Mrs. Faso the First was concerned, and that was making him uncommonly attentive. Which is code for *jealous*. And yeah, I was determined to enjoy it while it lasted.

For the record, I've never been the kind of woman who plays one guy off another, or plays hard to get—but dang if it doesn't work! Of course, it would have been nice to get that memo before I was racing headlong toward forty candles. I say that, but the fact is, I've never been comfortable playing games with people's emotions. It's not who I am. If that means a lifetime marked by few casual relationships and fewer meaningful ones—and most depressingly, no children—then so be it. In the immortal words of my role model, Popeye: I yam what I yam.

Dom gave my hand a quick, hard squeeze. And yeah, it felt good. So sue me. "I'm around if you change your mind," he said in that quietly intense way he darn well knew turned me all gooey inside.

I thought, *And I'm around if you decide to end your engagement—for real this time.*

Maybe.

"I almost forgot, I have a gift for you." He reached into his breast pocket and extracted a five-inch spike.

"Thank you, Dom. This will come in handy next time I'm laying railroad tracks."

"It's a self-defense tool." He dangled the thing by a little loop attached to it. "It hangs from your keychain. Weighs almost nothing. Feel."

Obediently I took the spike from him. It was made from shiny purple aluminum and had finger grooves all down its length, the better to hold it steady while you gouge out your attacker's eyes. "And you bought this for me why?" I asked.

"You have to ask? Considering the sketchy characters you deal with on a daily basis?"

There was one sketchy character in particular my ex would just as soon I jettison from my life. I suspect he purchased this adorable self-defense spike with the padre in mind.

He took it from me and tucked it into the pocket of my gray suit jacket. "Promise me you'll attach it to your keychain. Do it today."

"You know, you can be a real pain in the—"

"Promise me," he insisted.

"I'll think about it."

"I MEAN in the *hot tub*?" Allison's face on my computer screen was tear-streaked, her voice hoarse from crying. She crushed a damp tissue in her fist. "Can you imagine anything more clichéd? Well, actually, I can. Try this on for size, Jim. Grieving widow falls for hunky younger man before the love of her life is even cold. Hunk cheats on her with one of her own friends. That's the very definition of *cliché* right there."

She collapsed against the back of her easy chair, breathing hard, as if the effort to process her husband's infidelity had sapped all her strength. I was breathing hard along with her, outraged, angry, hurting for her. Hurting for a woman I'd never really known but had come to consider a friend after watching about two dozen of her video diary entries.

It was Thursday night, or rather Friday morning, around two a.m. Sleep had eluded me, and little wonder with images of Wondrous Wendell and his seven of spades invading my mind every time I began to nod off. Only, in my dream Wendell wasn't sitting still, and his mouth hadn't been superglued shut. *Pick a card and remember it!* he ordered, and *Don't let me see the card!* and *Don't take your eyes off that card!* I'm telling you, it was the most exhausting dream I ever had. All that work! And for a dead guy.

The date stamp on this video was December 11. This was the story Poppy had told me on Monday, how Allison had discovered Nick and Skye *in flagrante* and, rather than confront them then and there, had instead worked "behind the scenes" to quietly disinherit her husband and begin the divorce process. That conversation had left me with the impression of a woman who, if not coldly calculating, at least had her emotions battened down.

That was not the Allison I was witnessing in this video.

This was a woman in the throes of heartbreak. Nick's betrayal had cut her deeply.

Allison wore a pale blue bathrobe that might have been quilted silk. She dragged her fingers through her hair, which was loose. She grabbed a couple of fresh tissues, then mopped her face, blew her nose, and cleared her throat. "I went directly to Sten's office. He saw me immediately. I could barely get the story out, I was so…" She bit her lip. "He was very sweet. I never knew he had that in him, that level of compassion and understanding. No judgment, no 'I told you sos.' I always thought of him as this distinguished old guy who never lets down his guard, but he was… exactly what I needed just then."

I wasn't surprised to hear this. I knew Sten Jakobsen better than most, and knew there were depths to him his casual acquaintances never saw.

Allison dragged in a deep, shuddering breath and let it out slowly. "Thank God Sten had insisted on that prenup. I—"

A knocking sound interrupted her. She looked to her left, where I knew her office door to be. "What?" she called. I heard an indistinct male voice. It sounded like a question. "I'm just editing some pictures. I couldn't sleep," she told Nick. Her calm voice betrayed none of her roiling emotions. He said something else. "I don't know why I locked it," she said. "Habit. Go back to bed. I'll be up in a while."

She waited a few moments, listening for his departing footfalls, before turning back to the camera. "I'd fought Sten on the prenup. Mitchell hadn't asked me to sign one. I would have, though, if he'd wanted me to. I mean, I understand the concept behind it. Mitchell had started with nothing and had made millions with his ski resort. And believe me, he worked hard for every nickel. And here he was, marrying this girl who started with nothing and—" a wry smile "—still had nothing. But to him, our marriage wasn't about that, it was a loving partnership from day one."

Allison pulled her legs up and wrapped her arms around her knees. Her gaze drifted, as if she were reluctant to face the camera lens. "But that's not the only reason I didn't want to make Nick sign a prenup. After everything… well, you know, that whole mess you and I went through. It left a bad taste in my mouth, to say the least."

You and I? Was she still talking to the mysterious Jim?

"The last thing I wanted," she said, "was to make my second marriage about who had less and who had more, the difference in socioeconomic status and all that. Well, all I can say is, thank goodness Sten was so persistent. When I send that cheating son of a bitch packing, he's going to walk away without a penny of Mitchell's money."

"LET ME TAKE your coat," I said.

"Thank you, but I can't stay." Joleen Gleason looked ill at ease, standing in my foyer with melting snow dripping off her navy wool coat onto the macassar ebony floor. "I just stopped by to ask a favor."

"Of course," I said. "Name it."

"Well, this is somewhat awkward, so I'll come right out and say it. It seems that two detectives from the Crystal Harbor Police Department have been asking questions around town. Questions about Allison."

My stomach knotted. "Mrs. Gleason—"

"They want to know if she had any enemies. Did anyone ever stalk her. Did she ever express fear for her life. That sort of thing."

"I can explain that," I said.

"Doug and I already figured out that you're behind it," Joleen said. "I have to ask you to… to call them off. To get them to stop this. Our daughter's death was an accident, nothing more sinister than that." She swallowed hard. Her eyes were shiny.

So were mine. Shame welled up within me. "I never meant to cause you distress," I said.

"It's not me so much as… This has been especially hard on Doug," she said. "He holds so much inside. He feels he has to be strong for me. Losing his little girl, well… And now to have the police treating it like a crime…"

"It's not like that," I said. "It's not an official police investigation."

"I know that," Joleen said. "The authorities—the experts—they examined her death from every angle and they found nothing suspicious. We have to trust that they know what they're doing."

It would seem Joleen had not been told about the decapitated doll someone had left in her daughter's mailbox, and I had no intention of enlightening her. I'd caused her and her husband enough needless pain. The doll had been a stupid prank, the brainchild of some neighborhood thug in training. I'd had no business bringing it to the detectives' attention, sticking my nose where it didn't belong and causing the Gleasons more grief in the process.

In hindsight, I'd been primed to see evil where there was

only blameless tragedy, my dark suspicions nurtured by two decades in my bizarre career, not to mention the town's recent history of murders, for which I'd had a ringside seat.

Allison's mother was right. Her death was accidental. End of story.

"I'm so sorry, Mrs. Gleason," I said. "I'll call Detective Werker right away. No one will be asking any more questions."

JOLEEN'S VISIT HAD made me wish I'd never accepted the mushroom-shaped salt shaker, had never found Allison's flash drive and viewed her video diary. And yet, thinking it through, I realized that presenting the flash drive to her parents now, as if I'd just discovered it, would do little to ease their distress. They'd probably feel compelled to crack the password, which wouldn't take long—I mean, hey, if *I* could do it—and then they'd come face-to-face with their daughter's most private thoughts, the lows as well as the highs, not to mention that nasty headless doll. So then, what do I do with the thing? I certainly wasn't going to present it to the young widower.

These thoughts bombarded my brain as I began playing the twenty-seventh and final video. I mean, after all, I'd viewed all the others. I couldn't *not* watch the last one, right?

Oh, don't be like that. You can't tell me you're not even a teensy bit curious.

The date stamp on this video was December 17. In nine days the beautiful, composed young woman staring back through my computer screen would be dead. The realization sent a shiver through me. She wore the same pale blue bathrobe I'd seen several times previously. Apparently she made most of these videos late at night when Nick was asleep.

"I've been thinking about you a lot, Jim," she said. "Maybe it's because of what's happening to my marriage, how it's all gone to hell. But really, it goes further back to when Mitchell died. That's when I began to kind of... sense you. I've been feeling your presence, especially when I'm really blue. My guardian angel." A small smile.

"I know it doesn't make sense to still feel this close to you. I know I'll never set eyes on you again. But it helps to imagine you beside me, quietly supporting me. Sometimes I even sense your touch, your hand on my back." The smile turned crooked. "That's how far gone I am. Pretty pitiful, huh?"

Emotion constricted my throat. It didn't sound pitiful to me, it sounded touching, and all too similar to what I myself had experienced following my divorce from Dom. Not for the first time, I wondered about Allison's relationship with Jim, and how long ago he'd died.

"Do you remember how dorky I was when we first met?" Allison grimaced at the memory. "Fourteen years old, starting school in the middle of the year, a shy, awkward kid fresh from Superior, Texas, population three hundred seventeen. Okay, let's be honest. 'Awkward' doesn't come close. I was downright ugly. The acne, the dumb haircut, and my *clothes*! No wonder the popular girls all made fun of me."

She laughed at the memory and ratcheted up her mild accent. "Oh, and let's not forget that West Texas twang! The icing on the cake. Teenage girls can be so cruel, and the boys aren't much better. Except for you, Jim. If it hadn't been for you befriending me those first few months, protecting me, I don't know if I would've made it."

Allison had had her share of misery during her short life. Being uprooted and moved across country at an awkward age, leaving her at the mercy of her new school's mean girls. Then came the losses. First Jim, who'd obviously meant a great deal to her, then Mitchell, whom she'd called the love of her life. Then Nick's betrayal with a woman who was supposed to be Allison's friend. And if that wasn't enough, there was the horrible accident that had taken her life—horrible and ironic considering her love of the outdoors.

I tried not to think of how it had been for Allison at the end, struggling in vain in the freezing water, trying to scramble onto solid ice and feeling it give way beneath her, feeling hypothermia encroach and finally knowing there was nothing she could do, that she would die alone in that lake.

I gave my head a vigorous shake, trying to shed the unwelcome thoughts, the picture of Allison lying under the ice as if placed there as part of some grotesque museum display.

Now she was half rising from her seat and reaching for something offscreen. She settled back down and examined it in her lap. It was a small framed picture, no doubt one of the cluster of family photos that sat on her desk. She wore a sweet, enigmatic smile.

Finally she said, "Nick wanted to know who was in this picture with me. I told him you're my cousin. He's not the kind of guy that can handle looking at a picture of his wife's old boyfriend every day. Mitchell, on the other hand, was mature enough, self-confident enough, to get it. He didn't feel threatened by my memories of you."

Allison kissed her fingertips and tenderly pressed them to the picture. "Do you remember when this was taken? That time we went to that little amusement park with the other theater-club kids? Nunley's—it's still there. We'd been building sets and we were filthy, covered in paint."

She got up and brought the photo closer to the camera lens. A color snapshot filled the screen. Two teenagers on side-by-side wooden carousel horses, laughing as they tried to push each other off their mounts. Allison was easy to recognize, with her dark ponytail and violet eyes. The boy had medium brown hair that brushed his collar. His eyes appeared hazel or green. His face was distinctive if not particularly handsome.

I found myself leaning forward at my computer, eyes glued to the screen. When Allison pulled back and started to sit down again, I fumbled with the mouse and reversed the video a few seconds so I could freeze it on the photo.

I recognized this boy. But from where? The name Jim didn't help. The only Jim I knew was a pal of my dad's.

The thing is, this memory didn't feel old. It felt pretty darn fresh. I peered closely at the young man's eyes, his mouth, the shape of his face. I sat back, closed my eyes, and took a deep breath. *Where do I know you from, Jim?*

I opened my eyes and settled my gaze on his. "Oh." And I knew.

8

Shrooms Will Get You In

I'M NOT A social media type of person, by which I mean I don't *live* for social media. I do have a Facebook account because that's the only way some of my actual friends communicate, but I don't post much. I'm of the opinion that no one needs or wants constant hourly updates regarding my political views, snack status, or the weather outside my front door.

I don't go on Facebook every day, but I was on it now, searching for Skye's profile. It wasn't hard to find. She'd recently changed her cover photo to a selfie showing her glum face with Allison's casket in the background. I recalled watching Skye take this shot because she was the only one doing it. This wasn't Wondrous Wendell's wake, bizarre enough to justify a sea of clicking cell-phone cameras. This was the wake of a young woman whom Skye had claimed as a best friend. Which should have meant that Allison's wake was about, well, Allison.

But Skye hadn't restricted her photography to the wake. As I'd told Maia, she'd taken pictures at the cemetery too. Some of the shots were directed at the graveside service, but most were of herself, looking morose and missing her bestie. As it turned out, Skye had not locked down her Facebook profile, which meant all her status updates, all her pictures, her friends list, everything was open to public viewing. I'd been afraid I'd have to friend her and hope she accepted, but it was all right there, a click away, including the picture album she'd created just for the funeral.

When I'd finally recognized Jim in that picture from Allison's video, when the memory had clicked in, I'd known precisely where I'd seen that face. Attendance had been heavy at Allison's graveside service, not surprising considering her young age. One man had stood apart, some distance from the rest. Joleen and Doug's backs were to him, which I now suspected was deliberate, an effort to avoid being recognized by them. He hadn't stayed long.

Was it Jim? Was he alive? Or was I imagining things that weren't there, grasping at straws? At this point I gave it fifty-fifty odds.

The thing is, the man who looked like Jim had been standing behind Skye when she'd taken all those selfies. Was it possible she'd inadvertently recorded his image along with her own?

Skye appeared fond of Facebook's optional Check In feature, which uses GPS to stamp your precise location when posting an update from a cell phone. On the day of Allison's funeral she'd "checked in" at the Leonard T. Ahearn and Sons Funeral Home at 12:17 p.m., the Whispering Willows Cemetery at 1:52 p.m., and Allison's home at 3:22 p.m.

I scrolled through her cemetery pictures. She'd taken selfie after selfie, altering her expression slightly in each one, as if trying to achieve the ideal pretty, pouting mourning face. She'd shifted her phone this way and that, adjusting the angle.

I spotted him at last. He stood several yards behind Skye, his hands shoved into the pockets of his charcoal-gray overcoat, looking sober and sad and indisputably alive.

I stared at his image a long time. I'd been wondering what to do with Allison's flash drive, who should get it. Her video diary entries had been addressed directly to this man. It was as if she'd been whispering into his ear.

I knew what I had to do.

"HOW DID YOU KNOW I'm a vegetarian?" Jim Manning asked. We'd just introduced ourselves and claimed a blond-wood bistro table near the big picture windows of Janey's Place. It was two in the afternoon on Tuesday. The lunch rush was over and the after-school crowd had yet to descend. At the moment all the other tables were vacant.

This café was a pleasant refuge any time of year, but especially in winter, when it was like walking into your grandma's warm kitchen, perfumed with soups, stews, and various sweet concoctions. Okay, maybe your grandma never made vegetarian chili or tofu scramble wraps. She probably didn't whip up green smoothies in her blender or serve a thousand and one varieties of herbal tea. And I'm not saying I actually like this stuff—being your basic junk-food junkie, I usually stick to a single reliable menu item here—but it does smell awfully good and feel awfully comforting when it's close to freezing outside.

"I had no idea you're a vegetarian. I'm definitely not," I

admitted, "but I like this place."

He didn't ask whether Jane Delaney had any connection to Janey's Place, which was just as well. I didn't want to get into it. When people find out my ex-husband (who *is* a vegetarian) owns the successful Janey's Place chain of restaurants, they generally assume I'm rolling in dough from the divorce settlement.

Oh, Nice Guy Dom had offered me half of the business I'd helped to build when we'd split up all those years ago. At that time it had consisted of this one location and was still in the red. I'd opted instead to hang on to an adorable antique student desk we'd found at a flea market. I still have it. Meanwhile Janey's Place has made Dom a millionaire many times over. Yeah, that's me, Jane Delaney, negotiator extraordinaire.

I know you're dying to find out how I'd managed to locate Jim. I hate technology, except when it works. Did you know that nowadays many high schools are putting their yearbooks online? Neither did I, but I discovered it soon enough once I started looking for information about Allison's high school. I knew her family had moved to Massapequa from Texas when she was fourteen. She'd mentioned going to school with Jim.

I correctly surmised that Allison had graduated thirteen years earlier. It turned out she and Jim were in the same class. Their portraits had appeared in alphabetical order along with those of their fellow seniors. When I'd worked my way to the *M*'s, there he was, the same smiling youth I'd seen in the picture taken with Allison at Nunley's.

Contacting him had taken a little more effort, but eventually LinkedIn had come through. Turns out Jim is a civil engineer working in the nonprofit sector. I'd told him an abbreviated version of who I was and how I'd known Allison, and that she'd left something that should probably go to him. I'd told him that I didn't want to trust the item to the mail, which was true, but mainly I'd wanted to meet him, look him in the eye and talk with him, and then decide whether handing over Allison's video diary to a stranger was the responsible thing to do. I owed it to her not to get this wrong.

I'd brought along the little mushroom-shaped salt shaker, something of Allison's to give him if I decided not to hand over the flash drive. Yeah, it would be weird, but considering what I do for a living, it's not as if weird and I are strangers.

Cheyenne O'Rourke tottered over on her four-inch platform boots to take our order. Cheyenne was a local youth who'd had run-ins with the law, thanks to some astoundingly poor decision making. I'd call her disaffected, but that would imply an attitude of rebellion and grievance against authority figures, which in turn would imply that she believed in something outside of herself. Cheyenne believed in whatever would make her happy at the moment. This generally involved questionable associates, expensive toys, and glitter nail polish.

Today's manicure, sparkly black and yellow stripes, nearly caused me to leap out of my seat. *Enjoy your amuse-bouche of killer bees. I'll be back shortly with your scorpions en brochette.*

Cheyenne had paired the stratospheric platform boots with skull-printed leggings through which her thong panties were clearly visible. Her apple-green Janey's Place T-shirt was knotted over a stretchy purple athletic shirt. It was as if she'd woken up that morning and asked herself, *What can I wear that will display my prodigious behind and bulging muffin top to full advantage? Got it!*

Jim said, "I'll have the quinoa protein bowl."

"What do you want on it? There's, like, choices." Cheyenne scratched absentmindedly at a brand-new, raw tattoo on the side of her neck: the name *Brian*, inexpertly executed in script. The boyfriend du jour, obviously.

Yeah, more brilliant decision making. What can I tell you?

Jim peered at the wall menu behind the service counter. "Let's do hummus, almonds, kale, tomatoes, and olives. Cilantro-lime dressing."

That was sounding almost decent until I heard "kale."

"I haven't had lunch," Jim told me.

"No problem." I turned to Cheyenne. "I'll have my usual."

The girl just stared at me, scratching that red-rimmed tattoo. Okay, she was going to use gloves for the food prep, right? I mean, it's the law, right?

Apparently my use of the term "my usual" failed to trigger an association within her brain, despite my having ordered the same darn thing—and only that thing—approximately twenty million times.

"Papaya-ginger smoothie," I said, "large." I watched her wobble off in those preposterous boots, her long fingernails busy as bees. *Scritch, scritch, scritch.*

The day was clear and cold. Jim Manning sat next to the huge window in a patch of dazzling sunlight, as if inviting scrutiny. He was of average height and build, having filled out a bit since his lean teenage years. He was no Adonis, as I've said, but there was something compelling about his looks. Dark, peaked eyebrows and a dusting of old acne scars emphasized the strong lines of his face. His hazel gaze was direct and self-assured, putting me at ease.

He must have been comfortable with me, as well, to have ordered a whole meal rather than, say, a mug of peppermint tea. He could have simply asked me to hand over whatever I had to give him and hightailed it out of there.

The directness didn't stop at his gaze. "I checked you out online, Jane."

I smirked. "And you still agreed to meet me?"

"Are you kidding?" His smile was wide and appealing. "How could I resist?"

I keep track of what's said about me on assorted blogs and boards, although I've been known to regret it. Considering the unique services I provide and that I'd long ago been saddled with the nickname Death Diva, I tend to attract more than my share of wackos and Internet trolls. Chalk it up to the price of doing business.

His bluntness was contagious. I said, "So you were Allison's high school sweetheart."

"High school and throughout college. I went to Cornell. She was at Binghamton. We got together as often as we could."

"So this was a long-term relationship," I said.

He nodded, then turned to stare out the window for a moment at the pedestrian traffic a few feet away on Main Street's sidewalk. Finally he said, "My family didn't approve."

"Of Allison?"

"It was a simple case of snobbery," he said evenly. "A difference in socioeconomic status."

There was that word again, the one Allison had used in one of her last videos. How had she put it? *The last thing I wanted was to make my second marriage about who had less and who had more, the difference in socioeconomic status and all that.*

"My family is well off," he said. "Hers isn't."

I happened to know that "well off" was quite the understatement. I'd done my own Internet research before arranging to meet Jim. The Mannings' wealth went back generations. Jim didn't have to work if he didn't want to. I admired not only that he wanted to but that he used his skills as a civil engineer to help people in underdeveloped areas of the world gain access to clean water and sanitation.

I said, "She was from a small town in West Texas. Superior, I think it's called. Population three hundred something."

Those dark eyebrows rose. "You must have known her better than you say if she told you that much. Allie was pretty private."

"It's… complicated," I said. "So your family didn't want you two to be together?"

"My parents never understood how I could be attracted to, much less in love with, a girl from such a different background," he said. "I knew it was sheer elitism. I resisted it for a long time."

"All through high school and college," I said. "I'd call that a long time. And then?"

"And then—" He was interrupted by the return of Cheyenne, who clop-clopped back over with our food. She set the creamy, orange-colored smoothie in front of Jim, and the quinoa concoction in front of me. I managed not to recoil from it. He slid them into correct position and requested a fork.

"And a straw," I said.

Cheyenne sighed—*Will these oppressive demands never cease?*—and went off in search of eating implements.

"And then," he continued, "Allie and I made plans to get married right after college."

"Your parents must not have been happy about that," I said.

"They never let up. To them it was like end of the world. And you have to understand." He shook his head sadly. "I was close with my parents, still am. They aren't bad people. They have their faults, sure, but don't we all?"

I sensed where this was going. "So you listened to them."

"I held out as long as I could. They—"

Cheyenne returned, with her impeccable timing, to slap our utensils on the table and stomp away.

Jim sighed. "They kept up the pressure. Threatened to disown me. To end all contact with me."

"So you called off the wedding?"

"No. Allie and I were very much in love. She didn't care about my family's money, she just wanted to be with me, and I with her. We decided to elope. Somehow my parents got wind of it. Later I learned they'd hired a private investigator."

"Wow," I said, "they were serious."

"That's when they brought out the big guns. They got my whole family involved, my sisters, my grandparents. Even my best friend, Seth, who I'd known forever. Everyone telling me how much this would hurt them, hurt the family. They treated it like some damn intervention." He let out a long breath. "This was the night we were supposed to leave, Allie and me. She was waiting for me at her place."

I didn't want to ask, but... "Did you ever get there?"

He closed his eyes briefly. "She kept trying to call me, text me. 'Where are you?' I couldn't answer her and deal with my family at the same time, and eventually... I didn't want to answer her. I didn't know what I could say to her."

"Because it was over," I said quietly.

Jim nodded miserably and stared out the window again, for longer this time. He still hadn't touched his food. Finally he said, "I told myself we were just taking a break, Allie and me. Until I could get my head on straight, figure out what I wanted. But she knew even if I didn't that, yeah, it was over."

"What did she do?" I asked.

"She did what any self-respecting person in that situation would do," he said. "She told me to get lost."

"Did you try to get her back?"

He scrubbed a hand over his jaw. I could tell he didn't want to answer. "I was hurt. I thought she should… I don't know what I thought she should do. Sit on her hands and wait for me to come to my senses, I suppose. Anyway, there was this girl Seth had been trying to introduce me to. Tricia. I finally agreed to meet her, just to shut him up."

"Let me guess," I said. "Tricia was someone more 'appropriate.' Someone your family approved of."

"My parents knew her parents," Jim said. "They belonged to the same country club."

"Did you and Tricia get along?"

He offered a wry smile. "We've been married for eight years."

Yep, that qualified as getting along, all right.

"It was kind of a whirlwind thing," he added, "the kind of engagement that just sweeps you along until one day you find yourself standing there saying, 'I do,' and you don't quite know how you got there."

"Kids?"

"We have two sons," he said. "Two and a half and five."

I sucked down some of my smoothie, letting the creamy sweetness slide down my throat as I recalled Allison's stand regarding prenups. This is why she hadn't wanted to make Nick sign one. She hadn't wanted to be like Jim's parents, all about who has less and who has more. *After everything… well, you know, that whole mess we went through. It left a bad taste in my mouth, to say the least.*

I asked, "Did you ever see Allison again?"

"No. I was too ashamed to get in touch with her. And I'm sure she wanted nothing to do with me after the spineless way I handled the whole thing… But I never forgot her. I always kind of kept tabs on her from afar, just to see how she was doing, make sure she was all right. Nothing stalkerish."

"Following her on Facebook, that kind of thing?" I asked.

"Allie wasn't on Facebook. Instagram, yes, for her pictures. Google searches turned up gallery shows and stuff like that. And her wedding announcement was in the *Times*."

"No surprise there," I said. "Mitchell was a prominent businessman."

"When I found out she'd died…" His throat worked. His eyes were shiny.

I sipped my smoothie and waited.

Jim composed himself with an effort. "Don't misunderstand me, Jane. I love Tricia. I love my boys. I wouldn't give them up for anything."

And Allison had loved her first husband, Mitchell. Yet I suspected she and Jim had never stopped loving each other, as well, even during all their years apart and their marriages to other people. "I believe you," I said, thinking about Dom and me. "Life is complicated." After a moment I added, "Allison never forgot you either."

Jim's head came up. "Did she say something to you? About me?"

I guess I'd made the decision. "No, I meant it when I said I never knew her that well. But she left something behind." I reached into my purse and extracted the tiny silver flash drive. I set it on the table between us. "This is Allison's," I said. "It contains a series of short videos—twenty-seven of them. I guess you could call it a video diary."

He picked up the little device, turned it over in his hand. "Why me?"

"She… was talking to you in them," I said. "She said you're the only one she was ever able to open up to. She also said there was no chance you'd see them. I thought she meant… Anyway, I think she would have wanted you to have them. Oh! I almost forgot. The drive is password-protected. 'Shrooms' will get you in."

At that he smiled, that warm, wide grin. "Allie always did have a thing for mushrooms. By which I mean regular old fungi," he added, "not the magical variety."

"Oh, I know." I returned the smile. "I've seen her nature photos. Shrooms galore. It's how I guessed the password."

"Photography was always her refuge. She was really good, too. Even back in high school, that camera was always glued to her. I was happy to see she kept at it." He closed his fist around the flash drive and reached across the table with his free hand to squeeze mine. "You didn't have to do this, Jane. I'm glad you did. Thank you."

9

Geoffrey, No!

"WE ARE HERE to celebrate the life of Geoffrey T. Boatwright the Second." Father Kade projected his voice to ensure that no one present at the graveside service would miss a word. Not that he had to project far. Only seven individuals had shown up, including me, and I'd been paid to do so.

You guessed it, this was one of my Death Diva gigs. I'd made all the arrangements, which hadn't been too involved since there'd been no church service in this case.

"Geoffrey was loving and loyal," Father Kade intoned, as Agnes Boatwright began to sniffle, "and will always be remembered for his happy-go-lucky nature."

It was Wednesday afternoon and unseasonably mild for January, as it had been for the past couple of weeks. Today my usual funeral uniform—the gray suit, the faux pearls—was completely hidden under a sedate camel-colored coat. I could have paired a sexy leather corset with my ladylike black pumps, and no one would have been the wiser.

No, I do not own a sexy leather corset, and thank you very much for reminding me that I have no one to buy one for. Or to buy one for me. Oh, you know what I mean.

Agnes's sniffles turned to loud weeping. She was a small

woman of around sixty. Her grown daughter stood next to her, patting her back, murmuring words of consolation, and offering the occasional sunflower seed to the crow sitting on Agnes's shoulder. The inky black bird wore a little red harness attached to a leash.

Well, you don't want your crow taking off in the middle of a funeral, do you? I mean, be sensible.

Father Kade wore a black overcoat, his clerical collar visible in the vee of his neatly tucked gray scarf. He continued to sing the praises of Geoffrey T. Boatwright II. "His loved ones tell me he made friends easily. A better listener never lived."

The crow occupied itself by emitting the occasional caw and trying to snatch its grieving owner's eyeglasses off her face. Suddenly it screeched, "Geoffrey, no!"

I jumped. So did Father Kade, who shot me a reproachful look for not warning him about the bird. Well, how could I have warned him if I didn't know myself that Agnes would be bringing it? And yes, apparently crows can learn to mimic human speech. Who knew?

"Geoffrey loved physical activity," he continued. "His favorite pastimes were swimming in the pool and going for long walks. And I'm told he never met a tennis ball he didn't like." This prompted a warm chuckle of remembrance from the deceased's nearest and dearest.

"Geoffrey, no!" the crow cried again, as Agnes tried to hush it. The shells of sunflower seeds littered her hair and coat.

"Geoffrey was obedient," Father Kade said. "He never chewed furniture or did his business in the house."

On cue the crow screamed, "Geoffrey, no! Bad dog!" It flew off Agnes's shoulder and landed on the small, ornate casket next to the open grave, which was about three feet long. The tombstone was already in place. The deceased's portrait had been etched onto it, along with his name, the years of birth and death, and the words *Loving Husband of Agnes*.

Agnes tugged on the leash, to no avail. "Geoffrey, stop that!" she said. "Come back here."

Yes, the bird had the same name as the dead dog. Well, not exactly the same. The crow was Geoffrey T. Boatwright III. You see, it was the reincarnation of the deceased pug, who was Geoffrey T. Boatwright II, who in turn was the reincarnation of Geoffrey T. Boatwright, Agnes's beloved husband. The original Geoffrey, the human one, had died fifteen years ago. Does that clarify things?

Yeah, I know, but a girl has to make a living. So does a boy. Tending bar at Murray's provided the padre with a modest living, but just that. He supplemented his income by helping me out with the occasional Death Diva gig.

Oh, didn't I mention? When Martin is impersonating a priest, he calls himself Father Kade. He thinks he's being fiendishly clever since his full name is Martin Kade McAuliffe.

I almost had a real priest willing to do the service, but when he found out reincarnation was involved, that was the end of that. And I'm telling you, when Martin's wearing that collar and doing his priest shtick, you'd never know he wasn't the real deal. Agnes probably suspected, but she was so emotionally invested in a Catholic sendoff for Geoffrey II that she refrained from asking too many awkward questions.

Martin paused in his eulogy while Agnes and her daughter struggled to corral Geoffrey III, who was having none of it. He hopped into the neatly dug hole, which caused Agnes to sob and scream, "Geoffrey, no! It's not your time!" The other mourners got into the act, prompting the bird to try to fly off, still tethered to Agnes by its leash.

At this rate it would be dinnertime before I got home. My phone vibrated in my pocket. Using the escalating mayhem for cover, I discreetly checked the screen. It was Jim Manning. I'd handed over the flash drive to him just yesterday. Normally I wouldn't answer the phone in the middle of a funeral, but no one was likely to notice at the moment, and I was curious about Jim's reaction to the videos.

I moved a few yards away. The Best Friend Pet Cemetery was devoid of visitors except for our little group. I paused next to a row of three doggie headstones I was intimately familiar with, having arranged myself for their carving and placement, and having spent many years delivering flowers to these little graves on behalf of Irene McAuliffe. I'd started out pet-sitting for her when I was a teen, an after-school gig that gradually, through referrals, morphed into my Death Diva business.

Irene had been a movie buff. The markers I was looking at bore the names of her previous toy poodles: *Annie Hall*, *Dr. Strangelove*, and *Jaws*.

I answered the phone, keeping my voice low and one eye on the action at Geoffrey II's gravesite. Geoffrey III was cawing up a storm, pecking and biting anyone who attempted to grab him.

"Can you talk?" Jim asked.

"Um… only for a minute. What's up? Did you watch any of the videos?"

"I watched all of them," he said. "Once I started, I couldn't stop. I was up all night. I have to tell you, I'm a little disturbed. What's up with that Barbie doll?"

"Oh, that," I said. "Yeah, it bothered me too at first."

"It's sick," he said. "That someone would leave that thing for her to find."

"There was never anything else as far as I know," I said. "I mean, no other incidents like that. It was a one-shot deal."

"Is that supposed to be comforting?" he asked. "Someone tried to freak her out. Maybe threaten her."

"I know it looks that way, but the thinking is that it was just a kid playing a prank."

"Whose thinking?" he said. "Who did you talk to about this?"

"A couple of police detectives I know. They actually looked into it a little on their own time, asked around to see if anyone had it in for Allison, that kind of thing."

"Why didn't you tell me about this yesterday?" he asked.

I continued to monitor the activity at the gravesite. It appeared that Martin had finally had enough. I watched him wade into the fray, and hoped Geoffrey III didn't decide to go for his eyes.

"Jim, I know it's upsetting," I said, "that headless doll, but what does it matter at this point? It had nothing to do with what happened to Allison."

After a moment he asked, "How can you be sure?"

"The detectives didn't find anything useful," I said. "Not that they spent that long on it, but it was clear—"

"What do you mean? How long did they work on it?"

"A couple of days," I said. "Um, Allison's mom asked me to call them off. It was causing her and her husband more grief, and really, she was right. Jim, listen. The cops who were at the scene, the medical examiner, all the experts, they looked at the physical evidence and decided Allison's death was an accident."

Somehow Martin managed to seize Geoffrey III. He took the leash from Agnes and prepared to resume the eulogy with a pet crow perched on his right arm. He shot me a pointed look.

Would you care to join us?

"Okay, I get it," Jim said, "but just tell me, could there be any more videos besides the ones on this flash drive? I'm asking because Allie maxed out the space on this drive, and the last video on it was made nine days before she died. She'd been making at least one a week since June, so I'm thinking we might be missing one or two."

"There are no more that I know of. Listen, I have to go."

"Do you think her husband would let you look around?" Jim asked. "You know, for a second flash drive. I mean, I heard what Allie had to say about him, I know the guy's not likely to be cooperative, but maybe it's worth a try."

What did he think, that if more videos came to light, all his questions would be answered? That he'd see Allison laughingly relate her discovery that a neighbor's mischievous kid had left the doll in her mailbox? Or perhaps he envisioned her horror at learning that a particular individual wanted her dead.

There was a desperate edge to his request. I understood his concern. I'd felt the same way until four days earlier when Joleen's visit knocked some sense into me.

Geoffrey III scooted up Martin's arm to his shoulder, where he promptly pooped, then screamed, "Geoffrey, no! Not on the rug!"

"If she left another flash drive, I'll find it," I promised Jim. "I'll figure out a way."

"WHAT AM I supposed to do now?" I asked.

"That depends," Martin said. "Do you think there's another flash drive floating around?"

"How should I know?"

We were in his 1966 Mustang convertible. Candy-apple red, natch. No, the top wasn't down—it was January, remember? But that didn't diminish the car's appeal. It might not be as sexy as the big Harley the padre customarily rode, but it was still one hot ride. We were driving through Crystal Harbor's residential back streets, having left the cemetery a few minutes earlier. I'd been telling Martin about my conversation with Jim.

I plucked a tissue out of my purse and started scrubbing at the white blob Geoffrey III had deposited on the shoulder of Martin's coat. "Jim does have a point," I said. "There's a nine-day gap after the last video, and she was making them more frequently than that. And since there was no more room on the flash drive she was using…" I shrugged. "Yeah, there very well could be another one. But if so, it would be well hidden, like the first one."

"You'll find it. I have faith in you."

"You'll excuse me if that doesn't make me feel all warm and fuzzy inside." I wasn't having much success cleaning Martin's coat—unless making a small spot into a big spot and grinding it into black wool counted as success. I wagged the dirty tissue. "Where can I put this? Do you have a trash bag?"

He snatched it from my fingers, lowered the window, and tossed it outside. Which, I must point out, is something I never, ever do. Not because I'm such a responsible citizen, but because I'm convinced that the instant the thing left my fingers, I'd be surrounded by a phalanx of cop cars, complete with screaming sirens and blaring bullhorns. *Hands where I can see them!*

Martin said, "Just get in there and look for it."

"What, just knock on the door of Allison's house and ask Nick if he minds me snooping through his stuff on the off chance I might stumble across his late wife's secret video diary? Dang, why didn't I think of that?"

"It isn't *his* house, though, is it?" Martin asked. "Doesn't it belong to Allison's folks?"

"Yeah, but they're giving him a decent amount of time to move out. That's how her mother put it."

"Good luck with that," he said. "They really think the guy's going to give up a cushy crib like this without a fight?"

Like *this*? I glanced out the window and saw we were passing Allison's house. I'd been so absorbed in our conversation I hadn't noticed where Martin was taking us. He made a couple of turns and parked on a quiet side street behind the neighborhood. The houses were spaced far apart, the backyards abutting a patch of woods.

Martin said, "It looked like Nick was home."

How could he tell that from one quick drive-by? There'd been no car in the driveway, no one walking past a window. This questionable skill came under the general heading of Things I Would Rather Not Know About Martin. I was at peace with my ignorance. Kind of. I suspected that if I ever got the full story about this man's mysterious and possibly felonious past—and present?—I'd run in the opposite direction as fast as my legs could carry me.

The padre pulled his cell phone out of his pocket and handed it to me. "You're going to call him and get him out of the house."

"Oh, I am, am I? Just like that. Hey." I looked more closely at the phone. It was smaller than the one Martin usually carried, cheaper looking. "Is this new? What happened to the last one?"

"Oh, I still have it." He patted a different pocket. "Trust me, you don't want to make this call from your personal phone, and I don't want it traced back to me either."

It took my wee brain a couple of seconds to figure it out. Then I gaped at him, bug-eyed. "This is a *burner phone*!" I dropped the thing as if it might indeed burst into flames. It was one of those prepaid, no-contract phones that criminals bought with cash, used for some nefarious purpose, then discarded, along with the phone number. Not trackable, no incriminating trail.

"Careful." He reached over and picked it up from the floor. "This thing won't take much abuse."

He tried to hand it back to me. I glued myself to the passenger door, palms raised. "Don't give that to me. I don't want it. You shouldn't even have it."

"You've been watching too much *Law & Order*," he said. "People buy these for a lot of reasons, most of them perfectly legit."

"Why did *you* buy it?" The question was out of my mouth before I could stop it. Burner phones definitely qualified as one more Thing I Would Rather Not Know About Martin. Fortunately, his selective deafness prevented him from answering.

"The goal is to get Nick out of the house," he said. "An hour should do it, with both of us in there searching. Forty-five minutes minimum. Put on your thinking cap."

"Um..." My thinking cap was on the fritz. What would

motivate Nick to run out of the house? I was coming up empty.

"Does he have family that you know of?" Martin asked.

"No one who was at the funeral. At least I didn't get introduced to anyone. I hope you're not thinking I'd call pretending to be from a hospital or something, like your mama's been in an accident."

"An oldie but a goodie," he said. "There's always Skye. It doesn't have to be an accident. Maybe his baby mama has a bad case of food poisoning. He'd go running to hold her hand in the ER."

"Forget it, Padre, that's just too mean. I won't do it."

He spread his hands. "Hey, I'm just brainstorming here. You're the one who wants to find out if someone offed Allison."

"Correction," I said. "I know no one offed Allison. I'm just trying to put Jim's mind at rest. I owe him that much. I'm the one who gave him the videos and got him thinking along those lines."

"Back to Nick. Let's look at it from his perspective. What does he want more than anything?"

That was easy. "Allison's money. But I don't see how we could use that to—Oh. Hmm."

Martin was staring at me. "'Oh hmm' what? What's going on in that devious little mind of yours?"

"My mind isn't devious."

"Yes it is, whether you know it or not." He wore a silky smile. "And I find it sexy as hell."

"Uh-huh," I said, fully aware that the blush warming my face contradicted my blasé tone. "Okay, so here's what I'm thinking. Sten Jakobsen's office is a good twenty minutes from here."

"Closer to thirty with rush-hour traffic."

He was right. It was a little after four. The roads were starting to get congested. I said, "Nick gets a call from Sten's paralegal saying, I don't know, we found a loophole in the prenup or something. A mistake in your favor. You stand to inherit oodles of money after all."

"But you have to get here right this instant or the coach will turn back into a pumpkin."

"Right," I said. "Think it'll work?"

"Depends how convincing you are." Martin shoved the burner phone in my face. "He'll recognize your voice, so find a way to disguise it."

I hauled my own phone out of my bag to retrieve Nick's number from my contacts, then took a deep breath, tapped the number into the burner phone, and waited for the young widower to pick up.

"Hello?" Nick said, with the suspicious tone of one who doesn't recognize the number on his screen.

I roughened up my voice and went all nasal. "Mr. Birch?"

"Yeah?"

"This is Sharon from Sten Jakobsen's office. I'm his paralegal." I let out a couple of coughs. "'Scuse me, I have a bad cold."

Martin gave me a thumbs-up for effective voice disguising.

Nick asked, "What happened to Jeanie?"

"Who?"

"Jeanie," he said. "Mr. Jakobsen's paralegal."

"Oh. She quit. I'm new." Before he had a chance to question the abrupt change in staff, I said, "Mr. Jakobsen would like to see you at his office."

"Forget it," he said. "Anything that old shyster has to tell me, he can say to my new lawyer. You guys have his name and number. Don't call me again."

Before he could hang up, I said, "Wait! Wait! Mr. Birch, this is about the prenuptial agreement you and your late wife signed."

"You mean the prenup I was tricked into signing? *That* prenup? Like I said, he can talk to—"

"Mr. Jakobsen made a, um, technical error," I blurted. "The prenup is invalid. It's like it never existed."

I waited while he digested that. "Really? Then does that mean I get my share?"

"It's my understanding," I said, "that in the absence of the prenuptial agreement, you would be eligible to inherit one third of your late wife's estate. We need your signature, though, on the paperwork."

Nick almost blew out my eardrums with, "*Yes!* I knew it would work out. Tell him I'll be in sometime this week."

"I'm afraid Mr. Jakobsen won't be in the office for the rest of the week, or even for the next…"

I cast about for an appropriate time frame. Martin held up six fingers.

"For the next six days," I said, and watched the padre smack his forehead. "*Weeks!* He's going away for six weeks, to… to Mongolia for a, um, an international legal symposium. He's leaving for his trip in a half hour, and he has to be present to witness your signature, so you have to come in right now."

"I don't know… I just nuked a chicken pot pie. The paperwork will still be there when he gets back."

"Um, no, it won't," I said, thinking fast. "The deadline for filing the papers is five o'clock today—that's forty-seven minutes from now—otherwise the prenup stands and can never be undone. You need to get here pronto, Mr. Birch."

Radio silence as I imagined what was going on inside his handsome head. *Hmm… four million bucks or a chicken pot pie?* Yeah, I could see how he might be conflicted.

"All right, all right," he said, "I'm leaving now. Tell him to wait for me." The line went dead.

I tossed the burner phone at Martin and slumped back against my seat, feeling like I'd just run a 10K. Not that I've ever run a 10K, but I can, you know, imagine it feels something like that.

"You're a natural." Martin patted my thigh, his hand lingering just long enough to accelerate my pulse and supply a reviving boost of energy. He threw open his door and jumped out of the car. "Tick-tock, Jane, we have a home to burgle."

"Don't say that." I got out of the car, arranging my purse strap crossways, bandolier-style. "It's not like that, Padre. We're not burglars." Well, *I* wasn't. The jury was still out on Martin. "What we're doing is… well, all I know is it's not burglary."

He opened the car's trunk. "Sorry to burst your bubble, but once we get in, you're talking second-degree burglary."

"What if we leave empty-handed?"

"Doesn't matter," he said cheerfully. "Our intent matters, and we intend to take something that doesn't belong to us. You could get up to fifteen years in the slammer. Maybe more if they tack on criminal impersonation. Glad you asked?"

Well, they say you should try everything once, right? No, I don't know who says it—*they*, all right? The same *they* who tell me to exercise for thirty minutes every day and replace my mascara every three months. Both of which are as likely to happen as my trying everything once.

He closed the trunk and tossed something small at me. I fumbled the catch and had to bend to pick up the item, which turned out to be two items: a pair of latex gloves. I watched him pull on a pair.

This was getting too real. Up to that point, the only thought I'd given to fingerprints had been how to keep them off Irene's—now my—obscenely expensive glass-topped coffee table with a burl-wood cube base.

I started to whine about the gloves, but Martin had already taken off through the winter-bare woods. I struggled to catch up, picking my way cautiously in my impractical pumps. I stuck close to him as he located Allison's sprawling backyard and paused behind the cover of a large fir tree. Within moments I heard an unmistakable metallic rumbling. Peering through the branches, I spotted Nick hurrying from the back door of the house to the old carriage house, which apparently had been updated with an automatic garage door opener. Within moments a white Audi emerged and raced down the long drive to the street.

Martin peered at our surroundings for long moments, listening intently, as alert as a jaguar, before grabbing my hand and sprinting with me across the tree-studded yard to the back porch. We passed the covered hot tub, which should have been an inviting sight on a cold winter day, but all I could think, considering its notorious history, was *Eww...*

Opening his coat, he reached into a pocket of his black pants, part of his priest getup, and produced a credit card. Only, it wasn't a credit card. I knew this because I'd seen it before. It was solid black and a little thicker than an actual credit card, and when he slid the back off as he was doing now, one could see the five adorable little lock picks nestled inside.

"Possession of burglar's tools." He grinned. "Class A misdemeanor."

"Shut up."

"Well, aren't we grumpy," he said as he went to work on the lock. "I'm doing this for you, remember, risking serious jail time so you can—what's your story again?—oh yeah, so you can reassure this guy Jim, a virtual stranger, that there was nothing suspicious about the death of his old girlfriend, a woman he hadn't laid eyes on in, what, nearly a decade. Do I have that right? And we're in."

It took me a moment to realize that last comment had to do with the lock. "That was fast."

"There's probably an alarm. Stay here. And get those gloves on." Martin eased the door open. I expected a warning tone indicating an armed house alarm, but heard only silence. He stepped into the mudroom and glanced at the alarm pad near the door before beckoning me to join him. "He didn't set it."

I knew from experience that if Nick had set the alarm, it wouldn't have caused much of a delay in our breaking and entering. I myself had finally stopped installing newer, better, wowee kazowee alarm systems in my house. If the padre wanted to get in, he got in. This was both disturbing and strangely exciting. Disturbing because if he decided to slip into my home in the middle of the night, I had no way to stop him. Exciting because if he decided to slip into my home in the middle of the night, I had no way to stop him.

The padre strode swiftly into the kitchen, checking the time on his phone—one of his phones. I still couldn't believe he'd manipulated me into using a burner phone. Correction: using a burner phone to commit criminal impersonation so we could burgle the place. And I'd been worried about littering.

"Shake a leg, Jane. In thirty-nine minutes we're out of here, with or without that flash drive."

"If it even exists," I said.

He was yanking open drawers and cabinets, quickly pawing through utensils, dishes, pots and pans as Nick's uneaten chicken pot pie cooled on the counter. The darn thing smelled better than it had a right to. I wondered what the young widower would think if he came back to find a bite or two missing.

I went into the butler's pantry and opened the freezer, shoving aside a half gallon of rocky road and about two dozen chicken pot pies to peer into the corners. That's a favorite hiding place, right? The freezer?

We split up on the first floor. I emulated Martin, rifling quickly through every conceivable hiding place in the living room and sunroom while he took the dining room and den, both of us being careful to leave everything as we'd found it. We met up in Allison's office.

Martin checked his phone. "Twenty-seven minutes left."

"You know, there's a basement," I said. "Not to mention the second floor and the attic. This is a huge place." The subtext being: *There's no way we'll search the rest of this house in twenty-seven minutes and I'm getting really nervous, so let's get the heck out of here.*

Either he was oblivious to the subtext or he chose to ignore it. My money was on that second thing. He was rifling through Allison's desk drawers. "Did you check behind the pictures?" he asked. "Something that small could be taped—"

"Yes, of course," I snapped, in the wounded tones of a seasoned criminal whose expertise had just been challenged. I'd have to slip back into the rooms I'd searched and look behind the darn pictures.

"Ha!" he said.

My pulse leapt. "Did you find it?"

"Her phone." He displayed his booty, a sleek smartphone in a silver-pink case, and slipped it into a pocket. "Might be something useful on it."

"You can't take that."

"I just did." He closed the drawer and opened another. "Don't worry, I'll return it. Nick will never know it was gone."

"It probably doesn't even work," I said. "She must have had it on her when she went into the lake."

"I'll try to power it up later. No time to mess with it now. Shake a leg, Jane. Time's flying."

My heart was no longer in this project, if it ever was. Yeah, that's right, it was a project, not a burglary, so you can just save the judgmental attitude for a, you know, real burglar.

I made myself cross to the antique cherry-wood bookcase and start tipping back the books to check behind them. There were best-selling novels, anthologies of short stories and poetry, and volumes on photography and history—including, yes, the history of photography. Several shelves had been set aside for small framed photos and assorted souvenirs and tchotchkes, crammed together in sociable groupings.

An African figurine carved from dark wood. A small silver box encrusted with amethysts. A marble paperweight. A crystal hedgehog. Russian nesting dolls. An ornate Victorian teacup and saucer with gilded edges and an intricate floral design. A bowl carved from petrified wood and filled with small seashells and chunks of frosty beach glass in pastel tones.

I peered at a small, framed snapshot of a grinning Allison

standing on a crowded sidewalk—Times Square, by the looks of it. She wore a sundress and sandals. A camera hung from her neck by a strap, a serious-looking camera with a long lens. I smiled. She'd been doing what she loved best.

I poked my gloved finger into the bowl of shells and felt around for something the size and shape of a flash drive. As I did so, my gaze skated over the objects behind it and came to a startled halt on one object in particular, half-concealed behind a painted porcelain Buddha. It was a small piece of handmade ceramic, two to three inches tall, glossy black blending to an oatmeal-colored glaze at the edges. I saw a rounded top studded with tiny holes.

"Martin?" I said.

"Twenty-five minutes, Jane." He was digging around in a cardboard accordion file crammed with papers filed in alphabetical order. "More searching, less talking."

I reached behind the Buddha and picked up the little shaker shaped like a mushroom. I turned it upside down and shook it. No pepper came out. There wasn't a doubt in my mind that I was holding the missing mate to the salt shaker Joleen had given me. She'd assumed it had been broken.

My breathing quickened as I pried the tiny cork out of the bottom. A dab of poster putty had been stuck to the inside of the cork, and pressed into that—yes, I know you're way ahead of me, I'm so proud of you—was a tiny flash drive identical to the one I'd handed over to Jim yesterday.

10

A Couple of Gullible Nitwits

"MARTIN?"

He looked up from the accordion file, his hand jammed into the *N* section, his irritated frown only adding to his hotness quotient, damn his sexy hide. "What?" he barked, before focusing on the prize I triumphantly held in front of his face.

In one smooth movement he snatched the flash drive, pocketed it, and unceremoniously shoved me toward the doorway.

"Hey!" I dug in my heels. "Give that back."

"Later." He marched me down the hall and into the living room. "If we're caught, I don't want it found on you."

Oh my. A gallant gesture from Martin McAuliffe. I shouldn't have been surprised. It wasn't the first time he'd acted selflessly where I was concerned, but in the past it had been precipitated by a life-threatening situation.

We were passing the front vestibule when we heard the door lock turn. Nick was back! I froze. We had no hope of making it out of the living room, much less out of the house, before that door swung open.

Fortunately for me, the padre wasn't one to stand around

waiting to be caught in the act. As the doorknob began to turn, he propelled me across the living room to the staircase. He couldn't possibly think we had time to make it up the stairs. I started to pull back, only to have him grip my arm tighter, open the door to the little closet tucked under the staircase, haul us both inside, and shut us in just as the front door swung open.

The closet wasn't empty, as it turned out. We'd had to duck just to get into the cramped space and ended up falling on top of assorted stuff piled in there, impossible to identify in the pitch blackness. I thought for sure the noise would give us away, but at that precise moment a shrill female voice drowned out all else.

"Nick!"

It was Skye who'd entered the house, not Nick. Obviously the grieving widower had given his baby mama a key to his late wife's house.

The closet was tiny, a wedge of space with a sloping ceiling, impossible to stand up in even if it weren't half-filled with tennis rackets, balls, and other sports equipment, as I soon learned by groping around, trying to find a position in which to lie still and quiet. Martin was doing his share of groping too, and not the good kind, although we were pressed so close together that some of it ended up being the good kind just by accident.

The musty smell of the closet and its contents competed with the inviting scent of Martin's skin as I lay with my cheek nestled against his throat, trying to ignore the croquet mallet jabbing my ribs. Our limbs remained tangled from our fall—we didn't dare move. I felt the rise and fall of his chest, felt the steady beat of his heart right through his clothing and coat.

Never before had we found ourselves in such intimate proximity, an intimacy enhanced by the impenetrable darkness, not to mention the all-too-likely danger of getting caught.

I jumped when Skye screeched, *"Nick!"* right next to my ear. At least that's what it felt like. Belatedly I realized she must be standing at the foot of the stairs, calling up to the second floor. Martin pulled me tighter against him, if that was possible. I recognized it for the self-protective gesture it was. He didn't want me moving around, making noise, landing us both in the hoosegow. But I won't lie, it felt good.

Percussive blows shook the closet as Skye began to stomp up the stairs in search of Nick. I felt Martin tense and deduced he was preparing to vamoose as soon as she was safely out of earshot. I, too, got ready to bolt. Unfortunately, she halted halfway up the stairs. I heard some ripe cussing, directed at "that stupid SOB" Nick, as she banged back down the steps. Martin's frustrated sigh wafted over me.

She began moving through the living room, pausing here and there. An occasional clanking sound reached my ears, sometimes a dull thud, making me think of smallish items colliding. Her footfalls grew fainter and I pictured her entering the office and the other rooms off the hallway. Which didn't help us. As long as she remained on the first floor, we couldn't hope to sneak out of the house undetected.

Martin whispered in my ear, very very quietly, "Do you have Skye's phone number?"

I shook my head and felt him deflate. "Why?"

"I was going to text her," he said. "Something like 'This is Nick, I'm waiting for you upstairs, bunny. Good news about the prenup!'"

"But it wouldn't be coming from his phone," I said.

"'Lost my phone, bunny, this is a loaner.'"

Too bad. It probably would have worked. Clever Martin. Talk of phones made me realize something. I felt around for my purse and quietly withdrew my phone from it. I showed him what I was doing as the screen lit up and I silenced both ringer and vibration. His grunt was eloquent: *Good idea.* He did the same with both of his phones, muttering a curse when he saw how much time had elapsed.

Eventually Skye passed through the living room again, this time on her way to the dining room, by the sound of it.

"What could she be doing?" I whispered.

Martin replied with a shrug.

"Maybe she's collecting stuff she left here." I yawned.

"Maybe she's collecting stuff, period."

"What, you mean stealing?" I said. "From Nick?"

"From Allison's parents," he said. "They inherited the bulk of her assets."

I said, "Which probably includes all her physical belongings." The closet was unheated, which was just as well since we both still wore our coats, plus our combined body heat acted like a radiator in the small space. It was almost cozy. I yawned again.

The next thing I knew, Martin was gently shaking my shoulder. I woke up disoriented in the velvet blackness, demanding "What?" in a nice loud voice and trying to sit up.

The padre clamped a gloved hand over my mouth and pulled me tight against him, murmuring, "Shh…" into my ear. I struggled for a moment until my sleep-numbed brain caught on that this was not the best time and place to be creating a racket.

He withdrew his hand as I settled back down, still tucked

against him like a lover. I heard muted activity from a nearby room. "Where is she?" I whispered.

"Butler's pantry would be my guess."

Where the crystal and china were stored, not to mention plenty of sterling silver flatware and serving pieces. I'd admired them during the funeral reception. Martin was probably right. She was swiping all the small valuables she could carry.

My jaw was damp. So was the shoulder of Martin's coat, where the jaw in question had recently rested. "Please tell me I wasn't drooling in my sleep," I said.

"I didn't mind until you started snoring like a wood chipper," the padre said. "I had to wake you then or we'd have been busted."

Jane Delaney, paragon of grace and refinement. Oh, and here's another fun fact. I'd fallen asleep with my face pressed to his right shoulder, the shoulder that, though I couldn't see it in the dark, I knew to be adorned with ground-in crow feces. I tried to shift away from the spot, but there wasn't all that much room to shift.

"Look at it this way," he whispered, far too cheerfully. "From now on I can tell everyone that you slept with me."

Did I say he was gallant? I take it back.

"What time is it?" I whispered.

The glowing screen of a phone illuminated his face for a second or two. "Five twenty-two."

"Uh-oh," I said. Nick had headed out to Sten's office at 4:13. He could be back any—

"Skye?" Nick called from the vicinity of the kitchen. "I saw your car out front. Where are you, bunny?"

This was followed by his girlfriend's rapid footfalls hightailing it from the butler's pantry into the dining room.

He took off after her, catching up with her in the living room before she could make it out the front door.

"Hey, where are you going?" he said.

"Nowhere." She sounded out of breath. "I mean, I have to be somewhere."

Their voices came through loud and clear. They had to be standing right next to our hiding place.

"Listen," Nick said, "I'm sorry I wasn't home when you got here, but I got this call from, like, someone at that lawyer Jakobsen's office, only when I got there they had no idea—"

"I have to *go*," Skye insisted. "Like I *said*. Let go of my arm."

"What are you doing lugging around something this size? Wow, it's heavy."

"Give me that!" she cried.

"What do you have in here?" I heard loud clanking as he set her tote bag, or pillow case, or whatever it was on the rug. "You shouldn't be lifting heavy stuff in your condition."

"That's mine!" Skye yelled. "Give it back!"

An ominous silence ensued, several long seconds during which I pictured Nick taking in the contents of Skye's bag.

"What the hell?" he said.

"I *earned* it!" she screamed.

"This stuff doesn't belong to you." It was the first time I'd heard him raise his voice to his girlfriend.

"It does now," she said. "I'm not walking away from this with nothing to show—"

"What are you talking about?" he said. "Walking away from what? We're in this for the long haul, you and me. We have a baby on the way."

"*Oh my God, there is no baby!*" she screamed.

Nick was suddenly grave. "Oh, bunny, did something happen?"

"How dense are you?" she said. "There never *was* any baby."

The padre breathed a nearly inaudible "Whoa."

"What, you mean…" Nick sounded wounded. "You lied to me? About the baby? Why would you do something like that?"

"It was *my* turn!" she said. "She had everything. This place, all this stuff, all that *money*. What did I have? What did I *ever* have? *It was my turn!*"

"I don't see how that gives you the right to trick me." He sounded really steamed now. "To lie to me. Not about something like this."

"I knew you wanted a kid."

When he spoke a moment later, he sounded guarded. "I never told you I wanted one with you."

"Yeah, well, *she* sure as hell didn't want one with *you*. You bitched about it all the time." Skye did an insulting imitation of said bitching. "'Allison wanted Mitchell's baby but not mine, boo-hoo.' Face it, she was never going to have your baby. The last thing she wanted was to bring a brat of yours into the world."

"So you thought, what, I'll just lie to him? Make him think he's going to be a daddy?"

"Big deal," she said, "I would've gotten knocked up soon enough. But it didn't matter, did it? Even when you thought we had a baby on the way, you were never going to do anything about Allison."

After a moment, he said, "You don't know that."

Her response was a snort of derision. "Just my luck to rely

on a couple of gullible nitwits. I sure can pick 'em."

A *couple* of nitwits? She must mean Nick and Allison. No question Nick was a gullible nitwit, but his late wife? Then I realized that from Skye's perspective, it probably made sense. Allison had, after all, allowed Skye not only to get close to her, but to sneak around with her husband. Far more comfortable to blame the victim for her gullibility than to accept that you're a coldblooded, money-grubbing user.

"Is that why you pretended to be pregnant?" he asked. "To get me to leave her?"

"If so," she said sneeringly, "it worked like a charm, huh?"

"I would've had nothing if I left Allison. I mean, we weren't married that long. Four months. No way was I getting alimony or a settlement or whatever, even without that prenup."

"You only wanted to put a baby in her so she'd keep you around," Skye said, "keep you on easy street. It had nothing to do with wanting to be a daddy. Admit it."

Nick sighed. "It's not that simple. Sure, I'd like a kid. Why not?"

"But with *her*, not me. That way you would've had the kid *and* the money, am I right?"

"*We* were going to have the kid and the money, *you and me*," he said, "until Jakobsen threw that damn prenup in my face. That's why I hired this new lawyer, to get that thing overturned so the two of us… well, I thought it would be the three of us. You, me, and the baby."

"Yeah, and how's that going?" Her tone oozed disdain. "With the lawyer?"

"Not so good. He says he can't do anything until I cough up the eighteen grand for dispensations."

"*Disbursements*, you moron, and it's up to eighteen now? Last week he said fifteen. The guy's a rip-off artist. Whatever, I'm out of here."

I heard more clanking—the sack of loot being lifted, I assumed.

Nick said, "You're not taking that."

"I earned it, like I said."

"For services rendered?" There was a mean edge to his voice I'd never heard before, followed by a startled squawk from Skye and a violent clatter. I pictured Nick yanking the bag out of her grasp, pictured the contents scattering across the rug.

Martin half rose onto an elbow. I sensed his readiness to intervene if Nick decided that what his duplicitous girlfriend had actually earned was a black eye. If so, I imagined the mere sight of an avenging priest leaping out of the under-stairs closet would be enough to make him reconsider.

What we heard, however, was Nick yelping in pain as Skye screamed, *"You're calling me a whore now? Huh? Is that what I am, you sorry-ass loser?"*

"Stop it!" he bleated. "Skye, stop! Jeez, I'm sorry, all right?"

"Go to hell!" The whole house shook as the front door slammed.

11

So, Marty, When Do You Get Off?

"...SO THIS TIME tomorrow I'll be on my way to Canberra," Allison said from my computer screen. She was happy and excited, looking forward to her upcoming trek on horseback through the Snowy Mountains of New South Wales, Australia—or the Snowies, as she called them.

There was just one video on the flash drive I'd found in her office. It had been made at 10:32 p.m. on December 25, Christmas night. I was watching it with Jim, having invited him to my house for that purpose. It seemed strange sharing Allison's most private thoughts with another person. I had to remind myself that not only had he watched the other twenty-seven videos but that she'd addressed them to him.

I sat at my little antique desk in the maid's room. He stood behind me. It was shortly after eight p.m. Martin and I hadn't had long to wait after Skye stormed out of Allison's house three hours earlier. Nick had immediately retreated upstairs, leaving an opening for the padre and me to skedaddle, and skedaddle we had. If Nick had happened to be looking out one of the upstairs windows at the back of the house, he would have seen us sprinting across the backyard. Since I'd heard from neither him nor the cops, I assumed our hasty exit had gone unobserved.

In the video, Allison had discussed Christmas at her folks' and how she'd tried to take some of the burden off her mother by doing more of the cooking and cleanup, but Joleen wouldn't hear of it. They'd given her some gear for her trip—toiletry kit, folding toothbrush, that sort of thing. She'd given them a much-needed new roof. Her parents didn't have much, but they were proud. Apparently the only time they'd accept anything of value from her was at Christmas. Last year she'd given them a furnace and new siding.

Of course, the Gleasons were now multimillionaires and could purchase a spectacular new home. I knew they'd far prefer to have their daughter back.

Allison mentioned her argument with Nick over the loss of his job at Vargas Sporting Goods, but spent most of the video talking about her trip to the Snowies. Apparently she was an accomplished horsewoman, which came as no surprise considering her love of outdoor sports.

Allison sat curled in the armchair in her office, as usual, wearing a pretty red sweater and looking straight into the camera lens. "The flight's twenty-six hours with two stops," she said. "You know how I hate long flights, Jim, but it'll be worth it once I get there. I mean, for the balmy weather alone. It's in the eighties there this week. Plus I can definitely use the break, considering everything that's going on here."

She kept talking while she rose from the chair and walked out of the frame. "And think of the amazing shots I'll get." She sat back down and displayed two cameras in turn, a compact one that looked like something even I could handle and a larger, professional-looking one with a wide neck strap. I recognized that one from the snapshot I'd seen in her office, the one taken in Times Square. "I'll have both these babies with me, the little Fuji point-and-shoot and, of course, my Nikon DSLR with a few lenses."

Jim had one hand on the back of my chair, and I felt the tension in his body. He had to be thinking the same thing I was: That flight to Australia had taken off without Allison, and no one even knew she was dead for twelve days.

"But I am getting in one last dose of winter," she said with a smile. "We're going for a walk in the woods tomorrow morning, before my flight. And it wasn't even my idea, if you can believe that."

I heard my own gasp, felt Jim's grip on the chairback tighten.

Allison hadn't been alone in the woods the day she died?

I sat dazed as she continued. "It's supposed to be our private time together, like it would spoil the magic or something if I told anyone else about it, so don't spill the beans, okay?" She put her finger to her lips, chuckling at the insistence on secrecy. "Maybe this means we'll be able to clear the air and move on. Then all this drama will be over and I can relax and enjoy the Snowies. I'll give you a full report when I return, Jim." She blew him a kiss and turned off the camera.

"Back it up," he said. "Play that last part again."

I did. We listened again as Allison said *we're* going for a walk. It wasn't her idea. They'd clear the air and move on. She and... who?

Neither of us spoke. Jim paced to the other side of the small room and back. Meanwhile Allison's words replayed themselves in my mind in a relentless loop.

We're going for a walk… it wasn't my idea… this drama will be over…

I'd told Martin my purpose in looking for a second flash drive was to put Jim's mind at rest, to help him accept that Allison's death had been an accident. I realized now what the padre had known yesterday, that I was doing it for myself. I'd wanted to believe the official version of events, but it had never felt right, not since the moment I'd found her lying under the ice, had gazed at her still, pale face. It was as if she'd been staring back at me, silently pleading for justice.

I stood, feeling shaky. "Have you had dinner?"

"What?" He probably thought he'd heard me wrong. How could I be thinking about food now?

Numbly I walked down the hall to the kitchen, where I dug out my bottle of añejo tequila and two snifters. I poured generous shots as Sexy Beast roused himself from his bucket bed, executed a luxurious stretch, sniffed the air, and grumbled something in Poodle that I was just as happy I couldn't interpret. I placated him with a doggie biscuit from a canister on the counter.

Jim joined me and nodded at the snifters. "What's this?"

"Dinner." I lifted my glass and took a healthy swig. The silky burn helped clear my head.

He examined the pretty bottle. I watched those peaked eyebrows rise. Clearly he was a stranger to fine sipping tequila.

"Try it," I said.

He did. He approved.

Getting to the family room a few steps away suddenly seemed a daunting hike. The living room beyond might have been in, well, Australia. I circled the granite kitchen island and collapsed into a seat at the round breakfast table. Jim did likewise. I could almost hear the gears turning in his head as he reached down to give SB the obligatory scritches.

"Okay," he said, "they were going to talk things through. Allie and whoever. Get stuff off their chests. I'll go ahead and state the obvious. She'd just had a fight with the husband. Nick."

"I can't see him suggesting a walk in the woods," I said. "He's not the outdoorsy type."

"But to appease his wife? Like, 'Here, honey, I'm doing this thing you know I hate for your sake.'"

"Maybe, but he told me he slept till noon that day and that she'd already left for the airport by the time he got up." I told Jim about my conversation with Nick during the funeral reception, his version of the argument he and Allison had had. Afterward she'd worked in her office, he'd said, editing pictures—in reality, as we now knew, making what would be her final video diary entry—and gone to bed, while he'd remained up until the wee hours, drinking and playing video games.

Jim sipped his drink. "In the videos, she says she kept her divorce plans secret."

I nodded. "She wanted to wait until she had all her ducks in a row before springing it on him."

"But now it's Christmas night and they're having this fight about him getting fired. Sounds like it was a doozy. I'm thinking she might've gotten so worked up that she spilled the beans about the divorce, you know, threw it in his face."

"I don't know," I said. "I was there when he found out she was planning to divorce him. It came as a total surprise. Either that or he's a better actor than he gets credit for." Which, I had to admit, was possible.

"But he was cheating with her friend Skye," Jim said, "and being pretty sloppy about covering his tracks, according to the videos. He really thought she didn't know?"

"Cheaters always think their spouses haven't a clue," I said. "Once in a while they're even right."

"Well, I still think she might have let it slip during their fight," he said. "That he was about to get dumped. Or at least that she knew about the affair."

"In which case he, what, made nice and suggested they take a walk in the woods the next morning before her flight?"

"To talk things over." He made air quotes. "So they could 'clear the air and move on.'"

I shivered, my mind involuntarily moving a few steps ahead. "But how would he have... I mean, the way it looked..." I took a fortifying sip, set down the snifter.

"You mean, how could it have been murder?" he asked. "Since all the evidence points to her accidentally falling through thin ice?"

"Yeah, about that ice. Doesn't that bother you? I mean, Allison was a seasoned outdoorswoman. Even I know to test ice before putting my weight on it."

"That does bother me. The only thing I can think is that someone chased her onto the ice, that she had no choice but to risk it."

"Like maybe the person had a weapon?" I said.

"Something like that." Jim spread his hands as if to say, *That's all I've got.*

"What about the Barbie?" I asked.

"What *about* the Barbie?"

"If Nick did cause Allison's death, why would he have planted a headless Barbie, altered to look like her, in their mailbox for her to find? That was back in November, more than a month before her death."

"Maybe it really does have nothing to do with all of this," he said. "Kids. A prank."

"That would be the simplest explanation, wouldn't it?" I said.

Jim sat back in his chair. "What about Skye?"

"You think she might have left the Barbie?"

"I think she might have been the one who proposed a nice, civilized stroll through the woods for the purpose of clearing the air," he said. "Sort of like, 'Sorry I was doing the nasty with your husband, let's be friends again.'"

"You have to remember, though, Skye and Nick didn't know that Allison had gotten wind of the affair."

"Unless—" Jim raised a finger "—Allie did indeed tell Nick about her intention to divorce him during that argument on Christmas night. Allie tells Nick. Nick gets right on the phone and tells Skye. Skye calls Allie and says it's time for a girls' outing to hash this thing out."

"And Skye tells her not to mention it to anyone? Maybe not even to Nick?" At Jim's quizzical expression, I added, "Allison said she was supposed to keep it secret, remember? 'Don't spill the beans.' Like whoever she was meeting at the preserve didn't want anyone else to know about it. Tell me that doesn't sound suspicious."

"Allie didn't think so." He frowned. "She was too trusting."

"Let me ask you," I said. "How much do you know about Brenda Yates?"

It took him a second. "Mitchell's daughter? Only what was in the videos. She thinks Allie murdered her father. Have you met her?"

"Yep. She was at the funeral. And then I went to see her last week to return a family keepsake the Gleasons wanted her to have. Do you recall what Allison said about the timing of Brenda's accusation?"

He frowned in concentration. "She made it after finding out her father had disinherited her, that he'd left everything to Allie."

I asked, "Do you know that a murderer can't inherit from his victim?"

"I've heard that," he said. "It makes sense."

"The slayer rule, they call it."

"I think I see where you're going with this," he said. "If Allie had been found guilty of murdering Mitchell, then his estate would presumably have gone to his daughter."

"Which means there might be more to Brenda's accusation than a daughter's desire to see her father's murderer brought to justice."

"Greed," he said.

"But if that's the case… well, when I met with her, she seemed to really believe Allison killed her dad."

"Maybe she does." Jim swirled his tequila, studying the golden vortex. "And maybe the timing of her accusation, coming after the reading of his will, is coincidence. Maybe the slayer rule never crossed her mind."

"Allison did something surprising," I said, and saw him look up in interest. "She left one third of her assets in trust to Brenda's kids, and took out a million-dollar life-insurance policy naming Brenda as beneficiary."

"Wow."

"Brenda considers it the act of a guilty conscience," I added.

"I'm glad I never met this woman. She sounds like a miserable human being. Let me ask you this. Could she have known about this bequest to her kids, and the life insurance, before Allie died?"

"I don't think so," I said, "but she's not the easiest person to read. I think she keeps a lot bottled up inside. Bottom line is, I can't be sure."

"Do you know whether Brenda got the authorities upstate involved in her dad's supposed murder?" Jim asked. "Allie didn't mention it in her videos."

"She did. She says the cops up there didn't take it seriously. She said she actually had evidence, but it didn't matter to the 'yokels' conducting the investigation. Her word, not mine."

"Did she say what kind of evidence she had?" he asked.

I shook my head. "She said Mitchell was getting ready to divorce Allison and that that's why she killed him, because divorce would have left her broke. Maybe that's what she meant by evidence."

Jim said, "I didn't see anything in those videos that would make me think Mitchell had threatened her with divorce."

"No, it seemed like a loving relationship. Of course, we're only getting her side."

"So Brenda thought Allie had gotten away with murdering her father," he said. "That's the sort of thing that might make a devoted daughter take matters into her own hands. Only, the devoted part doesn't really apply, right? Hadn't they been estranged for years, Brenda and her dad?"

I nodded. "But I get the feeling it's not that simple, that she has a lot of, I don't know, emotional conflict."

"Well, it's a messy situation," he said. "Psychologically, I mean. Daddy and Mommy split up. Daddy marries a beautiful, much younger woman. He's deeply in love with her, trying to have children with her. And then suddenly he's gone and you realize you'll never get a chance to mend fences. That's a big, juicy dose of guilt right there, I don't care who you are."

"Don't tell me," I said. "You minored in psychology."

He grinned. "Nope, I just talk a good game."

"You know," I said, "it could be that whoever was supposed to go for a walk with Allison canceled or didn't show. Or maybe the person's not on our radar. A friend we don't know, someone she might have been on the outs with."

"I wish we could get ahold of her phone," Jim said.

"Yeah. That might tell us who contacted—" I jerked upright. "Wait. We have her phone!"

He blinked. "We do?"

"Well, the padre does." I was out of my seat in an instant, causing Sexy Beast to leap out of his bucket bed and spur me on with rapid-fire barking.

"Who's the padre?" he called to my retreating back as I ran back to the maid's room, where I'd left my phone. SB trailed me there and back.

Martin answered my call as I rejoined Jim at the table. "It works," he said without preamble. I heard bluegrass music and pictured him behind the bar at Murray's.

"Her phone *works*?" I said. "After being in a frozen lake for nearly two weeks?"

"I charged it, turned it on, bingo. Salt on the rim?"

"There's salt on the rim?" I asked, as Jim frowned in confusion. "It's a freshwater lake—"

"Not you," he said, "I'm making a margarita. So here's the deal. I read her texts and emails from the days before her death, checked out her calendar entries. Nothing relevant. But she did get a few calls on Christmas day."

"Was one of those calls from Skye?"

"It sure was," he said. "They spoke for three minutes and thirty-nine seconds. On the rocks? You know, they have a name for shoes like that, babe, but I'm too much of a gentleman to say it." The wicked smile in his voice told me he wasn't too much of a gentleman to think it. I imagined him leaning over the bar to get a better look at his customer's dome pumps, no doubt worn for his benefit. He said, "I'd ask how you manage the snow in those, but I don't really care as long as you wear 'em in here."

I heard a female giggle and a muted query I couldn't quite make out but that sounded an awful lot like *So, Marty, when do you get off?* How the man was able to simultaneously hold a phone conversation, mix drinks, and flirt outrageously with all the female customers was a mystery on the order of, well, how a drowned, thawed-out smartphone still managed to wink on and spill its contents.

Like I said, I hate technology, except when it works.

How I wished I knew what Allison and Skye had talked about during their last phone conversation. A suggestion to meet in the woods and clear the air, perhaps?

"What about Brenda?" I asked him. "Did she call Allison?"

"A Brenda Yates called her on Christmas afternoon," he said. "Who's she?"

"Allison's first husband's daughter. Her stepdaughter, I guess you could say. How long did they speak?"

"Hold on," he said, "I'll check. Hey, buddy, how's it going? I'll be with you in a sec." I waited a few moments as Martin located the call in Allison's phone. "They talked for four minutes and seventeen seconds at two p.m. on the button."

"Okay, thanks. And you'll get that phone back into her house like you promised, right?" I said.

"I'll do it tonight."

While Nick was asleep upstairs? *You don't want to know*, I reminded myself. I said goodbye as the padre took an order for a Moscow Mule.

Jim said, "I'm not even going to ask who that was or how he got Allie's phone."

"It's better that way. So it occurred to me that if she was in trouble in the woods, she would have called nine-one-one, and she didn't."

"Maybe she never got the chance," he said. "And here's what occurred to *me*. Allie never would have gone into those woods without—"

"A camera. She took one everywhere. You said so yourself."

"I did?" he asked.

"You told me that even back in high school, she always had one with her. Beau said the same thing." At his quizzical expression, I added, "A friend of hers. She was pretty close to him and his wife, Poppy."

"I think I saw them at the cemetery," he said. "Tall guy with a beard? She has blonde dreads? She was pretty broken up."

"That's them. Anyway, yeah, if Allison had a camera in the woods with her that morning—and she almost certainly would have—where is it now?"

"At the bottom of the lake would be my guess," he said, "if she was holding it when she fell in."

"Maybe she put it in a coat pocket," I said.

"Would it fit?"

"The little one might. The one she called a point-and-shoot."

"In that case the cops would have returned it to Nick." Jim studied me. "You think Allie might have taken a picture of whoever she was supposed to meet."

"You think so too or you wouldn't have mentioned the camera," I said.

"A long shot, but…" He gave a little shrug.

"You know, when it comes to the sheer volume of photographs," I said, "Skye probably had Allison beat, and I don't think she even owns a camera. That woman is the undisputed queen of the selfies."

"Yeah, I saw her at the cemetery." Jim's mouth tightened. "Looked like she was posting the pictures online. During the service."

"She chronicles her entire life online. Her social media is filled with—" I sat up straight.

So did Jim. "What?"

"I just remembered. She checks in. On Facebook. She clicks that Check In thing to say exactly where she is when she posts some of her status updates." I was on my feet now, moving back toward the maid's room, with Jim bringing up the rear. This time SB raised his little head, grumbled something that sounded like *Knock yourself out*, and went back to sleep.

"Are you thinking what I think you're thinking?" Jim stood behind me and watched while I took up position at my laptop, navigated to Skye's Facebook profile, and began scrolling backward in time through dozens—make that hundreds—of status updates, many of which included GPS-generated "Check In" location stamps.

"The gas station? Really?" Jim asked, as a recent update posted from a local Mobil station came into view. It featured a photo of Skye's yellow Kia at the pump and the words: *Running on fumes. Just made it!* He shook his head in wonder. "I mean, who cares…?"

"Don't you know? Everyone cares when and where Skye Guthrie fills her tank, or buys a Big Gulp," I said, as an update stamped *7-Eleven* rolled past and others took its place. "Or gets her nails done… or tosses back a couple of beers… or gets her roots touched up…"

With glazed eyes I scrolled past update after update, a seemingly endless stream of words and pictures documenting Skye's quotidian existence in reverse order during the past few weeks. Fast-food meals. Shopping malls. The local tanning salon. Bars. Murray's Pub appeared to be her second home.

Just think of it. All those satellites orbiting our planet, working in concert to triangulate the precise location of Skye Guthrie—or more accurately, Skye Guthrie's cell phone—at any moment in time. I'm telling you, it's a damn miracle.

Another gas station. Another fast-food joint. Another few belts at Murray's. The monotony was interrupted by a trip to Atlantic City the weekend following Allison's supposed departure for Australia. Eating, drinking, strolling the boardwalk, gambling in the casinos. One grinning selfie taken in front of a slot machine—*Ding! Ding! Ding!* Fifty-four-dollar jackpot!—amid a whole slew of frowny, thumbs-down selfies taken in front of evil, money-gobbling slot machines.

Nick's face didn't appear once, though I suspected he was the owner of the odd male arm or leg I spied in some photos.

Skye might not be the most sophisticated femme fatale who ever lived, but she was canny enough not to advertise her illicit affair with her "best friend's" husband. In some of the updates, she tagged other Facebook friends, but never Nick.

Poppy had told me Skye worked part-time at a cell-phone store, but I saw no evidence of it on her Facebook timeline. Obviously her job was not scintillating enough to compete with pumping gas or deciding which Pringles to buy: Ranch or Sour Cream & Onion?

Jim mock-whined, "Are we there yet?" as the parade of tiresome updates marched past.

"Almost," I said. "We made it to New Year's." Skye had spent the holiday in a spangly, low-cut dress and do-me pumps. If Nick was with her, he never appeared in her Facebook timeline.

Jim said, "No trips to the library. Not one museum or Broadway play or concert."

"Well, except for the New York Philharmonic at Lincoln Center."

"What?" He squinted at the computer.

"Gotcha," I said. "That was too easy."

He yanked a lock of my hair. "Brat."

"Okay, we're at December twenty-sixth." I slowed my scrolling and studied the updates Skye had posted the day Allison died. Dinner at a gastropub in Oceanside. She'd ordered the gut-busting house burger—loaded with everything you could imagine heaping onto a slab of ground cow, and some you probably couldn't—a mound of fries, and beer, with cheesecake for dessert. My stomach gave me what-for. Maybe I should have had something else for dinner besides tequila.

In the afternoon she'd gone to the mall to return a

necklace, a hat-and-glove set, a sweater, a pair of boots, and a purse that she'd received for Christmas. Her updates included selfies in which she made grossed-out faces while displaying the unwanted gifts. *Another ugly sweater from Grandma*, she wrote. *Try cash next time! Save me a trip to the store!* I could only hope Grandma wasn't on Facebook.

Scrolling down a bit further, I saw that her lunch had been a fast-food burger at 1:23 p.m. I detected a culinary theme of the day.

That had been her first update on December 26. The one below it was dated December 25 and showed a photo of a lopsided Christmas tree, groaning under approximately a thousand pounds of ornaments, garlands, and lights, and standing sentry over mountains of unwrapped presents and discarded paper and ribbons. A white cat batted at a low-hanging plastic icicle.

Had the picture been taken in her parents' home? For the first time I wondered about the family that had produced Skye Guthrie. The post read: *Snowball trying to pull down the tree!* Like all her updates, this one had received scores of likes from her myriad Facebook friends.

"So much for a smoking gun." I sat back, deflated. "Not that I really expected her to 'check in' from the nature preserve the morning of the twenty-sixth if she was up to no good, but a girl has to dream."

"It was worth a shot." Jim peered into the dark outside the window, where swirling snowflakes glittered. "It's coming down heavier. I'd better get going."

I walked him to the front door and watched him brush off his car before steering it down the long cobblestone drive. It was after eleven, but I was far too wound up to consider sleep.

I grabbed a cold slice of pizza from the fridge and opened my laptop once more. I found myself continuing to scroll through Skye's Facebook timeline even as I recognized it for the sick compulsion it was. What did I expect to find?

The proverbial smoking gun, that's what. Some part of me simply couldn't fathom that a woman who shared practically every moment of her life with the world at large wouldn't have left some hint about her role in her friend's mysterious death—if indeed she'd played a role, and if indeed said death was mysterious and not the tragic accident the authorities considered it to be.

I raced through the timeline in a sort of halting reverse movie of her recent life, unslowed by the occasional bite of congealed Buffalo-chicken pizza. A golden-brown roasted turkey shot past the screen—Thanksgiving already?—followed moments later by a toothy jack-o-lantern, the holiday updates nearly lost amid a bottomless litany of shopping, eating, and drinking, with occasional side trips to worship the holy trinity of grooming goddesses: Haira, Nailos, and Orangish, Goddess of Spray Tans.

Beach selfies, fireworks, more beach selfies—and what appeared to be an honest-to-God, if sadly fleeting, summer tan. I bit off a chunk of pizza crust, wondering whether Skye's Facebook timeline would ever bottom out, imagining it continuing back through generations, through centuries, through the murky, formless eons of prehistory, and wishing I'd thought to grab a bottle of soda from the fridge, when an image zipping past my eyes triggered recognition, halting me in midchew.

I'd already moved past it, whatever it was. What had I seen? I reversed course, moving forward in time now, experiencing June 12 along with *Skye*. Here was a pouty, post-blowout, heavily made-up selfie. *Hot date. Will I do?* Here was a picture of two hot-date outfits laid out on her messy bed. *Decisions, decisions. Help me choose.* Her friends favored the purple bandage dress. Here was a full-length selfie taken in front of her bathroom mirror, showing off the whole package. *Think he'll approve?*

We moved on to June 13. Egg McMuffin. Bikini shopping. Brenda's living room.

My heart sucker-punched my rib cage. I grabbed the edge of the desk, suddenly dizzy.

Nope. Wrong. Impossible. That selfie backdrop had to be someone else's white fireplace mantel, not Brenda's. And the pale abstract seascape hanging over it? Definitely not the same one I'd seen eight days earlier in Brenda's living room.

Skye and Brenda hadn't know each other back in June. They knew each other now, kind of, having been briefly introduced by Porter Vargas during Allison's funeral reception last week. Before that, they'd been strangers.

Hadn't they?

I thought back to the reception, to when Brenda and Lou Yates had shown up. I'd taken their coats and the bakery box they'd brought. Since they didn't seem to know anyone there, I'd introduced them to the Vargases. Porter, in turn, had introduced them to the woman he'd been led to believe was Allison's best friend.

Skye and Brenda had both appeared ill at ease as they'd shaken hands and murmured their *Nice to meet yous*. I hadn't thought anything of it at the time, but now…

I peered closely at the image in Skye's Facebook timeline, the image she'd taken back in June, a half year before Allison's death. It wasn't stamped with a location, but I didn't need it. There, behind her smiling face, was the white mantel. There was the lower left quadrant of the boring seascape. And there, peeking out from behind her black hair, was the edge of the crystal sailboat positioned as if to sail off into the painting.

No doubt about it, it was Brenda's living room, all right.

"They knew each other," I breathed.

What had Skye been doing at Brenda's house back in June? What else had been happening in June?

Mitchell's death. His fatal hiking accident had occurred on June 8, which I knew from having been hired by Allison to arrange his funeral reception. Skye had no doubt uploaded this selfie to Facebook as soon as she'd taken it, at 3:13 in the afternoon of June 13. I imagined her impulsively posting the photo with no inkling that anyone would recognize the background and draw a connection between her and Brenda. Allison herself hadn't been on Facebook, according to Jim.

I used the Print Screen key on my laptop's keyboard to take a screenshot, capturing the image in case Skye wised up at some point and deleted it from her timeline.

And where was the lady of the house while Skye was immortalizing her drab taste in home furnishings? Ever the polite hostess, Brenda was probably in the kitchen pouring coffee and arranging homemade cookies on a plate.

Before uploading her latest selfie to her timeline, Skye had tapped out a few words to accompany the picture.

It's my turn now!

12

Something About the Whole Thing Stinks

"WHAT'S GOING ON HERE?" I asked, as Sophie Halperin and I crossed Main Street, heading for the entrance to the Rose Bookshop. Twenty or so people stood lined up on the sidewalk, waiting to get in, undeterred by the damp cold or the gray, swollen sky that presaged more white stuff to come. The snowstorm had ceased around daybreak and the town had plowed and sanded the roads, but it was a bleak day, too bleak to be standing outside waiting for… what?

The line continued inside the shop, snaking through the section that actually sold books and into the middle room, which was an offbeat café that also hosted musical performances and book signings. Beyond that was a large third room that sold children's books and toys. The Rose, which had occupied the same storefront since 1946, had survived, when so many other independent bookstores had not, by adapting.

Sophie and I were headed to the café for lunch and a long-overdue gab session. We hadn't seen each other since Allison's funeral reception nearly two weeks earlier, and we hadn't really had a chance to talk then.

"Don't hear music," Sophie said as we bulled our way through the crowd, exchanging greetings with friends and neighbors along the way. "Some celebrity must be signing books."

If there was a poster in the window advertising the signing, it had been obscured behind the line of people standing in front of the place. I wondered who had enough clout to get the Rose to agree to a weekday signing. They were usually reserved for evenings and weekends.

"Maybe we should have gone to Patisserie Susanne," I said, with visions of chocolate croissants cavorting in my cranium.

"Eh, I'm there all the time."

And little wonder. The patisserie was located on the ground floor of the Town Hall. Mayor Sophie Halperin's office occupied the fourth floor of the historic building, a onetime hotel that had housed a speakeasy during Prohibition. Her office had, in fact, been a gambling den and saloon back then.

"Make way for the damn mayor!" Sophie bellowed in her brusque, good-natured way. "I don't have all day."

I wondered how long Sophie would hold the office. She was up for reelection in March, and it was well known that Nina Wallace intended to unseat her. Nina did not fight clean, as had been amply demonstrated during her successful bid for the presidency of the Crystal Harbor Historical Society. Sophie was popular and she was tough, but was she popular and tough enough to prevail against Nina's penchant for mudslinging and dirty tricks? Fervently I hoped so. Crystal Harbor did not need Nina Wallace at the helm.

At last we made it into the crowded café, with its heavenly mingled aromas of coffee, grilled sandwiches, and new books.

The food-service counter was at one end of the room. There were a few small tables, all occupied. At the other end of the room, a young woman arranged stacks of hardcover books on a cloth-draped table while a middle-aged man I recognized as a store employee assured those at the front of the line that the signing would commence in a few minutes and counseled patience.

"Got one!" Eagle-eyed Sophie launched herself at a table whose diners were just beginning to rise, establishing squatter's rights by plopping into a chair before its previous occupant had fully relinquished it. To me she said, "Get me the eggplant and goat cheese panino. And some of their good potato salad. And a peach iced tea."

"You got it." For myself I ordered a chicken panino with tomato, arugula, and asiago, along with the café's yummy signature coleslaw and store-made raspberry soda. I ferried everything over to our table in two trips.

As I was peeling the paper off my straw, I heard, "Jane!" I looked around to see who'd called my name as excited squeals and a scatter of applause erupted from the crowd awaiting the book signing.

"Think I just lost my appetite," Sophie groaned.

I followed her disgruntled gaze and saw a woman hurrying toward me, enveloped in a cloud of outrageously expensive French perfume. She looked about forty years old, but I knew her to be fifty, the beneficiary of extensive plastic surgery, weight-loss surgery, and a head-to-toe makeover.

Leonora Romano, in the flesh.

"Hello, Lee," I said, as she yanked an unoccupied chair from a nearby table without bothering to ask whether it was taken, swung it around to our table, and deposited her trim bottom on it. Said bottom was encased in a royal-blue pencil skirt, which she'd paired with a peach bouclé jacket and matching silk blouse. My gaze zeroed in on her brooch, a big, glittery leopard—diamonds and sapphires, and I'd bet anything they were real—snarling over its shoulder as it crawled up hers. As always, her feet were shod in lethal-looking designer stiletto heels. Her blonde hair was pulled back into a neat chignon. More diamonds and sapphires adorned her ears.

She and Sophie exchanged chilly greetings.

I was about to ask Lee what had brought her to the Rose Bookshop at lunchtime on a Thursday when the answer smacked me upside the head. I took in the eager patrons queued up out the door, the excited whispers, the adoring stares directed at Lee.

"Oh," I said. "*You're* the one signing books today."

She laughed. I'd like to tell you it was a friendly, teasing laugh. I'd also like to tell you I'm a Nobel-prizewinning lingerie model, but I cannot tell a lie. Except when it's necessary for some greater moral purpose or, you know, really convenient.

"You just realized that?" she said. "I used to think you had decent observational skills, Jane."

Despite claiming a loss of appetite, Sophie was making headway with her lunch. Over a mouthful of potato salad she said, "Don't you have some books to scribble in, Lee? The natives are getting restless."

"Let them wait."

Her tone said, *I'm a star.* I wish I could say it was all attitude and no substance, but the weird truth was that Leonora Romano was indeed a star. The onetime chef and restaurateur now hosted *The Romano Files*, a sensationalist "news" TV show that had little to do with actual news and everything to do with Lee's abrasive personality and talent for eviscerating any individual or organization she deemed worthy of public humiliation.

The network had offered her the show several months earlier in the hope of enticing viewers away from the loathsome *Ramrod News*, hosted by the loathsome Miranda Daniels, which aired in the same time slot. They'd sweetened the deal by giving Lee a second show in which she eviscerated—yeah, more evisceration, it suited her—restaurants' signature dishes and taught their chefs how to do it right. She was uniquely suited to this starring role as well, being both a world-class chef and meaner than the proverbial junkyard dog. With rabies. And a really bad case of fleas.

Both shows had done extraordinarily well, quickly soaring to number one in their respective categories and turning Leonora Romano into the household name she'd been determined to become. As much as I disliked the woman, I had to admire the laserlike sense of mission that had turned her from a homely nobody into a genuine celebrity, one the viewing public couldn't seem to get enough of.

The book-buying public, either. I know you're wondering what kind of book she'd written. All those fans were lined up to purchase a copy of *Leonora's Kitchen*, a slick, hefty cookbook with a price tag to match. This wasn't Lee's first signing at the Rose. Last fall she'd sat behind that very same table, pen in hand, without scrawling her signature in a single volume. Now she had hordes of people waiting outside in the cold for the privilege of forking over forty bucks for a signed copy of *Leonora's Kitchen*. I wondered how many of these fans would actually read any of the recipes it contained, much less haul out a saucepan and attempt to replicate her famous arrabbiata sauce.

I pointed to the young woman arranging Lee's books in aesthetically pleasing stacks, angled just so. "Who's that? I've never seen her here before."

"Oh, my publicist assigned her to me," Lee said with a negligent flick of her manicured claws—the same pretty peach hue as her jacket and blouse. "She keeps the line moving so I'm not sitting there all day. Good grief, the way some of my fans prattle and gush, you'd think I was the Second Coming."

Lee could pretend to be irritated by the attention, but everyone at that table knew this was precisely what she wanted, what she'd spent years working for: to be recognized and revered by the public at large.

"And of course I have to be in the city in a few hours to tape the show," Lee continued. "Somehow they managed to squeeze this signing in, but it's tight. Thank God the limo has a fully stocked bar."

I swallowed a bite of my sandwich and forked up some slaw. "So what do you want, Lee?" I ignored her affronted look. She had to want something. We had a history, she and I, and that history had not turned us into gal pals, no matter how loose your definition.

After a few moments she gave up the pretense of friendship. Glancing around and lowering her voice, she said, "I want the Zaleski story."

Sophie and I exchanged a look. Neither of us liked where this was going.

"What story?" I asked. "Allison Zaleski's death was a tragic—"

"Accident. Right. Until some startling new fact comes to

light and it turns out to be something juicier." She leaned forward. "And if that happens, I have no intention of letting that talentless hack Miranda Daniels beat me to the story."

Juicier. As if a bright, creative, beloved young woman dying at the hands of a murderer amounted to nothing more than a swell way to boost ratings in the six p.m. time slot.

Sophie must have sensed me struggling to control my temper, because she responded for me. "What new facts, Lee? You know something about Allison's death the authorities don't?"

"Don't be deliberately obtuse, Sophie," she said. "It doesn't become you. It's the responsibility of any good journalist to be suspicious."

And to sell more cornflakes and drain cleaner on behalf of her network's sponsors, I thought.

"And I'm suspicious about Allison's death," Lee continued. "It's a gut feeling. Something about the whole thing stinks."

I wasn't about to tell her she might be right, much less to share what little I knew. Lee had described herself as a good journalist. As much as I hated to admit it, she did indeed possess some of the personality traits required of effective investigative journalism, including doggedness, skepticism, and distrust of authority.

I said, "If there *is* anything more to her death, what makes you think I'd know about it?"

"Well, you discovered her body," Lee said, as if stating the obvious. "I don't doubt you've been in touch with the authorities. And then there's the grisly way you make a living. Who knows what juicy little tidbits you're keeping under wraps?"

There it was again. *Juicy.* Before I could tell her where she could stuff her juicy tidbits, Sophie came to my rescue.

"I'm the mayor of this damn burg," she said. "Don't you think if there were anything to know about Allison's death, I'd know it? Why aren't you pumping *me* for info?"

Another dismissive flick of the talons. "You're a puppet, you don't know anything."

I jerked my thumb toward Sophie. "Aren't you concerned about burning off a valuable contact with that kind of talk?"

"This 'valuable contact' will be out of office after the March elections." Lee turned to Sophie. "I hope that doesn't come as too much of a shock, Mayor, but it's common knowledge. You'd be wise to prepare yourself."

I saw Sophie stiffen. Now it was my turn to step in for my friend. "You seem to think you know everything that goes on in this town, Lee, but—"

"Not everything." She rose and smoothed her skirt, lowering her voice further still. "I don't know all the facts about Allison Zaleski's death. If you can supply verifiable information that it was more than a simple accident, the show is prepared to make it worth your while. We're talking about a very generous honorarium."

Honorarium, huh? Well, la-di-da. "Forget it, Lee, I—"

"Don't say no yet. You have my number." And then she was off, striding through the crowd, accepting handshakes, hugs, and breathless declarations of devotion on her way to the signing table. Her obsequious fans did everything but kneel and kiss her ring.

Sophie pushed away her half-eaten meal. "Now I really have lost my appetite."

"Me too." Plus I had no desire to sit there and listen to Lee's fans fawn all over her while her publicist's assistant tried to hurry them along.

"Let's meet for a drink soon." She got to her feet. "I'm buying."

"I'll hold you to that. Go," I told her, knowing she had to get back to her office at the Town Hall. "I'll bus the table."

After I'd deposited our trash in the bin, I started for the exit, stopping when I spied Detective Cookie Kaplan waiting at the counter for her order. Today's earrings were red-and-black glass ladybugs.

After we exchanged greetings, I said, "I hope you're not thinking of trying to eat here."

"No, just picking up takeout. What a zoo."

"Lee Romano is a real draw," I said.

"Not for me." Cookie accepted her change and a white paper sack from the young man behind the counter.

I was glad to hear it, though unsurprised. Cookie Kaplan didn't strike me as a *Romano Files* kind of gal. "Listen," I said, "do you have a moment? I was thinking about giving you a call."

"Sure. Let's find someplace quieter."

We ended up in a small room in the back of the book section of the store, which had been turned into a sort of mini greeting-card shop, with hundreds of unique and artistic cards arranged in racks. We were the only customers in that area, and the relative quiet after the pandemonium of the café went to my head like wine.

I jumped right in. "It's about Allison Zaleski."

She pushed her glasses up her nose. "How did I know you weren't finished with her?"

I felt my face heat. Last Saturday I'd asked Cookie and Howie to stop questioning people about Allison, which they'd only been doing as a favor to me.

"I don't want you to do anything. I just have a question, and I'm thinking you might know the answer." I'd decided to approach Cookie with this because the two of us had hit it off so readily, and she seemed a bit more flexible than Howie. Don't get me wrong, I've known Howie a long time, I'm one of his biggest fans, but he can be a little too by-the-book. There are times when by-the-book doesn't really work for me.

The level look she gave me wasn't unkind. "It was an accident, Jane."

"I know. I know that." At this point I knew no such thing, but it would do me no good to share my unformed suspicions with her. I didn't want to be branded as a total kook this early in our friendship. Borderline kook was bad enough.

And what did I know anyway? That Skye and Brenda had been acquainted last June. More than acquainted—Skye had been inside Brenda's home. Which meant she and Allison's stepdaughter must have known each other fairly well before pretending to meet for the first time during Allison's funeral reception.

I supposed it was possible Allison had introduced them, but her video diary seemed to suggest that she and Mitchell had seen his daughter and her family only on the occasional holiday or birthday. These were, by her account, uncomfortable get-togethers and certainly not occasions when she would have brought along tiresome hanger-on Skye.

And in the unlikely event Allison *had* introduced Skye and Brenda back then, why the playacting when they met after her death? It didn't add up.

Cookie said, "Didn't Allison's mother ask you to stop looking into her death?"

I nodded. "I'm not, you know, doing that. Um, looking

into her death." You could have fried an egg on my cheeks, they felt that hot.

"Uh-huh," she said.

Yeah, I was lying to a detective, and doing a miserable job of it.

"I'm just curious about something," I said. "Do you know whether they found Allison's camera on her? After they, um, retrieved her body from the lake?"

Cookie looked like she didn't want to answer. Probably didn't want to encourage my delusions. But something tipped the equation in my favor, because she said, "After our conversation at Murray's, I read through her files. She had a few personal items in her pockets, but no camera."

"I've been told she always carried one," I said. "I mean, when she was anywhere she might want to take pictures. She definitely would have had one in the woods that day."

"Then it's at the bottom of the lake."

"Maybe. I know she packed two cameras for her trip." At Cookie's questioning look, I added, "It was in those videos she made. Remember, I told you about them?"

"Oh. Right. About those videos. How did you get your hands on—"

"One of the cameras," I quickly interjected, "was small. Compact, you know? A Fuji point-and-shoot, she called it."

"That was found in her luggage," she said, "in the trunk of her car."

"The other camera she was bringing on the trip was a Nikon. It had a neck strap, which she would have been using because it's a substantial camera, a lot bigger than the Fuji."

Cookie was already shaking her head. "We only found the Fuji."

"Then she almost certainly had the Nikon with her in the woods."

She shrugged. "Bottom of the lake, like I said."

"Even with the neck strap? I mean, I know she would have been struggling, trying to get out of the water and back onto the ice." I couldn't stand to think about it. What a terrible way to go. The panic. The desperation. "But unless she deliberately removed the camera from around her neck—and why would she waste precious seconds doing that?—I'm thinking it would have remained with her body."

"You're wondering where it is and what images are on it," Cookie said.

"Well… I'm curious, like I said." I didn't add what I'd been thinking, which is that a second person—her hiking companion, perhaps?—could have forced her to relinquish the camera before chasing her onto the thin ice.

"Nothing wrong with curiosity." The look she gave me was too knowing. "As long as it doesn't cause the curious to do something stupid."

13

#SnackStatus #CottageCheese

AFTER MY UNSATISFYING lunch at the bookstore, I went home but found it impossible to concentrate on the Death Diva assignment I was researching for a prospective client. Hank was a fortyish stockbroker who lived in a Crystal Harbor McMansion with his wife and twin toddlers. His dad had recently died and been cremated. Hank had decided that the best way to commemorate Hank Senior's life was to have a large portrait of him tattooed onto his own back. The photo he wanted the artist to copy was a snapshot taken in Vietnam decades earlier of a very young Hank Senior wearing army fatigues and leaning on a Jeep.

Why involve the Death Diva? you ask. Isn't that a job for a tattoo artist? Right you are, but not just any tattoo artist would do—not when the client wanted the old man's ashes incorporated into the tattoo ink.

No, I did not make that up. Turns out it's a *thing*! So that your loved one can be part of you forever and ever and all that. For obvious reasons, though, it's not a *thing* you'd want to entrust to any old tattoo parlor.

Oh, please. It's nowhere near the weirdest thing I've been asked to do. Not to mention it's legal, a big plus.

So there I was, sitting at my computer struggling to compile a list of tattoo artists who possessed not only oodles of talent but actual hands-on experience with this particular, um, ingredient, and all I could think about was Skye and Brenda, who'd suddenly morphed from being virtual strangers into... into I don't know what. Friends? Acquaintances?

Coconspirators?

Plus, where the heck was Allison's Nikon?

I checked the time on my laptop's screen: 3:36 p.m. The day was turning into a total waste.

I closed the computer, snatched up my jacket and purse from the day bed, and detoured to the family room to give Sexy Beast some scritches and admonish him to behave in my absence. SB reclined in indolent luxury in a nest of throw pillows on the ivory leather sofa, watching *Sesame Street* on the enormous TV screen. It was his favorite show. He didn't seem to mind that I kept the sound muted.

Suddenly he lifted his little head and emitted a low growl. I knew what had prompted it even before I turned to see Mr. Snuffleupagus shuffle onto the screen. The growls turned into outraged barks as Sexy Beast came to stiff attention and sprang off the sofa. He stood in front of the television, tail raised, giving the seven-foot-tall mammoth puppet what for.

"You tell him, SB." I pushed my arms into the sleeves of my cream-colored anorak and zipped it. "Don't let him get away with that. Who does he think he is?"

This prompted an even more frenzied burst of barking. Of all the puppets on the show, Snuffy is the only one that pushes my dog's buttons. It didn't take me long to figure out why. It's because Snuffy walks on four legs. In Sexy Beast's version of reality, four legs equals *dog*, and dogs are to be barked at.

Including ginormous, furry dogs with enviably long eyelashes and prehensile trunks.

It's not just Snuffy who gets this treatment. That rhino on the nature channel? Dog. Those wild pigs on *Let's Go Shoot Us Some Wild Pigs*? Dogs. Wile E. Coyote? Well, duh. The Roadrunner? Probably not a dog, but suspicious enough to warrant a strict warning.

He was still carrying on as I retraced my steps through the kitchen and back down the hallway. The entrance to the garage was opposite the laundry room. My red Mazda, which I'd bought used a few months earlier, looked lonely and, let's face it, a little shabby in this cavernous space meant to house three luxury vehicles.

I would have left the car in front of the house if it hadn't started snowing again by the time I left the bookstore. The forecast was for one to three inches, which didn't sound like much until you added it to the past days' accumulation. It hadn't been all that cold the past couple of weeks, just cold enough to keep the white stuff from melting. Spring couldn't come soon enough, I thought as I steered down the long cobblestone drive to the street.

I know you're wondering where I was going. I was wondering the same thing—until I realized I was driving toward Brenda Yates's house. It shouldn't have surprised me, considering how much I'd been obsessing about her and Skye since the previous night's surprising discovery of a connection between the two of them.

I rolled to a stop a couple of doors down from Brenda's house and contemplated my next move. Do I knock on the door? Would she even let me in? Probably not. Our last meeting had been strained, to say the least. Clearly I wasn't on her list of favorite people.

As I stared at her house, the garage door began to rise. Her husband was likely at work, which meant she was probably on her way out. Sure enough, a blue Volvo station wagon rolled down the driveway and turned onto the street, in my direction, with Brenda at the wheel.

I did that thing you see people do on TV all the time, scrunching down and averting my face so she wouldn't notice me. Because there's nothing at all suspicious about a driver scrunching down and averting her face. Happily, her car never slowed. She kept her eyes on the road, like a good, safe driver.

Once she'd passed me, I executed a three-point turn—okay, so it was more like a seven-point turn, whatever—and followed her car at a distance, turning whenever she did. At no point did I see her glance in her rearview. Well, most people aren't expecting to be followed, right? I mean, this was real life, and in real life you're generally in no danger of being tailed by frustrated, bored Death Divas who have nothing better to do. Or who do have something better to do but prefer to play Janey Delaney, girl detective, instead.

She gunned it at a yellow light, trapping me as it turned red, but I'd already memorized her license plate in case we got separated. Ha! I *so* could have been a private investigator. If the Death Diva gig ever gets old, maybe Ben Ralston will take me on as an apprentice.

I caught up with Brenda easily and watched her pull into the main parking lot of the local Long Island Railroad station, which is usually filled with commuters' vehicles by 6:30 a.m. A few spots tend to open up in the afternoon, though, and sure enough, a handful were available. I watched her pass three perfectly good spots in order to park under a lamppost. Clearly she anticipated returning after dark and felt safer approaching a well-lit vehicle. That's the sort of sensible planning I never do. Maybe it had something to do with Brenda being a mother. You start thinking, What if someone conks me on the head in the LIRR parking lot? What will happen to my kids?

This train of thought could reliably be counted on to depress yours truly, a childless woman on the cusp of middle age, so I forcefully expunged it and concentrated on my quarry. As I pulled into a spot some distance from her Volvo, I saw her exit the car, beep it, and make her cautious way over packed, sanded snow to the ticket machine sheltered next to the escalator under the trestle.

I waited until she'd taken the moving stairs up to the platform before getting out of my car. There are two main choices for train travel on the Island: points west, the most prominent being Manhattan, a ride of an hour and a half from Crystal Harbor; and points east, with myriad towns along the way, culminating in Montauk on the far east end of our very Long Island.

The chance that Brenda was taking a train somewhere east of us, when she had the option of driving, was practically zero. On the other hand, most Long Islanders who are headed to Manhattan for an evening out prefer to rely on public transportation than to drive in and deal with such delights as congested midtown traffic and ungodly parking rates—especially with snow coming down. I thus calculated there was approximately a 99.99999% chance she was headed into the city. At the machine I bought a round-trip ticket to Manhattan.

Once on the elevated, wind-whipped platform, I snugged my jacket's hood around my face, partly for protection against the elements but also to keep Brenda from noticing me. For the same reason, I avoided the heated waiting room, now occupied by a half dozen travelers. Keeping out of sight, I spied her in there, standing near the wall of windows, as if willing the train to come faster. I assumed she avoided the less-than-pristine bench seats out of concern for her pale blue overcoat. A navy wool scarf was tucked at her throat. She wore a navy slouchy beret and navy leather gloves, all very matchy-matchy.

The electronic sign that announces departure times told me the westbound train would arrive in nine minutes. Nine minutes doesn't sound like a long time, but it sure feels like it when you're standing out in the open, huddled against wind-driven flurries. Only two other people, a teenage couple, chose to remain outdoors rather than inside the waiting room, and they were actively keeping each other toasty.

After standing there shivering for what felt more like nine hours than nine minutes, I finally spied the train's headlight in the distance. My half dozen fellow travelers emerged from the waiting room to join me on the platform. I hung back, keeping my face averted as Brenda boarded. The car held about a half dozen people, well spread out. For those going in the opposite direction, from the city to the Island, it was rush hour, the train cars packed with commuters returning from work. But our westbound train was mostly empty.

Once inside, I made out the back of Brenda's head in the middle of the car. She'd chosen a seat next to a window on a two-person bench. As I passed her, I casually glanced down, pasted on *Surprised!* and *Delighted!*, and squealed, "Brenda! Hi!"

She appeared *Surprised!* and *Not Delighted!* as I shoved her purse aside and plopped my fanny on the seat next to hers.

"So," I said. "Fun evening planned in the city?"

She pulled her purse onto her lap and scooted a little closer to the window. "I'm meeting my friend Donna for dinner and the theater. *Les Mis.*" After a moment she remembered to be polite. "And you?"

"Oh, an old friend is coming down from Connecticut. We're getting together at a jazz club." Yeah, yeah, I know what I said about lying. Do you have to pay such close attention?

Brenda's response was a terse nod.

Now that I was sitting next to her, now that she was a captive audience, so to speak, and too ladylike to shove past me and move to another car, I had no firm plan for how to proceed. Which didn't stop me from charging ahead.

"It's so funny running into you like this," I said. "I've been thinking about you."

A stiff half smile. "Oh?"

"Well, I mean, you've been through so much the past few months. First losing your dad, then your stepmother. Oh, but I forgot. You think she killed him. Pushed him into the ravine, right?"

I wasn't worried about being overheard. No one was sitting close enough to hear our conversation over the rumbling of the train.

Rather than take the bait, she said, "I never think of my father's second wife as my stepmother. I am, after all, several years older than her."

"Yeah, that had to be awkward, am I right?" I said. "Your father marrying someone that young?"

"That was his business. He was free to live his life as he pleased." She opened her purse and withdrew a paperback book titled *Lose the Clutter and Love Your Life!* She opened it to a page marked with a pretty, bejeweled bookmark. "Excuse me, but I was looking forward to some quiet time to catch up on my read—"

"Why didn't you want anyone knowing about you and Skye Guthrie?" I asked. And yeah, it might have been better to gradually work my way around to it, but instinct told me that opening my big yap and blurting it out was the way to go. Staring into Brenda's startled eyes, I hoped I hadn't just blown it. Instinct can be such a pushy broad.

"I—I beg your pardon?"

"Skye," I said pleasantly, as I pulled out my phone and tapped the Facebook icon. "Allison's friend? You know, the woman you supposedly met for the first time at the funeral reception? I mean, how many Skyes do you know?"

"I met several of Allison's friends and relations that day," Brenda said stiffly. "I'm sorry, but I don't specifically recall—"

"This is the one you just *pretended* you didn't already know." My fingers were swiping my phone's screen so fast, it was a wonder the dang thing didn't catch fire. "Porter Vargas introduced you."

"I think I know who you mean," Brenda said, "but I can't imagine what gave you the idea we were already acquainted."

"*This* gave me the idea." I shoved my phone in her face. The screen displayed the selfie Skye had taken in Brenda's living room.

She gave it a brief glance. "I really don't—"

"Look closer. Notice anything familiar about the background?"

I watched her face as she took it in. The white fireplace mantel. The bland seascape. The crystal sailboat figurine. Her eyes bulged. She snatched the phone out of my hand and stared at it unblinking.

"Check it out." I pointed to the date displayed on the screen. "She posted this on June thirteenth. Seven months before the two of you 'met.'"

Brenda's face had leeched color, except for two deep red patches on her cheeks. "I… I remember now. Allison brought her over that day. Just for a few minutes. She didn't even… I mean, we weren't even introduced. It was so… and I mean, we were all so upset the day of Allison's funeral, it's little wonder I didn't recall having met her before."

"I know that Skye came alone to your place in June," I said, "and I know it had something to do with your father's death."

It was an educated guess on my part. Details that had appeared unrelated were beginning to slide together in intriguing ways. The timing of Skye's visit to Brenda, five days after Mitchell died. The Facebook message Skye had posted during that visit: *It's my turn now!* The fact that Brenda had accused Allison of murdering Mitchell only after learning he'd left everything to his young widow. And let's not forget Skye's blatant greed. I could easily see her trying to devise a way to monetize Mitchell's death.

Brenda pulled herself up. "You're bluffing. You know no such thing."

"That's okay if you don't want to talk about it." I took back my phone and let her watch me pull up my contact list. "I'm buddies with a couple of police detectives. They'll tell me how Skye was involved in the investigation into your father's death. They can call the cops upstate and have the answer in five minutes."

This statement had the advantage of being true. Brenda

gaped at my screen, which displayed the words *Detective Howie Werker*, along with an image of his handsome, smiling face. I tapped the green Call icon.

She reached over and ended the call with shaking fingers. She slumped against her seat, eyes closed, clearly struggling to compose herself. I waited as the train rumbled to a stop at a station. No one got off. A middle-aged man in a gray windbreaker and tweed golf cap entered the car and sat in the aisle seat two rows ahead of us on the other side.

After a few moments the train jerked to a start again, causing Brenda to open her eyes. She still didn't look at me. I was wondering how to proceed when she said, "Who else knows?" She sounded exhausted.

"About you and Skye?" I said. "Just me."

She shook her head sadly. "I wish to God I'd never met that woman."

"I'm guessing you're not the first person to feel that way," I said, and waited. It was a long train ride. I had time.

Finally Brenda said, "We met at my father's funeral. Skye introduced herself as Allison's best friend. Later I realized that was, well, an exaggeration."

"To put it mildly," I said.

"At that time I still believed the official finding that Dad's death was an accident."

I cautioned myself to tread carefully. "But then you found out he'd cut you out of his will and left everything to Allison."

She faced me, her gaze drilling into mine. "Even then, Jane. Even after I knew he'd disinherited me, I still trusted the official conclusion, that it was an accident. I had no reason to doubt it."

I noticed movement at the edge of my vision and glanced

over to see the man two rows ahead reach into a pocket of his windbreaker. He appeared to be digging around for something. His ticket, I assumed.

I asked, "So what happened to change your mind?"

"Skye Guthrie happened." She looked like she wanted to spit. "She called me a few days after Dad's funeral, after the reading of his will, and asked to meet with me. She said she had critical information about his death."

"Let me guess," I said. "She told you not to mention your get-together to Allison."

Her expression told me I'd guessed right. "It was very hush-hush. I had no idea what to expect, but I let her come over."

The man in the windbreaker captured my attention again. He'd withdrawn something from his pocket. Cottage cheese, by the looks of it. Right about now you're imagining one of those cute little containers and a plastic spoon. Think again. This man—in all other respects a normal, sane-looking individual—held a big glob of cottage cheese in his naked hand and was shoving it into his mouth.

When he reached back into his pocket for more, I managed to wrench my gaze away. Brenda couldn't see him from her vantage point.

Where were we? "Um… so Skye came to your house," I said. "What was this critical info she had?"

"She told me that Allison killed my father. She said he was planning to divorce her and that that's why she did it."

"So she could inherit his fortune rather than settle for whatever she could get in a divorce," I said.

"Right. Skye claimed that early in their marriage, Allison had made him disinherit me and the kids, and leave everything to her."

"*Made* him?"

"She, I don't know, beguiled him," she said. "Convinced him it was the right thing to do."

"According to Skye," I said.

"That woman played me. She knew it would be easier for me to believe he'd been bewitched by his gold-digging young wife than that he'd made the decision on his own. Because of how broken our relationship was."

The door at the far end of the car opened. The conductor, a skinny older woman with a graying blonde ponytail, entered and started collecting tickets. Meanwhile the guy in the windbreaker was still chowing down.

I said, "Did Skye claim to have proof? That Allison killed your father? You said there was evidence."

"Evidence in the form of Skye's testimony. She told me Allison admitted it to her. How she posed Dad in front of the ravine for a photo, made him back up..." She shuddered.

"You didn't think it odd that she was ratting out her best friend?" I asked.

"She claimed she could no longer live with herself," she said. "Keeping Allison's terrible secret was eating her alive."

"So why didn't she go right to the police?" I asked. "Why sneak a meeting with you, the victim's daughter?"

"The way she spun it was that she wanted to do the right thing, but this was her best friend, after all. She needed incentive."

"Incentive for Skye can only mean money," I said. "She wanted you to pay her for reporting what she knew to the police, right? How much?"

Brenda said, "Are you aware that if you murder someone, you can't legally profit from their death?"

"I believe I've heard that." Déjà vu. "So if Allison was convicted of killing her husband, she couldn't inherit anything from him, will or no will. Which meant his fortune would then go to…" We both knew the answer, but I let Brenda say it, which she did without hesitation.

"Me. Skye knew that, and she also knew my dad had disinherited me, because Allison had told her. Even so, under the slayer rule, once Allison was convicted, his fortune would have gone to me."

The conductor had reached the guy in the windbreaker. She didn't react in the slightest as he passed her his ticket with his clean hand while continuing to feed his face with the other. Taking in her stolid expression, I could only wonder what marvels and oddities this woman had witnessed in her years as a railroad conductor. For her, seeing someone eat cottage cheese with his bare hand might very well rank one and a half on the official one-to-ten weirdo scale.

Brenda and I produced our round-trip tickets, which the conductor punched and handed back to us before moving on.

"I think I see what Skye was trying to engineer," I said. "She testifies against Allison, who, as a result, is convicted of murdering her husband. Your father's fortune goes to you, his next of kin, and you very generously share it with the woman who made it all possible."

"Skye wanted a million dollars," she said.

"A fraction of what you would have inherited if her scheme had worked. Did you agree?"

Brenda looked away. "Yes."

"Okay, so what happened then?"

"She went to the police upstate, where Dad died," she said. "Told them all about how Allison had confessed to her."

"How long did it take them to realize she was making the whole thing up?"

"Not long," she said. "Her story didn't hold up under questioning. The details kept changing. The detective in charge of the investigation could find no one to corroborate any of her claims, including that my dad's marriage was on the rocks. He figured Skye had it in for Allison and was just trying to cause her trouble."

"So they dismissed her story," I said, "and continued to maintain that his death was accidental."

Brenda nodded. "That's right."

"And Allison never knew about Skye's involvement in all this?" I asked.

"No. It never got that far. She only knew that I had accused her of murdering my father."

"The cops rejected Skye's story," I said, gently, "but you didn't, did you?"

She shook her head. She took a deep breath, her eyes moist. "No. I swallowed it hook, line, and sinker. I was... in a confused state of mind. My relationship with my dad... well, we hadn't gotten along for years, decades really, since he and my mom divorced. I saw him as the guilty party."

"How old were you when they split?" I asked.

"Thirteen."

"An impressionable age," I offered.

"To me it was all black and white. He'd wronged my mother."

"Had he cheated?"

"Oh no, nothing like that. They'd grown apart. Outwardly I blamed him, but inwardly I knew it was all my fault."

"How so?"

"Theirs was a shotgun wedding," she said. "Mom was pregnant with me when they married."

"A lot of people get married for that reason," I said. "Some stay together, some don't. But it's never the kid's fault."

Her smile was sad. "Intellectually I know that, but try telling it to a young girl whose life has just been turned inside out. My mom didn't make it any easier, unfortunately. She was too busy ripping Dad apart to notice, or care, that I was hurting. She was too mired in her own pain."

"You can tell me to take a hike if this is too personal," I said, "but did you ever seek therapy?"

She shook her head. "Mom didn't believe in it, and later, well, I grew up and figured I was over it."

"And then he married Allison," I said.

"That kind of brought everything to a head again. Mom had calmed down a bit over the years—about Dad, I mean. His 'abandoning' us, never mind that he was very generous with alimony and child support. But when he married this beautiful, talented, much younger woman, Mom couldn't handle it. I was running over to her place almost daily, trying to talk her down off the ledge."

"She never remarried?" I asked.

Brenda shook her head again. "I knew Dad and Allison were trying to have a baby. I have to admit, it brought all those old feelings to the surface again. The rejection. Once he had a child with *her*, what would that make *me*?"

"But you and your dad didn't really have a relationship at that point, right?" I said.

"Right, but it seemed so final, somehow." Brenda's eyes were moist. "Like a new baby would… erase me."

I had an overwhelming urge to put my arms around her.

Her pain was so close to the surface. But instinctively I knew she'd balk. I settled for patting her shoulder.

"I shouldn't..." She swiped at her eyes. "I'm sorry."

"No apology necessary." I pulled a tissue out of my purse and handed it to her.

"Allison was—" She choked back a sob. "She was always nice to me. To my kids. She tried to heal the rift between me and Dad. It took me a long time to admit to myself that the rift was mainly my fault. I pushed him away for so long, even after I was an adult and should have known better. Finally he just—" She broke off for a moment to collect herself. "Finally he just gave up. I can't blame him."

I waited while Brenda took a few calming breaths and wiped her eyes. "And then he died," she said, "and it was too late to make things right."

"It must have hurt when you found out he'd cut you out of his will," I said.

"It hurt, but I wasn't surprised, all things considered."

"Until Skye paid you a visit," I said.

Her expression hardened. "I know now that she was lying about Alison getting him to disinherit me and my kids. But Dad had just died and I was still reeling and..."

"And you believed her."

She nodded. "I believed all of it. That his marriage was on the rocks, the murder accusation, everything. Even after the cops upstate dismissed Skye's claims. I thought it was lazy police work, that they were letting a killer go free."

"That must have been tough for you to live with," I said, "the thought that Allison had gotten away with murder."

"It ate me up for months," she said. "It was practically all I could think about."

"So you decided to do something about it," I said.

She jerked as if burned. "What do you mean?"

I'd been thinking about that day I'd visited Brenda in her home, about the scattering of children's toys I'd spied in a corner of her living room. A couple of Matchbox cars. A red plastic cell phone. And a teensy-weensy pink doll purse, barely bigger than a postage stamp. I recalled Brenda saying she had two sons and a six-year-old daughter.

"Did you buy Meghan a new Barbie after you decapitated hers and left it in Allison's mailbox?" I asked.

Her mouth hinged open to deny it—and stayed open as she stared at me for long moments. Something in my expression must have told her the jig was up. She sagged in resignation. "I still can't believe I did something so stupid and immature."

"What were you hoping to accomplish?"

"I wanted to rattle her," she said. "To let her know there was someone out there who knew what she'd gotten away with."

"But since she hadn't actually gotten away with anything," I said, "all you succeeded in doing was to freak her out. She didn't make the connection between the headless doll and your father's death." Before she could ask how I knew all this, I added, "You still believed she'd gotten away with murder when I came to your house last week to bring you the pocket watch."

"I was confused, trying to work through everything," she said. "At that point I still bought in to Skye's story. A part of me clung to it, needed it. It's hard to explain. But Allison had just left my kids all that money in her will. A third of her assets. And she'd left a life insurance policy that paid me a million dollars."

"You told me she did it out of guilt," I said.

She grimaced. "Like I said. I was trying to work through it, to find an explanation that fit with my preconceived ideas of this woman who—" She looked away, pulled in a deep breath. "Who'd never done anything bad to me. Who'd made my father happy."

"When did you realize the truth?" I asked.

"When I confronted Skye about it a couple of days ago," she said. "I asked her point-blank why, if Allison had murdered my father, she would have provided for me and my kids in her will."

"What did she say?"

"She laughed. At me. At my gullibility." Brenda's color rose. "She admitted it was all fabricated, everything she'd told me. Part of her plot to make money off Dad's death. She manipulated me, took advantage of my confused feelings. Out of greed." She faced me squarely. "Jane, I don't want you to think that's what motivated me, that I went along with her for the money. My only thought was to avenge my father's murder."

"I believe you, Brenda." I patted her hand.

"Skye convinced me I couldn't do it without her, without her testimony. I was so mixed up, I didn't see her for the heartless, moneygrubbing schemer she is." She closed her eyes briefly, shook her head. "I'm so ashamed. I made it too easy for her."

"Don't blame yourself," I said. "She saw an opening and took advantage, like you said."

"Naturally, after her scheme fell through, she decided I was to blame, that I'd messed up somehow. She refused to recognize her own incompetence."

Her words reminded me of what Skye had said to Nick yesterday while the padre and I eavesdropped from our hiding place in the under-stairs closet. She'd said it was just her luck to rely on "a couple of gullible nitwits." Nick was, big surprise, Gullible Nitwit Number One. I'd assumed the other one was Allison, but now I realized she'd been referring to Brenda.

I'd avoided looking at the man in the windbreaker, but now I couldn't help noticing that he was done with his snack and in the process of licking his hand clean. Well, that was it. No more cottage cheese for me. Not that it was high on my list of favorite foods, but up until that point I'd at least been able to pass that section of the supermarket without gagging. Those halcyon days were over.

Brenda said, "Skye's fallback scheme didn't work out any better."

"What do you mean?" I asked, although of course I knew.

"Well, her affair with Nick," she said. "Not that I knew the two of them were involved until that nasty scene at Allison's funeral reception."

"Yeah," I said, "that sort of made it public knowledge."

"It has to be clear to everyone why she went after her friend's husband. It wasn't for his looks alone. She thought she could get him to leave Allison and marry her, and that they'd live off the juicy divorce settlement."

"Well, she had to know he wouldn't get a settlement after only four months of marriage," I said, "prenup or no prenup."

"I don't know, is she that smart?" Brenda asked.

"Smart enough to engineer these schemes," I said.

"But not smart enough to think them through, to make them work."

Unless, I thought, Skye *had* thought it through this time. I tried putting myself in her place. You know your married lover hasn't a prayer of receiving a lucrative divorce settlement after a scant four months of marriage, but a bit of casual questioning reveals that he expects (wrongly, as it turns out) to inherit millions in the unlikely event his wealthy wife kicks the bucket. What would your next move be?

I guess it depends how ruthless you are.

"I'm curious," I said. "When's the last time you spoke with Allison?"

"Christmas Day. She sent the kids presents. I called so they could thank her."

Which explained why Allison's phone showed a call from Brenda that day. I mentally debated for a moment, then said. "What if I told you that someone arranged to be with Allison at the nature preserve the next morning, before she left for Australia?"

Brenda went pale as the implication sank in. She stared at me without blinking, then croaked, "Who?"

"I wish I knew." I thought fast and came up with a plausible-sounding fib. "She, um, mentioned it to her mom. Only that she was going to, you know, be with someone there, but not who. The person told her not to talk to anyone else about it."

"Well, it wasn't me," she said.

"I'm not saying it was. There's something else. Her camera is missing."

"Missing from where?" she asked.

"From her body." Just saying the words brought to mind a ghastly image I wish I could forget: Allison Zaleski staring up through several inches of clear blue ice.

"How do you know she had a—"

"Trust me," I said, "she wouldn't have gone into those woods without a camera. The one she had with her that morning was pretty hefty and had a neck strap." At her silent query, I shrugged. "My detective buddies. We talk." It was the easiest answer.

"So the police are involved?" she said. "I thought they considered it a cut-and-dried accident."

"Well, they can't ignore compelling evidence that points to a different conclusion, can they?" At least I hoped not.

"Isn't it possible the camera strap slipped off her neck while she was trying to, um, get out of the water?" Brenda asked. "That it ended up at the bottom of the lake?"

"Doesn't seem likely. So." I spread my hands. "Any ideas?"

She gave it some thought. "Well, I hate to say this, but..."

"Oh, go ahead," I said. "It's just the two of us. What are you thinking?"

"Well, you said that whoever met Allison in the woods that day told her to keep the meeting secret."

"Right," I said.

"It probably doesn't mean anything, but like I said, that's the same thing Skye told me before she came over last June. 'Don't mention it to anyone,' she said. 'It's strictly hush-hush.'"

14

Sit! Stay!

AFTER WE REACHED Penn Station, Brenda and I took the stairs up to the main LIRR level. There we separated, she to meet her friend Donna for dinner and *Les Mis*, me to join my fictional Connecticut pal at a jazz club. As soon as she was out of sight, I caught the next train back to Crystal Harbor.

Once the train had emerged from the East River Tunnel and I could count on decent cell-phone reception, I texted Martin, who was tending bar at Murray's, and asked him to alert me if Skye showed up. I already knew she was a regular at the pub—her Facebook profile was filled with boozy selfies taken there.

More than an hour later, as I beeped my car in the train station parking lot, he texted back: *She's here.* It was still snowing lightly as I drove toward Murray's. I tried to formulate a game plan. I'd gotten Brenda's side of the story and was eager to hear Skye's. But how to persuade her to open up to me? I had her pegged not only as irascible and self-serving, but innately suspicious as well.

As it turned out, I never got the chance to try. I parked a couple of doors down from Murray's and hurried toward the entrance, only to see a burly young man slam out of the place, with Skye in hot pursuit.

"Emilio, wait!" she screeched. "Come back!"

Within seconds the fellow had sprinted halfway down the block, where he jumped into a black SUV and skidded down the street, nearly ramming a pickup truck in his haste to vamoose.

Nick had followed Skye outside, looking like an abandoned pup that's been kicked countless times yet keeps coming back for more. Not exactly the image of a sexy alpha male, I don't care how good-looking you are.

Sure enough, she turned on him, shoving him hard in the chest and yelling, "You did it again, you worthless loser! Why can't you leave me alone?"

He mewled something I couldn't quite make out, though I was able to catch "lonely" and "need you" and "make it work."

Good grief, did the man have no pride? I'd assumed that scene yesterday in his house, when Skye had tried to make off with everything of value she could carry, had spelled an end to their affair. Yet here he was, back for more abuse.

Skye stalked across the street to her yellow Kia, parked haphazardly in front of a hydrant. Nick trailed her, whining and pleading. He narrowly missed getting his fingers broken as she slammed the door, after treating him to the affectionate little *adieu* she reserved just for him: "Go to hell!"

He stood in the middle of the street amid drifting snowflakes, staring after her car as it sped away and zipped around the corner. A red Cadillac rolled to a stop behind him. The driver leaned on the horn. Still Nick didn't budge.

"Nick." I crossed to him and tugged on his arm. "Come on."

He jerked out of my grasp. The driver's window of the

Caddy rolled down, and the old guy behind the wheel urged Nick to abandon his fruitless vigil, only he didn't put it quite so politely.

"That's enough, Nick." I seized the collar of his black leather duster and forcefully hauled him onto the sidewalk. "Let's go inside for a beer. I'm buying."

"I need to go after her—"

"No. You don't." I shoved him through the doorway and into the warm, and warmly lit, interior of Murray's Pub. The worn floorboards perfumed the air with the mild and not-unpleasant scent of a hundred-plus years of spilled beer. Bluegrass music played in the background at a volume compatible with normal conversation.

There were about as many patrons as might be expected on a snowy Thursday night. Two men sat at the bar, separated by a couple of barstools but enjoying a friendly chat about the football game being shown on the TV—blessedly silenced, with closed captioning. Two young couples occupied the booth closest to the door. Three middle-aged women sat at one of the wooden tables, drinking martinis and laughing tipsily.

Martin stood behind the bar, pouring a shot of bourbon for one of the guys and talking football with them. As I steered Nick toward the booth at the far end of the pub, I caught the padre's eye. To the casual observer, his expression remained unchanged. Nevertheless, the two of us managed to squeeze an entire conversation into that one silent glance. We'd both had our fill of the tiresome drama that was Nick Birch and Skye Guthrie. Martin didn't know what I was up to at the moment, but whatever it was, he had my back.

And yeah, you make a good point about our ability to communicate without words and doesn't that mean something and what the heck do I intend to do about it.

I don't know, okay? And I certainly didn't have time to think about it just then as I pushed poor, dejected Nick into the booth with a firm order to *Sit!* and *Stay!* I hadn't spent all those years training headstrong pups for nothing.

I crossed to the bar and greeted the football fans, whom I knew from around town, then asked Martin for a pitcher of beer and some fried calamari. Oh yeah, and some nachos, too. I'd skipped dinner, and something told me Nick would benefit from anything that wasn't a chicken pot pie.

"The food will be a few minutes. I'll bring it over." The padre pushed a full pitcher and a couple of glasses across the bar. Quietly he said, "You know what you're doing, Jane?"

"Nope, but I'll figure it out."

Back at the booth, I poured the brew and watched my companion drain three-quarters of his glass in one pull. As I gave him a refill, I decided Nick was not getting behind the wheel again tonight. I'd snatch his keys if necessary and either give him a ride home or put him in a taxi. As for myself, I intended to nurse the one glass.

He looked leaner than when I'd first met him a couple of weeks earlier. He was unshaven, his dark-blond hair lank and dirty looking. Those amber eyes I once thought so dreamy were now puffy and bloodshot, making me wonder if he'd gotten a head start on his drinking before going out in search of Skye.

I wasn't without sympathy. The guy might not have been Husband of the Year, but he was alone and hurting, having just lost both his wife and his girlfriend. The first loss was a tragedy, the second not so much. He didn't see it that way, of course.

"If she'd just let me talk to her," he said. "I know I could bring her around if she'd just listen."

Good riddance, I thought. *You should count your blessings.* But what I said was, "This isn't the way to win her over, Nick. Ambushing her every time she goes on a date."

"She's hooking up with these random guys." He took another long gulp. "She doesn't know anything about them. She's going to get hurt."

"How's it going with the prenup?" I asked. "Are you making any headway getting it overturned?"

He made a rude noise, dismissing the idea with a wag of his hand. "That lawyer doesn't know what the hell he's doing. He's a damn thief, like Skye said. I should've listened to her. See, this is why we need each other. We're *good* for each other. I just have to make her see that."

I needed to broach the subject while he was still coherent. "Can we talk about Allison?"

Something flitted behind his eyes, something dark that I couldn't pin down. "Allison..." he murmured. "It didn't have to be like that."

I willed my voice to remain pleasantly neutral. "Didn't have to be like what, Nick?"

He looked at me, then at our surroundings, as if to remind himself where he was. He shrugged and took a drink before answering. "She never loved me."

"Oh, I'm sure that can't be true." Allison had loved Nick, or thought she did, during those early days when she'd been reeling from Mitchell's death.

"She didn't want my baby," he said.

"Maybe she just needed time," I said. "I mean, you two weren't married that long."

"She'd wanted *his* baby." Nick's expression was harder than I'd ever seen it. "An old man's baby. They went to specialists. Fertility doctors. She wanted a kid of his so bad, she would've done anything to make it happen. But not my kid, nope. No interest." His glass was almost empty again. He lifted the pitcher and topped it off. "She didn't even want my name. She kept *his* name. Zaleski. She kept her dead husband's name when she had a live husband right there in her bed. You have any idea how that made me feel? It's like she knew all along I was temporary."

My invisible antennae twitched. "What do you mean?"

"Huh?" He struggled to focus on my face.

"What do you mean you were temporary?" I asked.

"Temporary, you know," he said. "As in she was going to divorce me."

As casually as I could, I asked, "When did she tell you that?"

I held my breath, wondering if he was tipsy enough to blurt out a truth that went counter to the official version: that he'd learned of Allison's intention to divorce him from Sten during her funeral reception.

Nick squinted as if to bring my face into focus. He rubbed his eyes. "What?"

"When did Allison tell—"

"She didn't tell me," he said. "She kept it secret. She was going to spring it on me when she was good and ready. You know that. You were there."

Was he telling the truth? Jim had speculated that Allison might have let her divorce plans, or at least her knowledge of the affair, slip on Christmas night when she and Nick had argued about his getting fired and covering it up. Jim had thought it possible that Nick had invited her for a walk in the woods the next morning—supposedly to talk things through, to clear the air, but in actuality to ensure he'd end up a wealthy widower instead of a broke divorcé.

Maybe I should have gotten him drunker before asking.

Martin appeared with our food, along with plates, forks, and napkins. The ambrosial smells made my head swim. Before leaving us, the padre held my gaze for a fraction longer than necessary.

When Nick ignored the food, I piled fried calamari and nachos onto a plate and plunked it in front of him, with a firm command to eat. Only then did I begin filling my own grumbling belly.

I watched him pick halfheartedly at the food, wondering how best to proceed. When he drained yet another glass of beer, I decided it was now or never.

"So here's the thing," I said. "I'm wondering who was with Allison at the preserve the morning she died."

He looked at me. His eyebrows knitted together.

"Because, you know, someone either went with her or met her there," I continued, as offhandedly as if I were discussing the weather. "I was just wondering if it was you." I popped a breaded squid tentacle into my mouth.

His words were slightly slurred when he said, "I'm not into that outdoors stuff. I tried to tell her. It's just not for me, you know?"

"She tried to interest you in things like that?" I asked. "Hiking?"

"Hiking, kayaking…" He waved away the memory, nearly knocking over his glass before I righted it. "I get my workouts in a gym. Climate-controlled. Lots of mirrors. Why do I need to risk my neck skiing and that crap?" He pointed to his own face. "This is a valuable commodity, Jane. It's my livelihood. I get it banged up falling down some mountain or something, what then? Huh? What then?"

What livelihood? One soda commercial. Well, plus a sideline in marrying wealthy widows.

I shrugged. "But a simple walk in the woods. No mountains to fall down." *Just a half-frozen lake to fall through.* "I'm thinking maybe you wanted to kiss and make up with Allison, you know, after your fight Christmas night."

He frowned. "How do you know about the fight?"

"You told me."

A pause. "Was I drinking?"

"Um, yes, but—"

"What else did I say?" His frown had deepened into a dangerous scowl, bringing to mind his argument the day before with Skye. I hadn't been able to see their faces then, but I'd heard him. The whipped pup had been noticeably absent. In its place had been a full-grown Rottweiler. Nick Birch had a temper, and he was fond of the sauce—always a winning combination.

Reflexively I glanced over to the bar. Martin was behind the beer taps, drawing a brew and chatting with the guys. His gaze flicked in my direction for a fraction of a second. It was long enough. I relaxed.

I said, "That's all you told me."

"You're lying," he said.

If the padre weren't keeping such a close eye on our conversation, I might not have leaned in and said, "Why? What are you worried you might have blabbed about?"

After a long, tense minute he sat back, picked up his glass, and took a deep drink. "What makes you think someone was with Allison? In the woods that day."

"Well, I'm friends with a couple of cops," I said. "Detectives. The ones who were here last week, remember? They know all kinds of things that aren't public knowledge."

There I was, playing the cop card for the second time that night. Well, what was I supposed to say? *I got ahold of your dead wife's secret video diary. It was chock-full of all kinds of interesting stuff you wouldn't want folks to know.*

Nick did not look happy. "How are the cops involved? I thought they already decided her death was an accident."

"Hey, they don't tell me *everything*. Oh, but here's something else, just between us." I leaned forward again. So did he. "It seems her camera is missing."

"She had a bunch of cameras," he said.

I watched his face, just as I'd watched Brenda's face a few hours earlier when I'd imparted the same information—on the alert for some kind of incriminating reaction. In both cases the results were inconclusive. I reminded myself that Nick was a trained actor.

"I'm talking about the one she had with her in the woods that morning," I said. "The big Nikon with the neck strap. They can't find it. It wasn't on her body and they don't think it's in the lake."

"So the cops are really looking into this?" he asked.

I shrugged again. "You'd have to ask them. I guess they figure if they could find her camera and, you know, look at the pictures she took, it might show them who was with her that day. Any thoughts on who it could be?"

He stared into the bottom of his glass as he drained it. "No idea."

15

Do Something with This Already, Will Ya?

THE NEXT MORNING I found myself, for the second time in less than three weeks, hiking through the frigid woods.

Okay, maybe *frigid* is an overstatement. That day Martin brought Sexy Beast and me to this preserve to go skating, it had been bitter cold. The temperature was much milder this morning, as it had been during most of January. I wasn't wearing a hat or gloves, just my cream-colored anorak. Unlike that previous visit, however, when the ground had been relatively free of snow, I was now breaking trail through several inches of the white stuff. Sometime during the night, it had finally stopped snowing. The sun peeking over the eastern horizon cast long shadows.

The only sounds were the soft crunch of my boots through the snow and my own huffing breaths as I made my way toward the lake. I was mentally exhausted, having lain awake for hours thinking about Allison, and her camera, and the final moments of her life.

What, I'd asked myself in the dead of night, would Allison have done that morning in these woods? If someone else had indeed been with her—by no means a certainty—and if that someone else had turned on her, how would she have responded? It really depended on who the mystery person was, and what he or she had said or done or tried to do. Multiple scenarios had presented themselves as I lay in bed trying to work it out. I was no closer to figuring out the first part, but I thought I now knew Allison well enough to deduce what she might have done if she'd found herself in danger.

I'd come here this morning to get a sense of the place where she'd spent her last minutes, where she'd made her crucial final decisions, to see if my suppositions felt right.

The frozen lake came into view, along with something new, a yellow and black sign on a post, installed by the Department of Better Late Than Never: DANGER, THIN ICE. I squinted against the early-morning sunlight reflecting off the surface of the lake. Unlike my previous visit, when the ice had stretched before me like a sheet of clear blue glass, a seductive invitation to skate, the entire lake was now blanketed with a thick layer of untrammeled snow, coaxed by the wind into wavelike drifts.

And unlike my previous visit, when I'd been thinking about Martin and the hot chocolate in his backpack and his stupid chainsaw and Sexy Beast's delicate little feet, this morning as I strolled along the edge of the lake, I thought only of Allison.

Let's say she's out here with someone she knows and presumably trusts, only to find her trust is misplaced. Does the person have a weapon? My gut tells me yes. He or she would have needed it to control her. Allison was in excellent shape. The same could not necessarily be said of her hiking companion, whoever that might have been. I was trying to keep an open mind on that score, but that mind kept closing around one individual in particular.

Okay, I'll just say it. No way could Skye overpower her taller, stronger friend. So we're talking some sort of weapon. I'm thinking a gun. A knife requires you to get up close and personal with your victim. Allison could simply run from a knife, confident that Skye would be unable to catch her. I was thinking of those triathlons she'd competed in.

I can hear you thinking, *What about Nick?* Maybe Skye couldn't outrun Allison, but *he* could, right? I wouldn't be so sure. Yeah, he lifted enough heavy things in the gym to maintain a pleasing physique, but his cardio workout was probably limited to sexing up Skye in the hot tub. Throw poor nutrition and a fondness for intoxicating libations into the mix, and I couldn't see him catching up to his athletic wife if she was determined to evade him.

But according to the cops, Allison hadn't been shot, or stabbed, or undergone any trauma aside from drowning.

You see how this whole thing gets twisted up in contradictory details? Now you know why I was awake most of the night, obsessing about it.

So anyway, Allison finds herself in danger. What would she do? She'd run. I'm thinking she'd run even if the person was holding a gun on her, assuming her assailant wasn't a practiced marksman. Allison was fast and there were plenty of trees for cover.

But what might she do first, before taking off? Think about it. She's got a camera hanging around her neck. Snapping pictures comes as naturally to her as breathing. Maybe she's thinking she might not make it out of these woods alive. Maybe she's thinking that if the worst happens, she has the means to tell the police whodunit, from beyond the grave.

This woman is levelheaded, remember, analytical. The kind of woman who quietly plans out a divorce before springing it on her cheating spouse. A chess player, according to Poppy.

I imagine Allison quickly lifting her camera and snapping a picture of her gun-wielding companion before turning and running for her life. This is an unforeseen complication for the attacker, who, in addition to whatever nefarious plans he or she has for Allison, must now get ahold of her camera and destroy the incriminating image.

Which would explain why the camera wasn't found on her body: Her assailant took it from her before chasing her onto the half-frozen lake. Maybe she never got a chance to run. Maybe her assailant forced her at gunpoint to relinquish the camera, then made her walk out onto the dangerously thin ice. The result? A clear case of accidental death, with no messy knife or bullet wounds to make the authorities commence an inconvenient investigation.

At face value, this explanation made sense, but it didn't sit right with me. I couldn't see Allison Zaleski, the rational, resourceful woman I'd come to know vicariously through her videos, meekly cooperating with her killer. Giving in without a fight.

As I made my way around the snow-shrouded lake, the exercise and fresh air recharged my exhausted brain. Coming here had been the right call, I decided. I was glad I'd resisted the impulse to turn over in my warm bed and catch up on my sleep.

What would I have done if I'd been Allison and my hiking companion had pulled a gun? Take a picture? Yep. Run like the devil, perhaps veering around trees to make myself, and my bright red jacket, a more challenging target? You bet.

Hide the camera once I was out of my attacker's line of sight?

I stopped in my tracks. The thought had arrived unbidden and fully formed, as if hurled there by my impatient subconscious. *Here! Do something with this already, will ya?* I batted the idea around, let my conscious mind take charge of it, turn it this way and that, examine it from all sides.

I pictured Allison pausing in her flight just long enough to shove the camera out of sight—under a rock, perhaps, or inside a hollow log—while gunshots rang out closer and closer. She'd have recognized it as her best chance to ensure that the incriminating image would outlive her, in case one of her pursuer's bullets hit its mark.

I stood there chewing this over for a minute, then blinked and refocused on my surroundings. I was on the side of the lake nearest to where Allison had been found. Shading my eyes against the dazzling glare, I thought I recognized the spot where they'd cut her out of the ice, some twenty or thirty yards from where I now stood. It was obscured by drifting snow, but I detected a telltale rectangular dip, like a slightly sunken grave.

My gaze traced an invisible line from the place where she'd plunged through the ice back into the trees, their bare limbs now laden with snow. In my mind's eye I saw Allison darting around those trees toward the lake, desperate to escape her pursuer. She would have known not to trust the ice to support her weight. Whoever was chasing her might have known it, too.

Without consciously planning to, I followed that invisible trail some distance into the dense woods. It was as if I were channeling Allison, wanting—needing—to be where she'd been that day, to see what she'd seen. At some point, provided my theory was more than the bizarre ramblings of a sleep-deprived imagination, she'd stopped long enough to hide her camera.

See, this is why I didn't mention any of this to Howie or Cookie. *Bizarre ramblings* kinda sums it up, don't you think? I respected my detective pals and wanted them to continue to respect me. I shuddered to think what would happen to that respect if I shared my untested hunches prematurely.

On the other hand, spring was a few short weeks away, and before long these woods would host an endless stream of hikers, nature lovers, and curious youngsters turning over rocks and exploring hollow logs. If the camera was indeed here, it wouldn't be for long. Would the person who found it make the connection to the woman who'd drowned in the lake the previous winter? And if so, would the images it held still be identifiable after months of exposure to the elements? I wasn't tech-savvy enough to even make an educated guess on that last point.

Gingerly I picked my way through the thick snow, conscious of hidden obstacles under my boots, imagining every unseen rock and dead branch to be Allison's Nikon. Finally I stopped and simply looked around, taking in my pristine surroundings. I was beginning to comprehend what had drawn Allison to places like this, what had driven her to photograph things the rest of us took for granted. I smiled, thinking of her beloved mushrooms.

I stood rooted in place for several minutes, thinking about her, thinking about my suspicions, wondering what, if anything, I should do about them. I closed my eyes, breathed deeply of the clean, cold air, listened to the woods breathe, registered the occasional snap of a twig under its burden of snow.

I'd like to say the answer came to me then, that I

experienced some sort of Zen-like epiphany, but I'm not really a Zen kind of gal and my lack of movement was sapping my body heat. I took one last look around, and that's when I noticed something that seemed out of place: a patch of disturbed snow through the trees off to my right.

The snowfall had ended in the middle of the night, and I had to be the only human being enjoying an early-morning trek through this winter wonderland. My best guess at what had pawed through the snow was a deer or coyote. I hadn't spied any deer, although I knew they inhabited the preserve. I'd been told coyotes had taken up residence here, too, but they were shy creatures and unlikely to show themselves during the day.

I turned to go but was halted by an abrupt sound some distance away beyond the churned snow. I stood stock-still and listened. The noise came again. Something was moving over there. Something bigger than a deer or coyote.

I knew there were black bears on Long Island. Had some of them decided to make these woods their home? And what about those rumors of mountain lions?

Then a more worrisome thought came to me. Yeah, that's right, more worrisome than lions and bears. All that stuff I'd told Nick last night. About Allison's missing camera. About someone being with her in these woods the morning she died—Nick himself perhaps. If that was the case, he might very well have decided to rush over here at first light and try to locate the camera with the incriminating images before someone else stumbled over it.

And if he *hadn't* been here with Allison that fateful morning? Who would be the first person he'd think of once he learned she hadn't been alone?

Yeah, that's what I figured, too. He was still hung up on

his onetime mistress, for some reason I will never be able to fathom. I could almost hear him thinking, *Skye must love me, after all. She killed to have me!* Yeah, to have him and eight million bucks, the amount the two of them had assumed he'd inherit if his wife died.

Skye's initial scheme—exploiting the slayer rule to convict Allison of murder and cause her to be disinherited—had been a spectacular failure, so it was on to Plan B: Snag the boy-toy husband and make sure he ends up a very wealthy man.

Skye had accomplished the snagging part, with the help of a fake pregnancy. As for making Nick a multimillionaire, they both knew it wouldn't happen through divorce. Which left Skye two options: manipulate Nick into killing Allison or do the deed herself. I could see her putting option one into action and finding her handsome boy toy too dim or too weak to get the job done. Which would leave her no choice (in her warped mind) but to fall back on option two.

It's my turn now!

After Nick and I parted ways last night, did he phone Skye and warn her about the camera? Was that her tramping noisily through the woods toward me? Or perhaps it was both Nick and Skye. Wouldn't he help her find the camera? What better way to earn the love of a reluctant lady than to save her from being arrested for murder?

I hadn't seen another car when I'd arrived, but there was more than one entrance to the preserve, so that didn't mean I was alone here.

A flash of movement through the trees galvanized me. I slipped behind the nearest thick tree trunk and tried to make myself very, very small. My breaths sounded like a locomotive to my own ears. I concentrated on breathing as slowly and silently as I could.

The person now sounded very close, and getting closer. I say *person* because there was no mistaking the sound of two, not four, human feet shuffling unhurriedly through the snow, pausing frequently. During those pauses I heard a different noise, a repetitive one that sounded like something being thrust into the snow and scraped against the ground.

The individual approached the very tree I stood cowering behind. I heard more of that percussive stabbing and scratching in the vicinity of the roots. And yeah, I know what you're thinking because I was thinking the same thing. Someone was looking for an object hidden beneath the snow.

Then sudden silence, broken only by the sound of a sharply indrawn breath.

I looked down and saw my own boot prints in the snow, leading right to my hiding place. Well, wasn't that perfect. Jane Delaney, master of concealment, invisible as a wraith. I held my breath as the person began circling the tree trunk toward me.

I was debating my next move when a clump of snow fell into my hair. I looked up to see a long stick reaching up to nudge a dark object dangling from an overhead limb.

I hollered as Allison Zaleski's Nikon bounced off my noggin. Automatically I caught it.

Brenda Yates hollered, too, in surprise. Clearly she hadn't noticed me, or even my boot prints, until that instant, so intent had she been on snagging the camera out of its high perch in the tree. I could only assume Allison had tossed it up there during her flight from her pursuer.

From Brenda.

We stood gaping at each other, separated by no more than a couple of feet. I saw Brenda's options chase one another across her features, recognizing the moment when she realized she wouldn't be able to lie her way out of this one.

She held out her hand. "Give me the camera, Jane."

In response, I slipped the strap around my neck. Yeah, I know, but it wasn't really me doing it, not entirely. It felt as if Allison were reaching out from the other side to lend me courage.

That courage nearly deserted me when Brenda tossed the stick aside and pulled a small revolver from the pocket of her pale blue coat. She pointed the gun at me. "I said give me the camera."

At this close range, an attempt to flee would earn me nothing but a bullet in the back. "And then what?" I asked. "What happens to me once you have it?"

She appeared to give that serious thought. "Tell you what. I'll make it worth your while to keep quiet about all this. Fifty thousand dollars."

My first thought was that Brenda couldn't afford to make an offer like that. Then I remembered. Allison had generously made her stepdaughter the beneficiary of a million-dollar life-insurance policy. Now Brenda intended to repay that generosity by turning a portion of the insurance proceeds into a bribe to ensure she'd never be held accountable for her benefactor's death.

Brenda noticed my disgust but seemed a bit fuzzy on the precise cause of it. "All right, a hundred thousand," she said.

You might be thinking, *Why all the yakety-yak? What's Brenda waiting for?* All she has to do is shoot me and take the camera. A simple solution, but a messy one. There's the bloody corpse, for starters. Do you leave it? Do you try to hide it? And even if she somehow managed to make my dead body go bye-bye, there's the awkward fact that your friendly neighborhood Death Diva has now gone missing. The trail could conceivably lead back to her, depending on how skilled she was at covering her tracks.

I said, "A measly hundred grand? You were prepared to pay Skye a million."

"What? Oh, for that other thing."

I nodded. "To testify against Allison, to falsely convict her of killing your father."

"I didn't think it was false at the time," she said, "and I'm not giving you the whole million. Dream on."

"I'm thinking a fifty-fifty split isn't out of the question."

"Seventy-thirty," Brenda said.

"Make it sixty-forty and we have a deal."

After a long moment she nodded. "An easy four hundred grand for you, just for keeping your mouth shut."

"I can live with that." The operative word being *live*. I hope you realize I had zero intention of claiming that hush money. I was just stringing her along, making the negotiation as convincing as possible. As soon as I was out of the woods— and yes, I meant that both literally and figuratively—my new partner would discover our deal had fallen through.

I nodded toward the gun. "You can put that thing away now." When she made no move to do so, I added, "Trust me, Brenda, I'm on board. You come through for me, I'll come through for you." I mimed locking my lips and throwing away the key. "Allison Zaleski's death was an accident. End of story. And what good would come of causing trouble for you? Nothing can bring her back, and I'm guessing you didn't come here that day intending for her to die."

Brenda stared at me for long moments, then pocketed the gun. "I just wanted her to admit what she'd done, that's all. Just to hear her say the words."

"But she didn't admit it," I said, "because she didn't do it.

She didn't kill your father. She loved him."

Her features tightened. "It infuriated me to hear her keep saying it, even at gunpoint, to keep denying she killed him, when I knew… well, I thought I knew, that she was guilty as hell." Her malevolent gaze zeroed in on the camera still hanging around my neck. "She shouldn't have taken my picture."

"Is that when she ran?" I asked.

Brenda nodded, her face now flushed, and not from the cold. "It happened so fast. By the time I realized what she was doing, it was too late. In less than a second she snaps my picture and—" She threw her hands wide, as if Allison had disappeared into thin air. Sadly, I couldn't hope to emulate Allison's speed and athleticism.

"I couldn't let her go," she said. "I mean, if it weren't for that picture, me holding a gun on her… I couldn't let her show that to the police, and she would have, I knew she would have. There I was, just trying to do right by my father, and she turns the tables, makes *me* the villain."

"So you tried to shoot her," I said, "and ended up chasing her onto the lake."

"She kept zigzagging. I couldn't get a clear shot."

"Did you know the ice was too thin to support her?" I asked.

"No, that was a… fortunate development. It solved my problem. At least I thought so at the time."

"When she fell in," I said, "you assumed she had this camera with her."

"I only saw her from the back," she said. "I thought it was still around her neck. I figured the water would destroy it, obliterate any images on it. Then yesterday when you told me they never found the camera and didn't think it was in the lake, I knew I had to get to it before anyone else did."

I pictured Brenda standing at the edge of the lake, watching Allison fall through the ice, watching her struggle to save herself, and making no effort to help her.

She said, "At first, after she died, I was glad. I thought she'd gotten what she deserved. But now... now I'll have her death on my conscience for the rest of my life. And it's all *her* fault."

"Allison's?"

"*Skye's!* If she hadn't made up that awful story about Allison killing Dad... She was so *convincing*. If Skye hadn't been such a horrible, conniving bitch, none of this would have happened."

What Skye had done, trying to convict an innocent woman of murder, was indeed horrible. And yet it wasn't Skye who'd phoned Allison on Christmas Day to suggest a walk in the woods. It wasn't Skye who'd brought a gun along on that walk.

Allison had had such high hopes for her stroll in the woods with her late husband's daughter. *Maybe this means we'll be able to clear the air and move on.*

Brenda was watching me intently. I schooled my expression, too late. She said, "You have no intention of keeping your mouth shut."

"What, are you kidding? And forfeit four hundred grand?" I almost said I'd kill for that kind of money. "My mouth is shut, and shut it's going to stay."

She produced the gun once more and pointed it at my chest. "Who else knows you're here?"

"No one. I swear." I started to remove the camera from

around my neck, a show of solidarity with my new partner. "Here, don't you want this—"

"Leave that on," she said. "I don't believe you. I think you told those detective friends of yours where you were going. And I think you're going to run right to them as soon as you drive away from here."

"Brenda, I—"

"Move." She jerked her head in the direction of the lake, out of sight now behind the dense trees.

"This is crazy, you know that, right?" I said, as I began to retrace my steps through the woods. "We have a good arrangement. It's a win-win. Don't blow it by doing something stup—" I yelped as she jabbed the gun barrel into my back, prodding me to walk faster.

"You thought you were so smart," she sneered. "How smart do you feel now?"

"I'm telling you, you have it wrong," I insisted. "Let's just stick to the plan."

"Jane was too nosy. That's what people will say. She was obsessed with Allison, got herself all worked up, convinced herself it wasn't an accident. She took the whole thing too far, and look where it got her."

"You know what?" I said as the snow-covered lake came into view through the trees. "You're right, I did tell the detectives where I was going. Howie and Cookie know where I am right now. They're waiting to hear from me."

"Then they'll be very sad when you go missing and they come here looking for you. It'll be too late then for their nosy friend."

Fear pitched my voice higher. "They'll know it was you, Brenda. They know you were the one here with Allison that day."

"Oh, really? She told her mother she was meeting someone, but not who. You said so yourself. No one knows I was here that day and no one knows I'm here now. I made sure of that."

"Our footprints." I gestured behind us.

"It's supposed to warm up today. All this snow will melt, or enough to erase the footprints." We were at the edge of the lake. She shoved me. "Keep walking."

"What? Out there?"

"You can take a bullet right here or you can take your chances on the ice," she said. "Your choice."

Naturally she preferred the latter. It all came back to that bloody-body thing. Why take a risk like that when she could make it look like I'd died the same way Allison had, a victim of my own self-destructive obsession?

I happened to know something she didn't, which is that the ice on this lake was now plenty thick enough to support my weight. Hadn't the padre and I skated on it less than three weeks earlier? It was true that temperatures had been mild since then, but mild enough to weaken seven inches of ice? I was no expert on the subject, but if I had to bet, I'd bet it was still safe.

Once I got out there, however, and Brenda realized her mistake, what then? I'd be totally exposed, a ridiculously easy target in that unbroken expanse of white.

I flinched as she tapped the back of my head with the tip of the gun barrel. "What'll it be, Jane?"

"Okay, okay." I commenced my trek onto the lake, hurriedly slogging through several inches of wind-riffled snow, trying to put as much distance as I could between my back and Brenda's gun. At any moment I expected her to realize her mistake and pull the trigger.

I was about fifteen yards out when I dared a peek behind me. Brenda's expression was a mixture of bafflement and alarm. She raised the gun and I ran.

Or tried to. It was slow-motion running, like those frustrating dreams where you're expending all this effort but making little headway. I tripped and fell, which is the only thing that saved me as the first bullet zinged past my right ear. She was a decent shot, at least at this range.

I got my feet under me and barreled on, stumble-running, hunched over, trying to make myself a smaller target. A bullet tore through my left sleeve at the shoulder.

Reflexively I glanced back and saw that Brenda had followed me onto the ice and was swiftly closing the distance between us. She stopped to aim and I flattened myself to the snow as two more bullets ripped through the space I'd just vacated.

How many shots did a gun like that hold? This was something else I knew little about. I did know that a revolver holds fewer bullets than a semiautomatic, which was good news unless she'd come prepared to reload.

Brenda was close enough now that I doubted she'd miss again. As I struggled to my feet, I recalled what she'd said about Allison—*she kept zigzagging*—and abruptly lunged to the right. Something punched the side of my left butt cheek, throwing me off balance and collapsing my legs.

I tumbled into a gentle depression in the snow and lay there panting, trying to orient myself, trying to *think*. I was shot, but how seriously? And how many bullets did she have left? She only needed one to finish the job.

I struggled to roll onto my side so I could get up and keep

running, if that was even possible. I had no idea how far the bullet had penetrated. Could it reach a major organ through my fanny?

I'd managed to get my knees under me when I heard Brenda's boots approaching in a leisurely fashion. Looking up, squinting against the blinding sunlight, I watched her halt a few feet away. I watched her raise her gun and take careful aim at my head.

The solid surface under me suddenly shifted, with an audible *crack*. Wildly I looked around and realized the slight depression I'd rolled into was the place where Allison had been cut out of the ice. It hadn't been cold enough since then for a stable layer to re-form in this spot. Before I could react, the thin ice I'd been lying on imploded, plunging me into the glacially cold lake.

I sank with startling speed, dragged down by the weight of my clothing, fighting with all my strength against the overpowering urge to gasp. My boots were anchors, as was the heavy camera hanging around my neck, the strap now twisted tight as a noose.

The camera would be useless now, the incriminating image destroyed—which, I belatedly realized, is why Brenda had made me hold on to it. Once I was dead, and that single piece of evidence obliterated, she could never be brought to justice.

My gunshot wound burned like a brand, competing with the knifelike pain of the cold water. I was disoriented, starved for air, flailing in terror. I had no idea which way was up.

A tiny, calm, self-protective part of my brain rose up to smack some sense into the big, passive, panic-stricken part that was insisting it would be a swell idea to inhale lake water. *Get a grip!* tiny, calm Jane ordered. *Find the hole you fell through.*

Looking all around as my air-starved lungs burned and I continued to sink, I spied rays of morning sunlight streaming through a patch of blue sky, vivid against the opaque expanse of pale, snow-covered ice. Without pausing to appreciate the *National Geographic* moment, I swam with all my might, my uncoordinated limbs frantically shoving at the frigid water, making such sluggish progress I expected my lungs to burst at any moment.

At last, miraculously, my head breached the surface. My noisy gasps rang in my ears as I grabbed hold of the edge of the ice, only to have it break off in my hands. A shadow fell over me as I struggled to tread water. I squinted up at Brenda, her gun hand hanging relaxed by her side.

"Brenda!" I gasped. "Help me!" I tried to move toward her as the thin ice splintered beneath my grasping hands. She stared down at me, a passive observer.

Too soon, my strength gave out and I went under once more. My body seemed even weightier than before, pulling me down. I had nothing left to fight with. Why battle the inevitable when it would be so easy, so natural, to simply let go?

An image came to me then. Martin's stricken face looking down at me, at my dead body under the ice.

Like hell!

Adrenaline kicked my heart and threw my muscles into overdrive. I swam hard, pushing the water away, aiming for the patch of blue overhead.

I broke the surface once more, thinking, *This is when I get a bullet to the brain. At least it'll be fast.* But Brenda was nowhere to be seen. She'd taken off, apparently confident I'd die here just like Allison had. After all, if strong, fit Allison

Zaleski couldn't save herself, what chance did lazy, exercise-averse, junk-food-loving Jane Delaney have?

I'd be lying if I told you I wasn't asking myself the same depressing question. But even as I asked it, I commenced bashing my way through the thin, recently formed ice, aiming for the shelf of solid ice beyond it.

By the time I reached it, I just hung on, exhausted, gasping for air. I knew better than to rest for too long. That lovely surge of adrenaline was ebbing. It wouldn't take long for shock to set in, with hypothermia not far behind. I had to keep moving.

Knowing I had to hoist myself onto the solid ice was one thing. Accomplishing the feat? Not exactly a given, considering my current depleted, wounded state. The ice was slippery and covered with snow, and that damn camera kept getting in the way. Finally I paused, holding on to the ice with one hand while untwisting the neck strap with the other. I pulled the camera off and tossed it onto the frozen lake.

That's when it occurred to me that I had an advantage Allison had lacked: reliably solid ice. The day she'd died, the entire lake was covered in thin ice. She'd managed to run this far before it gave way under her, but any attempt to extricate herself would have meant relying on an unstable surface that cracked beneath her weight. It was little wonder she'd perished.

I made another attempt to pull myself onto the ice, and actually managed to dig one elbow into the snow before sliding off again.

This isn't working, calm Jane said.

Yeah, no kidding, panic-stricken Jane answered. *Got any bright ideas?*

If only I had something I could jab into the ice to help me

gain purchase. My keys wouldn't be much help, they were too small. I needed something like an icepick or a screwdriver or—

Or that stupid self-defense spike Dom had given me, and which, humoring him, I'd obediently attached to my key ring. I shoved my numb fingers into my jacket pocket, extracted the key ring, fumbled and dropped it, but managed to grab it again before it drifted to the bottom of the lake.

The purple, five-inch spike had finger grooves all down its length. I got a fierce grip on it, raised my arm over the ice, and jammed it down as hard as I could, keys jangling. It penetrated a short distance, providing the leverage I needed to hoist myself a few inches.

Once I had both forearms and elbows on the ice, I pried the spike free and aimed for a spot a few inches away, heaving my body up a bit more. I got my legs into the act now, stretching them out behind me in the water and kicking, helping to propel myself forward.

In this way I managed gradually to inch my torso onto the ice, then my hips. Finally I dragged my legs out and rolled away from the hole, hollering as pain lanced my wounded caboose.

I lay there panting, staring up at the brilliant blue sky. I wasn't out of trouble yet. I was wet and weak, and shivering violently. Plus I was, you know, lying in snow.

Automatically I groped in my jacket, looking for my cell phone, praying that, like Allison's phone, it would be functional after its icy dunking.

I pushed the button and, don't you know, the darn thing lit up, displaying my home-screen icons. I actually chuckled as I tapped 9-1-1.

I still hate technology. Except when… well, you know.

16

The Ice Queen Cometh

"WHY ISN'T SHE still in the hospital?" Dom asked.

"Because she wanted to come home." Sophie gestured at our surroundings, at my huge, richly appointed master bedroom, designed and furnished by its previous owner, Irene McAuliffe. "You telling me this doesn't beat some crappy hospital room?"

His worried gaze settled on yours truly, propped up in the middle of my king-size bed, tucked beneath Irene's exquisite silk-and-linen bedspread, hand woven in shades of coral, pale green, and ivory. Well, of course I'd kept it, since the alternative would have been to replace it with whatever cheap thing I could afford. Sexy Beast lay curled against my side, his dark little gaze darting between my ex and the town's irascible mayor as they stood there bickering.

He said, "She needs professional medical attention. She could take a turn for the worse at any moment."

"From a grazing wound?" Sophie crossed her arms and stared Dom down. "It's been stitched. She's got her antibiotics. She's got her painkillers. She's got *me*. And I'm not leaving till she jumps up from that bed and chases me out of this house with a stick."

"She almost drowned!" he said.

I spoke up. "May I say something?"

"She *didn't* drown," Sophie said. "Her lungs are clear. Hospitals suck. They have germs. You're being an ass, Dom."

"Why, because I'm concerned?" he said. "Because I want the best possible care for my—for Janey? When the EMTs reached her, she was already in hypothermia."

"Yeah, and she got treated at the hospital and now she's not."

Sexy Beast emitted a long-suffering sigh.

"Um, guys?" I said.

Dom pulled out his cell phone and started tapping the screen. "I'm going to hire round-the-clock nurses to stay with her. Why take a chance?"

Sophie tossed her hands up. "She's fine! You're overreact—"

"Guys!" I shouted. They both turned to me. "*She* is capable of making her own decisions."

Sophie smacked Dom's shoulder. "Isn't that what I've been telling you?"

He raised his palms placatingly. "Of course you are, Janey, I know that. It's just that the hypothermia affected you more than you might realize. In terms of your judgment. Your decision making. You were pretty confused in the hospital, didn't even know where you were."

"Only until they got me warmed up and everything," I said. "That was hours ago. I'm a hundred percent now." Okay, maybe seventy-nine percent. Getting a full charge might take a while.

Dom had been there in the hospital with me the whole time. So had Sophie. And before you ask, no, Martin had not made an appearance there. I wasn't sure how I felt about that.

Oh, who am I kidding? I knew precisely how I felt about it.

It was close to six p.m., more than ten hours since the first responders had descended on that frozen lake. By that time, I'd been pretty out of it. I remembered little of the rescue itself, a blur of people and activity. I don't want to think about what would have happened if my cell phone hadn't worked. Turns out those gadgets are more resilient than I'd assumed.

He said, "Janey—"

"If you're going to keep this up, I'm gonna have to ask you to leave," I said. "But I'm keeping the soup."

Dom had brought me a gallon of homemade chicken noodle soup, conveniently divided into serving-size Janey's Place takeout containers, currently crowding my fridge. Well, except for the bowlful I'd wolfed down as soon as he'd arrived, despite the filling dinner Sophie had made me, plus the guacamole and chips her housekeeper, Maria, had sent along. SB turned out to be a big fan of the soup too. I drew the line at sharing the guac with him. Suffice it to say, I was grateful for the forgiving drawstring waist of my jammie bottoms.

What's that? You recall my informing you my ex is a vegetarian? Right you are. Apparently he still cared enough about me to set aside his personal dietary convictions and make me a batch of chicken noodle soup with his own two hands. His Janey needed some of the proverbial Jewish penicillin, and he was going to make sure she got it, using the very same recipe she herself had used during their brief, ill-fated marriage. It was an involved recipe and I hadn't made it once during the intervening years. Even the mouthwatering smell of that soup brought back bittersweet memories of our time together.

And yeah, I'm pretty sure he was counting on that. The

man was devious and endearing in equal measure.

Sophie gave a brisk nod. "Okay, that's settled. No more hospital talk. Long as you're here," she said to Dom, "I'll leave the patient in your capable care and get a little work done. Just have a couple of calls to make, then I'm finished for the day."

She'd installed herself in the guest room at the end of the hall, which Irene had turned into a beautifully appointed home office. I never could concentrate in that room, distracted as I was by Irene's ghostly, hovering presence. And no, I don't believe in ghosts, but just for the sake of argument, if Irene *was* now a ghost, her old home office was where she hung out.

No, it does not have to make sense. My house, my rules. Anyway, I felt more comfortable working in the little maid's room near the kitchen.

As Sophie was leaving the room, I heard a phone vibrate. "Is that mine?" I asked. She'd commandeered it so she could run interference. So far she'd fielded dozens of phone calls, many from the press, and about a million texts. I'd let her put a few concerned friends through, including Jim Manning.

In addition, she'd turned away a bunch of well-meaning visitors who assumed I'd be thrilled to have them waltz in unannounced and set a spell. The only people I'd allowed inside were Sophie and Dom.

The advantage to having her deal with my would-be callers and visitors is that, whereas I would have felt obligated to humor each one, she was no slave to diplomacy. With few exceptions, her side of these conversations went something like this: *You won't be getting past me, it's nonnegotiable, sayonara.*

An exception had been Leonora Romano, who'd started leaving voice mails the instant the story broke that morning. Once I'd been able to form a coherent thought, I'd told a surprised Sophie to hand me the phone next time she called.

She looked at my phone's screen now, and grimaced. "Nina Wallace again. I'm not answering it."

"I'd question your sanity if you did," I said.

She stabbed a finger at the screen, dumping the call. "She just wants to pump you for all the juicy details. See you in a few," she added as she started down the hall.

Dom sat on the bed next to me. He stroked Sexy Beast, who sniffed him avidly, no doubt detecting traces of Bonnie's prizewinning standard poodle, the urbane and charismatic Frederick. SB snorted in disdain.

I started to scoot over a little to give Dom more room, only to wince in pain at the sudden movement.

He was instantly alert. "Is it bad?"

"It's… just a little sore." A lie, but if he started in again about the hospital, I'd seriously have to get Sophie to kick him out. And she could do it.

"When's the last time you took something for it?" he asked.

"About an hour ago."

"Where's the prescription? Let me see." He looked at the floating nightstands, crafted from the same rich mahogany as the sleigh bed. The bed's headboard and footboard were upholstered in ivory leather. He picked up the bottle of ibuprofen. "What, just this over-the-counter stuff? Didn't they offer you something stronger?"

"I don't need something stronger." Okay, maybe I did, but I had no desire to drift on back to la-la land. I'd spent enough of the day there already. I snatched the bottle out of his hand and placed it on the nightstand. "The bullet grazed me, Dom, it didn't penetrate. It just kind of…" I made a skating motion with my hand.

The wound was about three inches long and located on the outside of my left buttock. I couldn't help thinking that if I hadn't taken a cue from Allison and zigzagged just as Brenda pulled the trigger, the bullet might very well have severed my spinal cord.

"I talked to the doctor," he said. "You lost a chunk of flesh. You needed stitches."

"Yeah, like I can't stand to lose a little back there. Wait." I frowned. "The doctor talked to you about my medical stuff? What about privacy?"

He nibbled his lower lip, a sure sign he had something to hide. "He might have, uh, thought I was your husband."

I stared at him. "Really. And where would he have gotten an idea like that, Dom?"

"Well, I *was* your husband." He gave me the charming little smile he knew I couldn't resist.

I resisted it. "Doesn't your fiancée mind that you're spending the whole day with me?"

Sexy Beast chose that moment to yawn, and I could swear it sounded like, *Oh, snap!*

His mouth tightened. "It's not up to Bonnie how I spend my time. And anyway, why would she have a problem with it? It's not like I'm slipping around behind her back."

"She doesn't know you're here, does she?" I asked. "She thinks you're at work."

He sighed in frustration. "Why are we talking about her?"

"You told that doctor we're married."

"Okay, I admit I crossed a line," he said, "but I was worried about you, Janey. You'd have done the same thing in my place. Admit it."

"No," I said. "I wouldn't have."

"You're saying that if it were me lying in some hospital bed, wounded, disoriented, you wouldn't have pulled out the stops to find out my condition? Even if it meant stretching the truth a little?"

"That's a pretty big stretch," I said, "considering our marriage ended nearly two decades ago."

"You're exaggerating," he said.

"Not by much. It'll be eighteen years next month, Dom. Do the math."

He did. "Wow," he said softly. "It doesn't seem that long."

"Not to you," I said. "You've been busy." We both knew what I meant. Busy with two subsequent wives and a fiancée. Busy raising three children. For my part, I'd keenly felt every day of those eighteen years we'd spent apart.

After a moment he said, "Bonnie's getting antsy. She's been trying to pin me down. About a wedding date."

"Can you blame her?"

"I'm just not ready to commit to a date."

"Okay, for the record, you *committed* the day you proposed to her," I said. "The rest is detail."

"But this time it feels so final somehow," he said.

"This isn't like you, Dom. You're the Marriage Guy. When you don't have a significant other, you get hives. Are you telling me it doesn't feel right with Bonnie?"

"It feels fine." He shrugged.

"Try to restrain your enthusiasm," I said dryly. "Listen, if you don't love her—"

"I love her," he said quickly. Too quickly.

A few months earlier I'd spied Bonnie in the Rose Bookshop perusing wedding-planning books. She might not be my favorite person, but no woman deserved to start married life—in her case, for the first time—with a spouse whose commitment was lukewarm at best. I said, "It sounds like you have to ask yourself some tough questions."

"I told you, I love her," he snapped, then took a deep breath and shoved his fingers through his dark, curly hair. "I shouldn't be laying this on you after what you've been through today."

"After what I've been through *today*?" I knew I shouldn't, but I couldn't help myself. "Try what I've been through the past eighteen years."

Dom studied my face, his expression uncharacteristically sober. This was the thing we never spoke about, never acknowledged, although, to my shame, I knew he was well aware of it: my continued emotional attachment to him, my pain watching him fall in love with a series of other women, settle down with them, make children with them.

A year ago I would have shied away from his searching gaze. Now I met it unflinchingly, baring it all. The longing, the loneliness. The emptiness I'd been so certain only he could fill.

He squeezed my hand, held on to it. I let him. Neither of us spoke for a long minute. When at last he broke the silence, his voice was raw. "When I heard what happened to you today, how it almost ended…" He shook his head, at a loss for words.

"It was your spike that saved me," I said.

"My what?" One dark eyebrow rose. "That sounds vaguely dirty. Okay, not so vaguely."

"You know, that self-defense thingy you gave me for my key chain. I used it to stab the ice and haul myself out of the water. If I hadn't had it on me…" I let the rest go unsaid.

"It's a sign," he said. "About you and me."

"Since when do you believe in signs?"

"Since I almost lost you," he said.

I made myself say, "You can't lose what you don't have, Dom."

Slowly he nodded. "I blew it last summer, asking you to marry me again and then not giving you enough time to think it over."

"I hope you're not angling for a do-over," I said.

"I know I don't deserve one."

"You got that right."

It wasn't what he'd expected to hear, I could tell. After a few moments he said, "What if I were a free man?"

"Then you'd be miserable," I said. "It's in your nature to be in a relationship, like I said."

"You know what I mean. Would you give me a second chance? If Bonnie and I weren't together?"

"I think we're on third chances at this point," I said. "Maybe fourth."

"Why are you being so difficult, Janey?" he said. "I'm opening myself up to you here."

"What you're doing," I said, as I reclaimed my hand, "is hedging your bets. Asking for a commitment from me before you break things off with her."

He opened his mouth to object, then closed it again. With a sigh of resignation he said, "I can see how it might look that way."

"It looks that way because it *is* that way."

It probably hadn't occurred to him that while he'd just professed his love for his fiancée, albeit unconvincingly, he had yet to tell me he loved me. I lifted Sexy Beast and cuddled him close to my chest, needing something, someone, to hold on to. Pushing Dom away felt so wrong, after all those years needing him—or thinking I did.

"You're not yourself," he said. "It's still messing with your head, the hypothermia."

"I'm not—"

"The aftereffects," he said. "You know what I mean."

"Let me be clear, Dom." I locked my gaze with his. "And this is *me* speaking, not the hypothermia or exhaustion or any of that. If breaking up with Bonnie is right for you, then that's what you should do. But don't assume I'll be waiting to take her place."

He took that in. I could tell he wanted to press me, to extract some kind of quasi-promise. Finally he muttered, "Fair enough."

Sexy Beast abruptly sprang off the bed and raced across the room, barking in welcome. Martin stood in the open doorway, a pair of cut-crystal snifters dangling from the fingers of one hand, a brand-new bottle of my favorite añejo tequila in the other.

How long had he been standing out there in the hallway? Had he overheard any of our conversation? Certainly the padre would have removed himself from earshot once he realized Dom and I were having a private conversation.

That's a joke.

He said, "Bad timing?"

"No, it's fine," I said. "Come in."

"How did you get in the house?" Dom demanded. The doorbell hadn't rung, and Sophie hadn't gone downstairs to open the front door.

The look I gave Dom said, *How do you think?* Before he could work up a head of steam on the subject of dangerous men and their lock picks, I turned to Martin and said, "You better not have swiped that from the pub."

"Would I do such a thing?" He sauntered to the night table and set the bottle and glasses next to the ibuprofen.

"If you could get away with it?" I said.

He didn't challenge me on that point. "It just so happens I came by this bottle legitimately, as in I spent my own hard-earned cash. Maxine only buys one at a time for the pub, and only for the single patron who drinks it."

Meaning me. "But I never order it," I said. "It's too expensive."

"Yet the level in the bottle keeps dropping," he said. "It's an enigma."

I gaped at him. "Are you telling me Max *knows* you've been sneaking me high-end booze and charging me for the cheap stuff?"

Martin shrugged. "She likes you. And it's not like you're in there every night guzzling it." He knelt to give Sexy Beast some love. My dog was doing his I-am-unworthy thing, bowing and crawling toward the padre, begging for a scrap of attention from the alpha male. I'm always a little embarrassed by SB's self-abasement, but I suppose it's better than him thinking *he's* in charge. Martin gave the little poodle a final pat before rising and uncorking the bottle.

Dom edged a little closer to me. He placed a hand on my thigh over the comforter. "Janey can't have any of that. She's on medication."

The padre poured two fingers of tequila into both snifters, and told my ex, "I would've brought another glass if I'd known you were here. You can run and get a bathroom cup."

"Did you hear me?" Dom said. "She shouldn't—"

"I'm not on any narcotics," I said, perhaps a bit too testily. "Chill, Dom."

"To happy endings." Martin clinked his glass against mine and we sipped.

Sophie ambled into the room, her sharp gaze zeroing in on the newcomer. "Thought I heard you in here. Afraid I wouldn't let you through the front door?"

"I didn't want to make you run the stairs, Mayor," he said. "I'm too much of a gentleman for that."

Her snort of derision told him what she thought of that claim. She eyed the drink in his hand. "Where's mine?"

Martin smoothly topped off his own glass and handed it to her. I'd seen him do this before, play the gentleman when the occasion called for it, and suspected it came more naturally than he was willing to admit. Those touches of civilization could be traced back to his grandmother Anne McAuliffe, whose efforts to civilize her bastard grandson had met with mixed success.

Anne had had this very house built to her specifications decades earlier. She and her husband, Arthur, had lived in it for twenty years until Irene had broken up their marriage. Eventually Irene had inherited the house along with the bulk of Arthur's other substantial assets. I knew Martin was still sensitive on the subject—the manipulative Other Woman ending up with his beloved grandma's dream house and then leaving it to her poodle!—although he hadn't brought it up in months.

Sophie carried her drink to one of a pair of overstuffed armchairs set before the large windows overlooking the back of my property, their ivory silk drapes drawn against the darkening sky. The chairs were upholstered in pale green and separated by a round, padded coffee table covered in ivory leather. Not the most practical choice, perhaps, but again, it was Irene's taste, not mine. I did approve of the muted coral walls. It's not a shade I would have chosen myself, but I have to admit that Irene, or her decorator, had known what she was doing there.

"Here." I held my snifter out to Martin. "I can't finish all this. You gave me too much."

"We'll share." He took a sip and handed it back.

Dom made a show of ignoring this cozy little exchange. Turning to Sophie, he asked, "What's the latest?"

Nothing happened in Crystal Harbor that she didn't know about, and not just because she was the mayor. Sophie Halperin absorbed local news as if by osmosis. It was spooky.

"Brenda was arraigned this afternoon," Sophie said. "Bail set at a million bucks. Last I heard, she was still in jail."

"What did she plead?" I asked, as if I couldn't guess.

"Not guilty," she said, "even with the evidence stacked against her."

Dom said, "What evidence do they have? I mean, besides Janey's testimony."

"There's the ballistics, for one thing." She sipped her tequila.

"I didn't think of that," I said. "The cops probably found spent bullets on the ice and, what, matched them to her gun?"

Sophie nodded. "Dug a few slugs out of the trees, too, from when she was shooting at Allison. Gun was still in her car. They figure she was planning to ditch it somewhere after dark, maybe take it apart and put the pieces in dumpsters or something."

Dom said, "But why would she bother doing that now and not after Allison died?"

Martin answered that one. "Because Allison hadn't been

shot. Brenda had known her death would be considered a drowning accident. No reason for ballistics testing."

"But I *was* shot," I said. "She'd have figured that once my body was found, sporting a gunshot wound, the cops would be scouring the crime scene for bullets."

"And trying to identify the weapon they came from," Sophie said.

Martin said, "But the picture is what's really going to sink her."

I jerked upright, and regretted it. "*Ow.* Picture? You don't mean… The only picture I know of is the one Allison took right before she died, and that's history. The camera got soaked."

"Yeah, so?" he said. "The memory card survived. The cops have a beautifully framed, time-stamped photo of Brenda standing in the woods, pointing a gun."

"Really? I just assumed…" I was grinning now. "I mean, Brenda was so certain the lake water would destroy the camera and every image on it. I just took her word for it." Turned out she knew even less about this technical stuff than I did.

"Can she afford to post bail, do you think?" Dom asked.

"Yes and no," Sophie said. "She has the money because, get this, Allison left a million-dollar life-insurance policy naming Brenda as beneficiary."

Again, I wasn't surprised Sophie had the inside scoop. Years ago she'd worked as a paralegal for Sten Jakobsen, and the two of them were still tight. If anyone could get the closemouthed attorney to spill, it was her.

"And she gets to keep it?" Dom said. "That doesn't sound right."

I said, "I don't think she *will* get to keep it, because of something called the slayer rule. You can't profit from murdering someone."

"That'd be pretty sick," the padre said, "if they let her post bail for Allison's murder with the proceeds of Allison's life-insurance policy."

"So then who gets that money?" Dom asked.

Sophie said, "Allison named three contingent beneficiaries—Brenda's kids. Plus I know she left gobs of cash in trust for them. Doubt any of that'll be affected. *They* didn't do anything wrong."

My phone vibrated again. Sophie checked the screen, grinned, and heaved herself out of the chair to bring it to me. "You'll want to answer this one."

I looked at the phone's display and felt my own face relax into a smile. I pushed the green Answer icon. "Victor!" It was my French hottie, calling all the way from Paris. Out of the corner of my eye I saw Dom doing his imitation of someone who couldn't be less interested. The padre crossed the room to pour more tequila into Sophie's glass. She did not object.

I mentally debated whether to request privacy or let Dom and Martin stay and hear my side of the conversation. Hmm… which would make them suffer more? Staying and listening, I decided. Plus it would let me sneak peeks at them to gauge their reactions.

Oh, like you wouldn't have done the same thing. We're talking about Mr. Hedge My Bets and Mr. Won't Make a Move While She's Still Hung Up on the Ex. These guys do not deserve your sympathy. *I* deserve your sympathy for putting up with them for so long.

"What a sweetie you are for calling," I cooed into the phone.

"Jane, *mon Dieu*," he said. "I'm so relieved to hear your voice. Sophie called this morning. She said you'd been shot."

Ah. So that's how he'd found out about my little adventure. "It's just a grazing wound," I said, "in my rear end of all places. I'll never race horses again."

"You race horses?"

"Forget it," I said. "Stupid American humor."

"I'm astonished you can joke about it," he said. "You also nearly drowned, yes?"

"I'm afraid so." He sounded so concerned that I added, "But I'm okay now, Victor, totally on the mend. I have my dog and my friends and some amazing tequila. Oh, plus about a gazillion chocolate croissants."

"Four dozen," he said. "I know it's your favorite. They freeze."

Victor had phoned Patisserie Susanne that morning and ordered the pastries to be delivered to the house, in gut-busting quantities.

I said, "This is a conspiracy between you and all the other people who are feeding me. I know what you're thinking. If you get me fat enough, I won't be able to fit through a hole in the ice. Or I'll float like a beach ball until help comes."

"I wanted to fly out as soon as I heard," he said, "but Sophie insisted it wasn't necessary."

"You were going to *fly all the way here to be with me?*" I said, for the benefit of the gentlemen in the room. Sophie smirked. "Well, I can't tell you how much that means to me, but Sophie's right. I'm being well taken care of."

Sophie called out, "He's in India."

"What are you doing in India?" I asked him.

"My firm is opening a branch in Mumbai," he said, "and

I'm helping to set it up." Victor was an architect. His firm was headquartered on the Champs-Élysées but handled many international projects, including a bunch in the U.S. When he'd been in Crystal Harbor last fall to look into his brother Pierre's murder, he'd worked for a while out of his firm's SoHo office.

"You're on an important business trip," I said. "You're needed there. You can't be running off to Long Island to change the dressing on my derriere."

Dom, who up until now had done a creditable job of acting nonchalant, looked up sharply. Martin, now occupying the chair next to Sophie's, appeared not to have heard the comment. Which I didn't buy for an instant.

"Well…" Victor's accented voice was smooth as silk. "I don't have much experience dressing derrieres, but I have some experience *un*dressing them, if that counts. Not to mention boundless energy and a willingness to learn. I'll simply keep trying until I get it right."

I giggled like an adolescent, feeling my face heat. And no, I wasn't putting it on for the guys' benefit. Victor was seriously hot. Have I mentioned that?

"Jane." His tone became more serious. "I can't stop thinking about you. And about that kiss, too, if I'm being honest."

"Me too," I breathed. I wasn't lying. This flirtatious conversation notwithstanding, that one perfect, heart-stopping kiss we'd shared in my car when I'd dropped him off at the airport was the extent of our physical relationship. So far. Reliving that kiss was my go-to happy place whenever I was tempted to wring the neck of one of the clueless dudes closer to home.

"I still want you to visit me in Paris," he said, "and my family's B and B in Uzès. You promised, and I intend to hold you to it."

You can hold me to anything you want, I thought, remembering how this man had looked wearing nothing but a pair of snug black boxer briefs.

Oh, stop, it was perfectly innocent! I'd happened upon him in the kitchen when he'd thought he was alone in the house. Which didn't mean I wasn't allowed to relive that moment, too, whenever I felt like it.

My house, my rules, remember? Sheesh.

"I'm not sure how long they'll need me here in Mumbai," Victor said. "Looks like it could be a while. But when I get back to Paris, let's make plans for you to come over. I miss you, Jane."

"I miss you, too," I said, not caring who heard.

Sophie glanced at the bedside clock and shot to her feet, tapping her bare wrist in the universal sign for *It's later than you think.* I nodded at her as Victor said, "We'll speak soon. I know Sophie will take good care of you. And don't get shot again."

"I'll try," I said, "but no promises."

"Irritating woman."

While we were saying our *au revoirs,* Sophie was adjusting the position of the television, which was located in the corner to the right of the windows, attached to one of those articulating wall mounts.

She tossed me the remote. "Show's already started."

"What show?" Dom asked.

"The Romano Files." I turned on the TV and switched channels. To Sophie I added, "Don't worry, I DVR'd it. If we

missed anything, we can catch it later."

Martin got up and moved closer to the bed for a better view as Leonora Romano's brittle, nip-and-tucked features filled the screen. She was yammering on about Crystal Harbor's deadly Ice Queen (that would be Brenda), who'd caused the gruesome death of a beautiful, talented, vibrant young woman and come close to doing the same to the weirdo who bills herself as—get this!—the Death Diva!

Okay, she didn't say "weirdo," though considering our history, I'm sure she was tempted.

Sexy Beast, once again nestled against me, lifted his head and snarled at the television.

"That's strange," I said. "He only growls at creatures with four legs."

"Must be the horns and forked tail," Sophie said.

Dom said, "Please tell me she didn't talk you into an interview."

"No, no interview," I said. "As if I'd let that woman into my home with a TV camera." Plus, hello, with me lying here all puffy-eyed and straggle-haired? Yeah, that'd happen. "And I refused a phone-in too. We struck a deal, Lee and I."

Dom's "Hmm…" sounded just like SB's growl. We all had good reason to distrust Lee Romano, whose sensationalist on-air hijinks knew no bounds as she strove to entice viewers away from Miranda Daniels's *Ramrod News*, which aired in the same time slot.

Onscreen, Lee's face was replaced with jerky video footage from the crime scene—which is to say, the frozen lake where I came close to dying the same way Allison had. I saw myself at a distance lying on a stretcher, pale and bedraggled, surrounded by emergency personnel—cops, EMTs, firefighters—and covered with a reflective emergency blanket. Someone was holding an IV bag over me. I was grateful the video didn't show the part where they stripped off my wet clothing and bundled me in warm, dry blankets.

"Who took this footage?" Sophie asked. "Doesn't look like an official police video. Cops would never release that to the press anyway."

"I have no idea," I said. "I was so out of it by then, there could have been a whole darn film crew and I wouldn't have noticed."

Lee's voice-over provided a running commentary. "Death Diva Jane Delaney spoke to me from the hospital where she'd been resuscitated after having been shot and left for dead in an ice-covered lake."

"'Resuscitated.' Listen to the woman." I lowered the volume and hollered at the TV, "Try 'warmed up,' Lee. They warmed me up and bandaged my booboo."

Martin said, "So does this mean you're no longer frigid?"

I gave him a wry look. "You've been waiting all day to use that stupid gag, haven't you?"

"What gag?" he said. "I don't know what you mean."

"Children, try to focus," Sophie said. "Jane, I want to know about this deal you struck with Lee. On second thought, maybe I don't."

"It's no biggie," I said. "I agreed to supply her with a few insider details not available to the public, that's all." Lee had finally gotten what she'd asked for that day at the Rose Bookshop.

"And in return?" Sophie asked.

I know she was thinking about the "generous honorarium" Lee had promised me in exchange for "juicy tidbits" about

Allison's death. My friend's dubious expression said she knew me too well to think I'd jump at an offer like that. She was right. No filthy lucre changed hands.

"In return," I said, "Lee leaves Allison's parents alone. She doesn't harass them for quotes or background info, doesn't even contact them."

"Yeah," she said, "but you can bet they've heard from Miranda Daniels."

"I can't do anything about that aside from warning them not to talk to her, which I did," I said. "Look. I'm no fan of Lee Romano, but Miranda is Beelzebub incarnate. If I have to pick sides, I'm sticking with Lee."

Dom said, "So Lee gets to scoop her nemesis Miranda."

"And I get to retain a little control over the info she puts out," I said.

"Plus," Sophie said, "you're making this whole thing a little less horrible for Allison's folks. As close to a win-win as you're likely to get."

Even with the volume lowered, Lee's exclamations about the Ice Queen's shocking—*shocking!*—crime spree were intrusive. I pressed the Mute button.

"Wait." Sophie squinted at the TV. "Martin, is that you?"

I sat up straight, and cursed. I really had to stop doing that. Not cursing, which I reserve for deserving occasions, thank you very much, but bolting upright with a freshly stitched butt wound.

Peering at the TV screen, I saw Martin sprint across the frozen lake toward the stretcher. My mouth dropped open. I turned to look at the man himself, who now stood leaning against the wall with his arms folded, his face a blank mask. Clearly he wasn't pleased to have been caught on camera.

"I had no idea you were there," I said. "Why didn't you tell me?"

Instead of addressing my question, he answered an earlier one. "This footage was shot surreptitiously by one of the EMTs, on his phone—obviously to peddle to the highest bidder. I don't think anyone noticed what he was up to but me."

None of us asked him how he'd known what had transpired at the preserve. We all knew Martin had buddies on the police force, as well as his own police scanner. It wasn't hard to imagine him jumping on his motorcycle and racing to the preserve at insane speeds on back roads made treacherous by snow and ice.

Staring at the television screen, I saw Martin try to get to me where I lay on the stretcher, only to be thwarted by the people working on me. Meanwhile my addled, hypothermic self struggled weakly with my rescuers as they strapped me down. I might have been watching a Hollywood movie. I didn't recall any of it.

Sophie scowled at Martin. "So why the hell didn't you come to the hospital?"

"I did," he said. "They wouldn't let me in to see her because you guys were already there. Two people max, they said."

I repressed a satisfied little smile, which waned as a difficult question presented itself. If I'd been in a position to choose, which man would I have wanted with me in the hospital, Dom or Martin?

I hope you're not waiting for an answer, because I don't have one.

Onscreen, Martin pushed his way past the emergency

responders, more forcefully this time, resulting in a brief shoving match. I'd never seen him as he was in this video, beyond agitated, almost frantic. I have no way of knowing what words were exchanged as he raised his hands in a placating gesture. He must have said the right thing, because eventually they relented and let him approach me.

I stared at the television, transfixed, as Martin bent over the stretcher and tenderly brushed strands of damp hair off my face. My eyes appeared to be closed. He brought his mouth close to my ear and whispered something. Of course, I remembered none of this.

Finally a pair of burly firefighters succeeded in hauling him away from the stretcher, but not before he managed to do one last thing. I stopped breathing as I watched the padre, on the television screen, slowly lower his lips to mine and kiss me. As he did so, I saw myself struggle to open my eyes, to focus on him.

The bedroom was utterly silent. Martin hadn't moved a muscle. I wondered if I was the only one who detected the tension radiating from him. Dom's sullen expression left little doubt as to the direction of his thoughts. For her part, Sophie looked unsurprised by what she'd just witnessed. The deepening crinkles at the corners of her eyes gave her away, and I just knew she was going to be insufferable once she got me alone.

So now I had yet another kiss to relive in my imagination. It would have been nice if I actually remembered it and didn't have to rely on jerky video footage that had been shared with millions of fans of *The Romano Files*. On the plus side, I'd recorded the show, so I could watch it again, should the desire arise.

On second thought, that wasn't necessarily a plus. I flashed on an image of myself lounging in front of the huge TV in the family room, shoveling Cherry Garcia straight from the carton and pressing Rewind on the remote, over and over.

Oh, come on! I didn't say I was *going* to do that, only that it had, you know, crossed my mind as a possibility.

Sexy Beast picked up on the strange vibes zinging around the room, staring pointedly at each of us in turn. His whine said, *Guys! Someone want to let me in on it?*

I could no longer bear the loaded silence. Someone had to say something. It might as well be Leonora Romano, whose refined, store-bought features once more filled the television screen. I turned the volume back up.

"…I'd give anything," she was saying, "to know what that sexy Prince Charming whispered to the Death Diva right before he woke her with a kiss, wouldn't you?"

Indeed I would, I thought, but I wasn't going to waste my breath asking Prince Charming to elaborate. I already knew him well enough to know he'd deny having whispered anything in my ear, particularly of the sweet-nothings variety.

"Okay, fellas." Sophie made shooing motions, herding Dom and Martin out of the room. "You've brought your offerings, you've done your little courtship displays, now scoot so she can get some rest. Go mark your territories or something."

"I'm staying," Dom said. "Janey needs—"

"Git!" She propelled him through the doorway. "How are we supposed to gossip about you if you won't go away? And you!" She stabbed a finger in the padre's sternum. "Aren't you supposed to be mixing up girlie drinks for your adoring fans?"

"Max is covering for me," he said.

"Then go buy this one a beer." She jerked her head toward Dom, moping in the hallway. "Tell him you didn't mean to kiss her. It was an accident. Your lips slipped."

"What kiss?" Martin was all innocence as he and Dom started down the curved staircase. "Did someone get kissed?"

About the Author

Pamela Burford comes from a funny family. You may take that any way you want. She was raised in a household that valued laughter above all, so of course the first thing she looked for in a husband was a sense of humor. Is it any wonder their grown kids are into stand-up comedy and improv? Oh, and here's another fun fact: Pamela's identical twin sister, Patricia Ryan, aka P.B. Ryan, is also a published novelist. Patricia is the Good Twin, and yeah, Pamela knows what that makes her. But hey, Evil Twins have more fun!

It should come as no surprise that everything Pamela writes is infused with her own quirky brand of humor, from her feel-good contemporary romance and romantic suspense novels to her popular Jane Delaney mystery series, featuring snarky "Death Diva" Jane, her canine sidekick Sexy Beast, and a fun love-triangle subplot. Pamela's own beloved poodle, Murray, wants you to know that any similarities between himself and neurotic, high-strung Sexy Beast are purely coincidental.

Pamela is the proud founder and past president of Long Island Romance Writers. Her books have won awards and sold millions of copies, but what excites her most is hearing from readers. Swing by and say hi at pamelaburford.com.